Devil's Ways

AN ANTHOLOGY BY:

PERSEPHONE D'SHAUN
BEN LOORY
R.S.A.GARCIA
MICHAEL SWANWICK
ANDY DUNCAN
CURTIS C. CHEN
DARRELL SCHWEITZER
IMOGEN HOWSON
EDWINA HARVEY
NANCY KRESS
AVRAM DAVIDSON
J. M. SIDOROVA

DRAGONWELL PUBLISHING

This is a work of fiction. All of the characters, organizations, and events portrayed in this novel are either products of the author's imagination or are used fictitiously.

Edited by Anna Kashina and J. M. Sidorova
Design by Anna Kashina

Published by Dragonwell Publishing
www.dragonwellpublishing.com

ISBN 978-1-940076-49-2

Contents

Preface

There is no light without dark; no highlights without shadows; no good without evil.

No God without the Devil.

The Devil takes many guises, showing their face in every culture and religion. From the sovereign of the underworld, the Death Incarnate, to minor deities too mischievous to contain themselves when messing with humans is so much fun, the Devil has been with us for as long as we remember. It seems, the more benevolent and good are the people's gods, the more evil and depraved become their devils. And yet, even having created the Devil as the Enemy, the Destroyer, we can't help but peek behind this fearsome facade. It seems impossible to leave it alone, resist the forbidden. So sure we are that the Devil is always deeply interested in us humans, so drawn to the mystery that shrouds the embodiment of the ultimate Evil. Perhaps it is the mystery itself that makes it so irresistible to continue looking the Devil's way, portraying him in stories and lore – as a Destroyer, yes – but also as a trickster, a meddler, oh and a seducer, of course. Often, the Devil arises from something we did, created or awoken by our actions. As we peek long enough, we want to discern her soft and blind spots, personality quirks and personal problems – bits of humanity, in other words, that make the Devil more – relatable? Now the devil is an enemy, but a beatable one, a trickster, but semi-competent, a villain, but with a tragic back story. Sometimes the Devil is not what we expect. Every once in a blue moon the Devil even does something good.

Truth be told, the Devil is where things happen. Where stories begin.

This collection brings together stories from multiple cultures, featuring the Devil both as an abstract concept and a creature, a terror, a force of nature, an enemy, a trickster, and so many more. Step into the world of shadows, and travel through Devil's many incarnations spanning centuries of history and myth, from the Ancient Greece, African and Caribbean folklore, dark ages in Europe, all the way to the present day.

Anna Kashina

J.M. Sidorova

PERSEPHONE D'SHAUN

Nzembe

Last week all the nzembe-born children in town went into trances.

The week before that, leopards sat together on my grandmother's porch for an entire day, keeping her inside. Later, many women came to her for help, insisting they had fallen into sleep in the middle of the day and been violated by evil spirits in the shape of vulgar children.

And the week before that, Henriette claimed to have seen a sharp-toothed boy peeking at her from one of the thick clusters of palm trees that grow near Little River.

I do not want to think about these things, but today memories are thick and dry like wild grass in the place between towns, tinder in my mind, needing only the smallest spark to destroy the fragile peace I have built.

Today…

Nzembe

The nebulous halo that is the sun, hidden by a yellow-gray expanse of clouds, is halfway into the sky as I approach the house of the biomancer. A two-story building with a slanted tin roof and a covered porch, it is the largest house in the town; once a mission hospital, it has been rebuilt piece-by-piece many time since the X-HIV plague.

"Siabanda!" my grandmother calls. She is the biomancer, although her proper title is Priestess. Always she uses my full name, when everyone else calls me Sia. "You are late." Even though she is blind, my grandmother always knows the time of day. "Did you stop by Zaria's to remind her that her payment is due?"

Zaria owns one of the bunny houses in town and leases most of her nzembe from my grandmother. It is a lucrative business. My grandmother animates nzembe and leases them to the owners of the bunny houses.

I hesitate, certain I see a child smiling at the window of my grandmother's house. But when I take another step, there is nothing.

"Siabanda?"

"Yes, grandmother. She will bring it by tomorrow morning." I glance at the window one more time, but there is no small face between the gauzy curtains she has hanging inside.

"Good. Now come, tell me what you were doing that made you so late. Show me what you found."

The sack I carry is heavy; I am afraid the material will break, so thin from more than a decade of use. But it holds, and after I push an inanimate nzembe blocking the porch of my grandmother's house out of the way, I carry my burden up the stairs to where she sits in a rocking chair older than she is.

She is very old.

"What will you use that one for?" I ask about the nzembe.

"That one is empty."

"Ah." They are everywhere, these empties, moving only when prompted, for some reason unable to house the demons my grandmother summons to animate them.

"Now. If you are a good granddaughter, you will tell me that you were busy making a grandchild for me."

I don't answer, because she already knows I wasn't.

When I married my first husband, Gabriel, the idea of five or six children – preferably all girls – appealed to me; I wanted to be a mother, and oh! How powerful it would make me! And Gabriel!

Beautiful, smart Gabriel, with his wide smile and intense gaze.

I would do anything to have him back.

"Siabanda, where are you right now?" My grandmother breaks into my thoughts. "I feel your soul wandering."

I sigh. "Only further into myself. I have brought a story for the Priestess."

My grandmother straightens, but she is not surprised, motioning to me with her hand.

"This is the end of the story," I say after a moment's hesitation.

"What is it?"

"A head."

"Put it in my lap then."

No priestess is squeamish. I upend the sack into her lap, arranging the head it so it properly faces her. Running her fingers over it, she exhales softly.

I wait. The early afternoon is quiet, with fresh laundry and burnt sugar sweetening the air. Someone will be upset, sugar is hard to come by. Dusty streets are mostly deserted for the heat, the empty nzembe a familiar comfort dotting the landscape, silent, unmoving, vacant. That is why I do not like to visit Freetown. Lacking the presence of empty nzembe, the old city is eerie and unnatural.

Except.

Gabriel and I met on a salvaging trip into Freetown. His group came up from the south pulling a big flatbed, hoping to find toilets; my friends were out for copper wire and light bulbs. I was looking for inanimate nzembe on my grandmother's orders, even though people had stripped the city of them before I was ever born, making it a ghost town.

From the first moment we met, we didn't look away from each other, Gabriel and I, and my heart broke when he admitted after a stolen kiss that he'd promised to marry a girl from his town who was pregnant with his child.

My grandmother breaks the silence, shatters the memory. Her words have a different cadence to them, less sharp, more liquid. "It is time for the beginning of this story. You need me to be grandmother as well as Priestess, Siabanda. For this, you need both."

"First Husband argued with me today." It is the reason the past will not leave me alone.

"Everyone in the neighborhood knows you argued with First Husband." She pats the head and waves a hand wrinkled by time, but not as wrinkled as it would be if she were not a Priestess. Every summoned demon leaves a tiny spark of itself inside a priestess when she implants it into a nzembe; it is what allows her to control them, to give them instructions to carry out whatever function the demons have agreed to, in exchange for having a body. "We could all hear the shouting, if not the words. What was it about?"

I am certain she can hear me rolling my eyes when I speak. "The usual. He wants to come to my bed, the sex nzembe aren't warm enough, they aren't tight enough, the bunny house is too far away, they don't participate the way he wants them to, I am a terrible wife and mine are the only husbands who have never been allowed into my bed, whine, whine, whine. And *he* was arguing with *me*, grandmother, not the other way around."

She purses her lips, blows a sound of dismissal. "It is nothing new."

"No." I drop the old, bloody sack, kick it across the splintered wood and off the porch.

The man who became First Husband paid a bride price for me almost as soon as my Gabriel disappeared on the horizon, the day his people came and dragged him away. It was one month after my seventeenth birthday. At the time, First Husband was thirty-four, and like many older men, desirous of a wife not yet out of adolescence, something I could not, and do not, understand. What was okay between Gabriel and I, was not okay between that man and I. I have never taken him to my bed.

"It is not new," I agree. "But he also told me today that it was he who went to Gabriel's town to tell them of Gabriel's whereabouts. I do not know whether he spoke truly, for he often says cruel things to me. He said that I should be happy with him, for he and my other husbands are all I will ever have." I have four, although only Razi, my Fourth Husband, is not unwanted; he wants nothing from me physically and is my true friend.

The Priestess flattens a hand over the coarse matted hair on the head. "You did not keep your temper." It is why my grandmother does not speak of Gabriel to me. She understands that I am not rational about Gabriel. I will never forget her words from that day of punishment, severe and echoing with the power of biomancy: "It is a hard lesson, Siabanda. Every action is a purchase, every consequence a price that must be paid. This you have known; it is the first lesson I taught you when the demons told me you would one day be a priestess."

"Of course I didn't keep my temper! If he speaks truly, it is he who ruined my life!"

"You did that to yourself, Siabanda. When Gabriel came to town with three verified inhabitable nzembe and two breeding goats for a bride price, you did it to yourself. When he was here instead of there, giving himself to you instead of her, you did it to yourself. When you did not come to me for help, you did it to yourself."

I stare at the back of the head in her lap. The blood has soaked into her bright skirt, a slow, crimson spread that will dry into something dark, a permanent stain. My reply is bitter, because I know she has a point, and my heart is broken, and has been for eight years. "You have always believed we were in the wrong."

"He was promised. He acted dishonorably. How is that right?"

"It is more right than what was done," I say, clenching my fists. "You ruined three lives instead of just one." I remember our wedding, how in the sweet dark night we learned each other's bodies, and afterward I begged Gabriel to tell me his version of my favorite childhood tale.

A lot of people still believe that white people in the United States created the nzembe to kill off all the Africans, but it wasn't true. The nzembe apocalypse hardly bothered African countries at all, not the way HIV, and later XHIV, had.

Besides, nzembe came from Africa in the first place. That is why all over the world, old African magic let us evolve into what we are today. That, the beginning of biomancy, was the tale he'd told, making me giggle. I'd never heard a funny version of how biomancy came to Sierra Leone.

It was perfect, and I loved him.

I try not to lose my temper with grandmother. "I would have supported the woman and her child. Or I could have taken her as wife." It is rare, but not unheard of. "Now she is married to a man who will always make sure she knows that he does not love her. She is unhappy, he is unhappy, and I am unhappy."

"Are you certain? Men come to love the women they take to their beds, and forget the ones they don't."

"Maybe some men do, but Gabriel won't." I would never lose the image of that final desperate look on his face, before his feet unwillingly carried him one step too far for me to make out his features. He looked over his shoulder until the horizon swallowed him and the men dragging him away from me and he was gone out of my life forever. "Not ever," I add for emphasis, even as my control slips.

Remembering makes me furious and I and lash out, striking the head off my grandmother's lap. It hits the floor with a solid thunk. "So no, I did not keep my temper. I told First Husband I would see him dead and get Gabriel back if it was the last thing I did, and together we would piss on his grave." A useless threat, but I was very angry at the time.

My grandmother waits, slowly rocking back and forth. "Are you finished?"

"Did you know?" I challenge, although I pick up the head and she stops the movement of her chair long enough for me to put it back in her lap. I back away and take a deep breath. I am *not* rational when it comes to Gabriel. In a more respectful tone, I repeat, "Did you know?"

"Continue with your story." She does not answer my question, which is in itself answer enough: First Husband had reported Gabriel after our marriage. I try not to hate her, but I always have, just a little, since that day.

There will be no persuading her, however. "Well then, after First Husband went out, I went to see Nasratha. One of her kids wandered off when she sent him to the store. I found him outside of town, sitting quietly as they do, with vacant eyes and his mouth hanging open. He was all the way out near Little Hill."

They always go out into the woodland, those wandering nzembe-born. The result of nzembe copulating with one another and rescued before the demon in the maternal nzembe can force out the newborn soul and take over the body, nzembe-born are touched in the head, but human. Mostly. "When we walked back, the kid spoke at great length about what he saw and did in the spirit world. I thought to bring him back by way of the brick road."

"A pretty detour."

"Yes. But as we went, I saw one of your enforcers off in the distance." The day Gabriel and I were punished, my grandmother called up three demons, and before she put them into the nzembe, they each licked my soul, and Gabriel's. A more repulsive violation does not exist on all the earth. It meant they could track us forever, force us to follow the orders my grandmother gave them as part of our punishment. I could never leave the boundaries of our land, and Gabriel, although he made heated promises before they dragged him away, could never leave his. I can feel when they are close, those soul-licking nzembe, like sand in all the places you never want it. Usually I walk the other way. "It marched right toward us. Nasratha's boy became very excited, jumping up and down and laughing, and I had to hold him by the arm."

"And my nzembe?" The scrutiny of the Priestess is intense; she searches me with sight that does not use eyes, and sees everything.

"It carried the end of the story, dropping the head at my feet before it walked off. I picked it up and took the boy home. But on the way, he kept pointing into the grasses, the trees. I would see something, but then it would be gone."

A cryptic smile crosses the soft, wrinkled features of her face. "You are correct. It is not quite the end."

I cross my arms over my chest, lean against her porch railing. It shifts outward under my weight, but holds. I will replace it for her this week, I think.

She places her right palm flat atop the head. "You know I must ask you, Siabanda. Did you do this thing?"

This is why it is a story for the Priestess. I argued with my First Husband, threatened to kill him and piss on his grave, and now his head is in my grandmother's lap. I am strong, almost as strong as my grandmother. People will say I animated a nzembe and had it pull off my First Husband's head for spite. "I did not. Just because I said it doesn't mean I actually want him dead. Wanted him dead."

She thinks, and I know the flow of her mind, because it is the same as mine a few hours ago. "You did not see his body?"

"Your nzembe was... messy. Like a devil nzembe." The nzembe that necromancers take control of using devils are the only ones that roam anymore, mindlessly eating anything they can catch. They are surprisingly fast too, so although things with wings or four legs usually escape, people are not so lucky. And because devil nzembe are mindless, their feasting is sloppy.

Nzembe animated with demons by biomancy will eat flesh only if it is pertinent to their instructions in some way: if a nzembe is set to guard a husband's fidelity and he breaks it, the nzembe can rightfully eat him. If I go outside the boundaries of our land, the nzembe can eat me as well. There is one exception. They also eat flesh if they come across a body already dead. It is known and accepted. But demon nzembe are not mindless, and they eat neatly.

So it was that if someone found my First Husband's body cleanly eaten, it would not be so strange. But instead I was given his head and grandmother's nzembe looked as if it had eaten flesh in the wild way of a devil nzembe.

"Do you recall Henriette's tale of the sharp-toothed boy?"

I nod.

"And the vulgar children on the day of the leopards?"

Another nod.

"I think, Siabanda, that we are dealing with those we did not rescue."

Those we did not rescue. The Un-rescued Ones, the babes carried off by paternal nzembe, the demons housed in a new body that cannot be controlled by a Priestess, leaving the empty maternal shell behind.

As far as I know, no one has seen any of those children, but it was always only a matter of time. After all, demons are not tame. They are not grateful. And while, unlike their dead counterparts – devils – they are capable of kindness, usually they aren't. They are leashed by the Priestess's power, and like any wild thing, will escape whenever they can.

"If they grow like normal children, the Un-rescued ones should become full adults...but do they?"

The Priestess tugs on the lips of First Husband's head in her lap. "We do not know. But these sightings...my nzembe, eating like a devil, yet mindful enough to bring you a neatly severed head. It does not matter how they grow. This speaks of power unbound by any biomancer, and only the Un-rescued ones may have such power. Go fetch your remaining husbands. We will need a fourth to witness for First Husband. I will ask the demons for a vision." She levers herself out of the rocking chair, keeping hold of the head, ambling into her house.

I walk east through the town, navigating small roads and tightly packed shacks, pushing empties out of my way. I know where Razi is, and I find him first, cleaning rifles in the dusty front yard of his lover's house – a secret Razi entrusted to me long before he was my husband – and tell them both to come. Next year I will take his lover as Fifth Husband, but until then, I only hope they do not get caught. For now, the man can witness in place of First Husband.

We split up to check the bunny houses, which is where Second Husband spends much of his time if I do not give him work to do. He is at Zaria's. Before I go down the hall to retrieve him, Zaria tells me he must not come to her house for a while; he is in love with his favorite bunny. It happens that way sometimes and never ends well. The bunnies are nzembes, after all, and men are fools.

Men are fools. It makes me think of grandmother's question, and I do not like it. Men are fools, but not Gabriel.

We cannot find Third Husband, and I do not care to look hard for him. Neither do the two husbands I did find. They are more concerned that they too might end up headless and eaten by nzembe.

It does not matter, however; by the time we all reach my grandmother's, twilight is falling and Third Husband is on her porch. He looks at me nervously. He must believe I really did have a nzembe pull off First Husband's head.

"You are in no danger from me," I say gently. "If you become too unhappy, we will talk and I will find you a wife." He is surprised, I think, exchanging looks with Second Husband.

I am prevented from saying more when my grandmother opens her door and comes out onto the porch, carrying First Husband's head. It is drying, and is beginning to stink. "I had a vision," she says.

"What did you learn in the vision?" I ask.

"That your heart is what made this possible, Siabanda." She holds the head out to me. I take it woodenly, dread wrapping itself around me like copper coils. "It is part of your price."

"Price?" I frown. I want to drop First Husband's head, kick it into the bushes where some nzembe will find it and eat it. "What have I done that First Husband losing his head is a consequence?"

"This is a price you began paying when you acted dishonorably by marrying a man promised to another." My grandmother's words are sad. I wonder if she has seen my death, and a look at the men tells me they believe she has. Why else make me find them, but to witness me going to my death?

I am tired of paying prices, especially this one. "What must I do?"

"You must take the head and find the nzembe who brought it to you. Ask it to take you to the Un-rescued One who has done this thing."

A shiver of apprehension runs through me. It is not what I expected. "I don't want to do this. That nzembe licked my soul. It is unpleasant to be around, and may eat me." It is easier for me to be afraid of the demon I know.

"Then you had better run fast, Siabanda, daughter of Nasratha, daughter of Mariama." It is not a fleeting notion that prompts my grandmother to list my lineage; it is the Priestess's way of calling on the Ancestors – and her own spirit – to aid me. If they can.

She has seen my death then.

I look pleadingly at my grandmother. She has the power to recall those nzembe that pose a danger, but she is resolute, arms crossed over her chest. "It is the cost; I will not change it. Deals with demons are deals with demons." It is true. In exchange for demon visions, a priestess agrees not to interfere with the outcome.

I set the head down long enough to hug each of my husbands and Razi's lover. I hold my grandmother the longest, and there are tears in her dark eyes when she pulls away. "Visions are never permanent," she tells me.

I nod, pick up the head, and turn to walk away from the life I've hated for eight years. Now that I might lose it, I am not sure it is worth it.

A nzembe comes with me because the sun sinks quickly in this land, even the haloed sun behind clouds left over from the Time of War and the Time of Famine. The nzembe carries a flashlight haphazardly patched together and manually powered; the whir of its crank sounds like a creature of the night.

There is no way to know where the nzembe I am looking for is right now. I have no idea what the three who licked my soul do as they wander the land, ever prepared to eat me in case I attempt to leave. So I go back to the brick road. It is as good a place as any to start.

"You came!"

The exuberant greeting, coming out of the tall grasses to my left, startles a small scream out of me. Without a rustle, a child steps out of the darkness onto the path.

It is the face I saw in my grandmother's window, and my question is answered.

Nzembe children, the Un-rescued Ones, do not grow like regular children. They are not children at all.

This one mostly has the appearance and size of a healthy six-year-old girl, with dark, sparkling liquid eyes and an uncombed mop of wool on her head. She is naked, her pale brown body adorned with large, well-formed breasts. It is obscene, a little girl's body with a woman's breasts.

"Was I hard to find?" she asks, putting a hand on her hip.

"Yes."

"Good! I hid for a very long time."

"How old are you?" I need to know. I do not like looking at her, it is so vile a twist of anything natural.

And for all that, she is not ugly. Equally disturbing.

"I've eighteen years in this body, although I was my mother for thirteen before that. I am older than you."

"Yes, you are." I hold out the head, because that is what I am here for. It is never a good idea to get side-tracked with demons. "Did you send the nzembe that brought me this?"

She steps closer to me, and I see that the sparkling in her eyes are tiny pinpoints of gold light. A window, the eyes.

"I did. As a show of goodwill. I hope you will always cherish it. But come now, I have been sent to bring you far away."

Bring me far away. Hope is a hawk's cry in my heart, swift and sharp, and fades just as quickly. It is not possible.

"Stop that," the demon-child says abruptly, and the whirring of the flashlight in my grandmother's nzembe's hands slows, stops. The nzembe obeys this child-thing immediately, although it is my grandmother's. It is a chilling thing to see.

A moment passes. I can still see, although I don't know how. She does not glow, this girl-thing, but the light belongs to her somehow.

"I will cherish your gift," I say slowly. "But I cannot come away."

"Why not?" Indignant.

"I am not permitted to leave this land."

"Why not?"

"Because the Priestess animated nzembe to keep me from leaving. They will eat me if I try."

"Oh, that." The demon child comes to my side, takes my hand, caked with dried blood and dirt. "As long as you hold my hand while we run, they will not catch us. They cannot go where we are going."

It seems a sure thing, then, that I will lose hold of her hand and get ripped to bits before we are safely away, but I nod and begin to run, a demonic child-thing on one hand and a head in the other. It does not feel as if I am moving any faster than I normally would, but when we flash by my grandmother's nzembe trying to head us off, I know that we are.

Terror makes itself comfortable in the pit of my stomach. These child-things, whatever they are, are incredibly powerful. It is no less than expected, but far more than imagined. They are changed in unfathomable ways from the demons they were when summoned to animate a nzembe under the control of a Priestess.

In that part of me that has the gifts of a priestess, there is the whisper of foresight. They herald the changing of the age once more, these creatures, the shape of which will be unlike anything seen before.

"Why are you doing this?" I ask, because running does not make me tired – another effect from the child-thing, I think.

She grins up at me. "A deal was made."

Who is crazy enough to make a deal with this creature?

Who is crazy enough to make deals with demons at all, a small voice inside me whispers.

We run until the sun comes up, stopping in a jungle as different from my own lands as this girl-thing is from a real child. I ask if we are still in Africa at least, and she asks me where else anyone would anyone bother to go.

It is a good point.

After making a wide berth around a very large snake wrapped around an antelope of some kind – well, I make a wide berth; the girl-thing lets go of my hand to take a flying leap right over it – she leads me to a village.

A village of child-things.

The boys are equally as abominable as the girls, with oversized genitalia that do not belong on a child's body. Some of the girl-things, impossibly, are pregnant. Others hold babies that may or may not have once had human souls.

It makes me sick, and I think of First Husband, who first solicited me just after my cutting, when I was thirteen. He had to wait until I was seventeen to marry me, and never got what he wanted. He would like these child-things, I think, so small and young-looking, indulging whatever desire it is men like that have when they want to have sex with young girls.

Almost, I throw up.

The child-things cheer when they see me. Child-sized hands push at my legs, herding me toward a house that, though small, is disturbingly beautiful, a structure of graceful curves and polished wood, the jungle given practical form.

"Why are we going here?" I ask.

"The deal." As if that explains everything.

Perhaps it does.

Inside is a large room, perfectly round and well lit. Benches curve the entire circle against the walls, some made of stone, some of wood, some of animal bones.

Gabriel sits on the far side – eight years older, but as beautiful as the day he went away.

My muscles still, throat locking mid-swallow. It seems I cannot breathe, and then I am breathing too fast.

Quickly, the benches fill with child-things, and several argue for a place on either side of him. Gabriel. When the furor settles, I am still in shock.

"I can hold your head," says one of the boy-things.

I nod, and the nearest one snatches First Husband's head out of my hand, passing it down until it reaches the volunteer.

"Siabanda," mouths Gabriel. No sound emerges.

"I don't understand." Although I do. My Gabriel. He had promised to make deals with devils. This, this is so much worse.

The girl-thing dances away from me. "A deal!"

"Deal!" "Deal!" "Deal!" The shouts ripple through the room, and I feel as if I am in a perverted version of a preschool class.

I cannot look away from Gabriel. I want to go to him, want to run from him, want this to be a dream, never want to wake up. Over the cries, the girl-thing says, "Your husband made a deal."

My husband, yes. No matter that grandmother nulled the marriage.

But this…? What has he done?

My silent prayer to the Ancestors is pointless. They cannot find me here, so far away from home, even if they could help me. "A deal." Corporeal demons are still demons, and deals are their currency. They *always* make a profit.

"Yes! It is a good deal too, one that is very beneficial to everyone involved. In return for my bringing you here, your husband agreed to lay with me ten times. It was wonderful, although sadly, I will have no child from him."

Finally, I throw up, but it isn't much; I haven't eaten since before going to find Nasratha's runaway.

As if I have not made a mess, she continues. "If you agree to the same – not with me, of course, but a man – and you lay with him until he impregnates you, after the child is born, you and your husband may go away together. We will eat the baby, for it will have your biomancer ability, and then we too shall have it!" She is gleeful. Already, I shake my head, refusing. Man? These things are not men! I will not look at the face of a six-year old between my legs, will not give them a child of my body!

"If you do not, we will eat your husband."

Tension sings through me. I stop shaking my head. "No..."

"No?" Cheers go up around the room, along with demands on who will get which parts of the man I love. Even knowing what he has done to bring us back together, I still love him, will always love him.

Part of me understands, after all. The other part does not.

"I meant, no, that can't be right," I correct myself immediately. The cries die down to regular conversation level; to my left, several child-things huddle together, debating whether an accidental "no" is legitimate, or whether it is simply haggling on my part.

"It is right! That is the deal!"

"Gabriel, why did you do this?" My throat feels like it has rocks in it when I ask. I never thought to see him again, yet here we are, separated by the madness and death that are the only outcomes of this thing he has done, this thing my heart made possible.

He opens his mouth, but nothing comes out.

"He is not allowed to speak. Deals are not subject to last minute influential intervention."

I frown. "That is not how demons..."

"We are more than demons." She is scornful. "We are *new*. Now choose. Do you pay the price, or does your husband?" There is a quality to her voice, a warning that she is about to get annoyed.

Choose. Have a child with a boy-thing and give it over so they can eat it, or let Gabriel die. It is that simple, and that hard.

My heart does not break, it shatters.

The volunteer is doing something pornographic with First Husband's head, making those around him laugh. The girl-thing pulls a boy-thing off the bench, showing me what I will get if I so choose; he stands proud, a child's body with a man's sex at ready, not a child at all, not human at all.

I cannot. Will not.

I must.

It is not really a choice at all.

It is a horror.

Oh, my Gabriel. We never looked away from each other from the first moment we met.

BEN LOORY

Death and the Lady

A lady goes to church one Sunday morning and notices Death sitting beside her in the pew.

Oh Death! she says, very much surprised. Why, hello – I didn't see you!

Hello to you too, miss, Death says with a smile. And what are we praying for today?

Oh, says the lady, long life – and happiness!

Ah, says Death. Sounds nice.

When the service is over, the lady gets up to leave.

I'll see you later, Death, she says.

Indeed, says Death, I certainly hope so.

And he smiles and watches her walk away.

The next week the lady returns to church, and Death is sitting there again.

Death and the Lady

Afternoon, miss, he says, with a smile.
If you don't mind, she says, I'm actually a ma'am.
Oh? says Death.
He looks a bit surprised.
I know, isn't it strange? the lady says.
She raises her hand and wiggles her wedding ring.
Well! says Death. Lucky man!

Are you all right? the lady says, after a moment. You're looking a little pale, you know.

Working hard, says Death. Just working hard, is all.

Well, let's get some lunch, the lady says.

But..., says Death, motioning to the service.

Oh, don't worry about that, the lady says.

She rises from the pew and motions for Death to follow.

They have those all the time, she says.

The lady takes Death to a nearby cafe. They sit at a table and eat bread and sausage.

Feel better? says the lady.

Oh yes, says Death. In fact, I do – very much!

For a moment, the two of them just sit there and smile.

Do you have any children? the lady says.

Oh no, says Death. Marriage is not for me. My career has to come first, you know.

I understand, the lady says, with her best understanding nod. I have a cousin like that. Wait, I think I have a picture in here.

She rummages around in her purse.

That's my husband, she says, passing Death a photo, and that's my sister, and my cousin. And that's my daughter, and those are the twins.

Handsome boys, says Death. You must be proud.

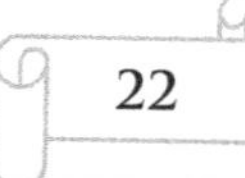

Just then a bell tolls in the distance.

Goodness, says the lady, I have to go! We're having a dinner party tonight and I still have so much to do.

Quite all right! says Death. I hope it goes well. And don't worry, I'll get the bill.

Are you sure? says the lady. I had a wonderful time.

Absolutely, says Death. I did too!

The next week, the lady arrives at church to find Death sitting out front in a convertible.

I thought we might go for a drive, he says. After all, the weather's beautiful.

What a marvelous idea, the lady says, climbing in.

Is this yours? she says. The car?

Oh no, says Death. I took a vow of poverty. My uncle let me borrow it for the day.

Ah, says the lady. That's very nice of him! Well, on with it, Jeeves, let's go!

And Death laughs and puts the car into gear, and onward the two of them roll.

Death drives the lady up into the hills that stand overlooking the city. They park by a cliff and spread out a blanket and open up Death's picnic basket. They unpack a feast and lay it all out, and then they drink a toast.

To you, says Death.

No, you! says the lady.

Well then, says Death. To us both!

The two lie on the blanket and laugh and talk. Death tells the lady about his job.

It's okay, he says. But sometimes I get lonely.

I know how you feel, the lady says.

You do? says Death. I always thought you were happy. Dinner parties and photographs and all.

Well, says the lady, things are different now. What with everyone gone.

Gone? says Death. But where did they go?

Well, my husband, you know, the lady says. And my daughter's married and in Sweden now, and the twins have moved to Maine.

Maine? Death says. But last week they were four.

Oh, that wasn't last week, the lady says. Maybe time moves differently for you. But I haven't seen you in ages.

But, says Death, gazing at her in awe. But you look exactly the same.

But even as he says that, he sees the old woman, like a ghost there moving beneath the skin.

Well, says Death.

He blinks and looks away.

You look the same to *me*, he says.

It's nice of you to say, the lady says, with a smile. And I still *feel* the same, on most days.

And what have *you* been up to? she suddenly says brightly, as if to change the subject.

Me? says Death. Oh well, not too much. Running up and down upon the earth.

Well tell me all about it, the lady says. I've never been anywhere in my life.

Nowhere? says Death.

Just here, the lady says. Is the rest of the world as nice?

Nice? Death says. I never thought of it that way. I like it best in Asia, I guess.

Did you see the Great Wall of China? the lady says.

Oh yes, says Death. Of course.

So he tells her about his time there, about the houses and the domes, about the sunsets and the spires. And he tells her about Egypt, and Iceland, and Norway, and Antarctica, and everywhere else.

It all sounds so nice, the lady says, with a sigh. I

always meant to see the world, but there wasn't time.

Well, says Death, it's never too late. We can go – and if you want, you can drive.

He raises a hand and motions to the car.

Oh, I couldn't, the lady says. And besides, don't you have a job to be at?

I could take some time off, Death says.

The lady looks at Death and Death looks back. Then, with a smile, she starts to nod.

All right, she says, you got yourself a deal. Now please, help an old lady up.

So Death stands up and takes the lady's arm, and he walks her slowly to the car. He helps her in and then climbs in himself. She turns the key and the engine roars.

Okay now, says Death. Are you sure you want to do this?

I do, says the lady. But first, a kiss.

So Death leans in, and they close their eyes.

And they kiss.

Then she floors it off the cliff.

R.S.A. GARCIA

Fire In His Eyes, Blood On His Teeth

He comes to me with fire in his eyes and blood on his teeth. Sometimes the blood is his enemies. Sometimes it's mine. Eventually, it's mine. Always.

He is different today, striding across the sandy soil toward my home with scuffed, much-mended boots. Often, he's charming and beautiful, like the first time I met him. Smooth brown skin and white smiles, smelling of freshly scraped coconuts. Sometimes he is fierce and tall and smells of the salty sea, with a glorious shining beard braided around the fuses he hides beneath his battered hat. His teeth are longer, yellow, and his skin burned from the sun. They call him a pirate then, and men on land and sea tremble to speak his name. He has harsh words, but there are no teeth for me yet. They come later.

Devil's Ways

They come with the fire and a shadow on the sun.

He has seen much. Done much. He forgets, and then the hunger comes and the call to be free and he wrenches himself from me. Tears us apart with fists and teeth and hate for all my kind. What used to be my kind.

(...what is my kind? Women? Women like me? Human? I no longer know. I no longer care...)

He wears purple today. A royal color. His color. The waistcoat is battered, the once gold buttons faded, the shirt beneath grimed as his patched pants. But the purple is bright; bright as he becomes when the shadow is on the sun.

The daylight is beginning to shift; the time is drawing near. I had no real hope of staying hidden. I left our home, but not the islands. There are many of them here, scattered like broken pieces of jade across the Caribbean Sea. I found one with water, one with food, and I built my own place. Sometimes my hands bled from the work, but at least it was my blood shed for me.

For her.

Not him.

A shadow falls on the village, but I can't see the cause. There are clouds, but the sky is blue and clear above the forest clearing. I hear a strange wind, but feel no breeze. People run and scream. We feel fear, but we don't know why. There is nothing to see. Then he lands, with a crash of wings and broken trees, and belches fire, and I drop my bucket of water from the river and run too.

We all hide in the forest for days before we go back in small groups. When I do, he's in my undamaged hut, alone and naked and smiling, smelling of faraway places. He holds out his arms and I go straight into them without a thought. He whispers honey in my ears and I'm lost and found, awake and aware. I see the world with new eyes and he is the beauty in it. We sneak out of the village that night. He's dressed in the clothes I stole for him. I carry what food I have. I never go back. I have a new home now.

His skin is black as night now. His head is tied with a faded red cloth and there are gold loops in his nose and ears. Rings crowd fingers and chains rest on a sweaty neck. His stomach is barrel-round beneath the purple waistcoat, his bare arms corded with muscle. He has a knife in his belt. It's all he needs.

He smiles. "Beloved," he says, and though he is still to reach me, it's as if his hands have grasped my shoulders. I can feel their warmth and calluses scrape my skin. Orange light dances in dark eyes but his teeth are still white and too many for his mouth.

Beloved is what he calls me. I call him my heart. I give him everything. Body, soul. He is mine and I am his. I'm young then. I do whatever he wants. I leave my people behind for him and his sweet words. I have nowhere to turn after that, of course. He wants that too.

He is not like other men. He changes when he pleases, leaves without a word. But he always comes back and I always know him. Wherever he leaves me, I wait. I have no choice. He has my heart and I can't go without it.

We walk for long days, through Cockpit Country and past towns and plantations. We never see people. He knows when they are coming and we go the other way. When we reach the sea, the salt smells like life. This is him. Too vast to contain, too wild to resist. He settles me between his thighs, sand sliding beneath my skirts, and pulls me back against his chest. He's oven-hot, his arms silky-smooth and strong as metal bands.

"My beloved," he says. "My treasure."

When the moon rises above us and I see its glowing, colour-shifting beauty – see its true splendour for the first time between swaying palm leaves – I am distracted.

It's then that he reaches down and pulls my heart from my chest.

I look up, but the sun is still there. The shadow is not yet on it. And I am blessedly clear of mind as the sky is clear of clouds. I've been waiting here by the river for days, knowing he would come. Feeling it.

Running was never the plan. Not after I met the Queen.

Not after I had her.

I wait for him to come nearer. Near enough to try to take it from me again.

Near enough to fail.

The first time he fed on me was the worst because I didn't know it was coming. He needed it, he said. He had no choice. He was tired, spent. He had long searched for a special woman like me. Someone who would take the pain and love him for it. Someone who could be with him wholly and feed him as he needed.

I was proud to be her. Scared to be her. But after that first, unimaginable pain it was easier. He called me his girl, and was tender with me until I healed. And we went on. But I was different inside. I needed his warmth to fend off the cold. Needed his will to strengthen my own.

He went away for a while and came back with a fierce beard and a ship of his own. I was glad when he held out rough hands and I put my own in them. It had been unbearable without him. Cold and lonely. Empty and slow. The colors drained from the edges of things. I knew he'd come back when I saw the red of his teeth. But the tiniest bit of fear

(...the pain, dear God, the pain...)

tingled along my skin in the moments before he reached into my chest. The fear left me when he took my heart, but he knew it was there. Of course, he did. After that, he locked my heart in a chest he kept in his cabin and I had no fear at all, no matter what he did to me.

No matter what I did for him.

He smiles and speaks again. Words that enchanted before. Words that told me how beautiful I was. How incomparable I was. How special.

Words that told me how ugly I was. Words that told me how weak and clingy and boring I was. How lucky I was to have him. To have anyone.

Words, words, words.

When we are good together, we seldom speak. We don't need to. I know what he wants and I do it; he knows what I need and he gives it to me.

Words are love and pain and everything hateful in-between.

Now, they're a prelude to something I no longer need.

"Beloved," he says.

"No," I say to him. "I'm not your Beloved. I've loved you. You never loved me."

(...not the way I love her. Not the way she deserves...)

The sea is our home. The sea is our life.

I scheme with him. Pillage with him. Murder with him. I like the way colors leave people when they die.

How they turn gray and small. I like the spill of blood, of gold, of rich cloths and glittering jewels. They are bright and alive in an otherwise drab world. I stab and shoot and laugh and fuck and feel nothing but euphoria. I have no fears and no hopes. No needs but him.

I lose track of how long we stay this way. Of the shapes he takes and forms he makes me wear. Sometimes I'm his first mate, sometimes his love; always his other half, always there. He doesn't care what others think, and neither do I. All we care about is the treasure we take and the need to feed. It doesn't happen often, but there is always a time when the moon is full and he forgets he loves me. Then he draws from me the screams and the pain until my heart is full and crimson and beating and he can eat. After, he locks my heart away and I'm something else again.

Perhaps it would have gone on forever, if I hadn't met the old woman and the one-armed slave.

He's barely two feet away. Far beyond him is the merest glimmer of the sea between the swaying coconut trees, bluer than the sky. I draw strength from it. From the wide river rushing to its ocean destination beside me. From the darts of light filtered between the wind-swept palm leaves. From the birdsong that trills out in the forest on my right. Behind the hut I used to pray to Mami in.

Where her Children first came in answer to my prayers, their tiny hooves scraping on the sea-salt and sand crusted wood of the floor.

It is hot and smelly, like all ports. Noise everywhere, and the clamour of men loading and unloading, ships rising and falling, fish guts and scales and sweat and rot clogging every throat. But it's been years since I left this land and its treacherous Cockpit Country and I walk away from the ships for a while, into the town, hearing the water slapping the stone piers behind me, no matter how far I go. I have an idea to find a place to drink until he is finished trading for supplies for the men, but I end up walking the damp dirt between a dry goods store and an inn.

When the old woman appears at the end of the path and stares right at me, I know *she*, not drink, is what I sought. We both stand still and take stock of each other. I don't know what she sees, what form I wear for her, but I see a small, thin woman. Her skin is dark, and wrinkles kiss her eyes and bracket her mouth. A flowered wrap covers her hair. Cheekbones jut as proudly as she carries herself. Her dark eyes see through me, into me. I know I can deny her nothing. She crooks a finger at me.

"Come, 'gal."

I go, stand quietly as she looks me over, runs hands along my arms. Power trails in the wake of her fingers, pebbling my skin. Out of the corner of my left eye, I see two men approach, cutlasses at their waist. One of them is short and dark and carrying two sacks; the other, tall and brown with one arm. I look at the tall one directly and he stops dead as the other walks on.

"Who that?" he asks in patois. His deep voice prickles my nape.

"A slave," the old woman says, and her voice is strong and kind. I meet her eyes again. She smiles and there is just us in all the world.

Girl, she says in my mind, *how long ju like this?*

It is perfectly natural for me to answer the same way. *I don't know.*

Him tek ju, or ju tek him?

I don't know.

She sighs. The one-armed man is next to us now. The other looks confused.

Devil's Ways

"We must go, Queen Nanny," the one-armed man says in English. "We stay here too long, they will find us."

I've heard this name before. She's Queen Nanny of the Maroons. She's led slaves against the planters and won.

She nods at me, never breaking eye contact. "Una wait."

I don't know what she does next. Fire flashes over me, under my skin. The coldness flees before it. Suddenly, I am warm again. I breathe again. The breath I take shudders in my throat and there is coolness on my cheeks.

What have I done? I think. *What have I done?*

"Nutting," she says in a fierce whisper. "Him the 'wan do it. Tek it back, gal. Go tek it back."

"I don't know how," I say and for the first time in a long time I have thoughts. Thoughts of my own that I cannot escape from. Questions and fear and so much else. I'm free, I sense, but only halfway. I can leave, but he will find me.

The one-armed slave is more than he seems. I sense him the way I sense Queen Nanny. He draws closer now, and dark eyes narrow at me. He mutters under his breath in a language I don't know and Nanny answers him. He shakes his head and says to me, "That one is strong. You cannot do this alone. What of your Gods?" he asks.

"I never knew them," I say. "My people were taken."

He sighs. "We were all taken. But some of us remember the old Gods. Know the old ways." He and Queen Nanny look at each other. She nods at him. He pulls a tiny wooden figurine from the pocket of his battered pants and presses it into my palm.

"She is of my people. I ask her to free me from my British master. He bring me here from Barbados. Now I am with Queen Nanny. Pray to her. Give her loyalty. Give her something precious. She will give you what you need most."

I look at the faded red carving. It's a woman with the tail of a fish. I know her name from other peoples who were taken from the motherland, like my people. "Mami Wata can do this?" I ask. "She can free me?"

Queen Nanny chuckles briefly. "*Ju* free already, mi done say it true."

She's right. I can feel it. Queen Nanny has freed me, as she has so many others. I am myself.

And, I became aware, something more. Deep within me is another rhythm. Another heart.

One he doesn't have.

One I can never let him have.

She nods, eyes bright and unsmiling as I place my hand over my stomach.

"Tek it back," she says and walks away.

I never see any of them again.

Sometimes, even when we do not know it, we pray. And if we are desperate and forsaken enough, sometimes the Gods choose to hear us.

I remember when I prayed. When the pain was so great, I called out to something bigger than myself. Anything larger than the never-ending waves and the power of his shadow.

No flash of lightning told me I was heard. No voice boomed from above. Gods almost never do their own work.

And it wasn't the God he hates and fears that heard me anyway. The God of the planters who they say helps those that helps themselves.

She's older – from the place Before. Before we were shipped in our own filth across a cruel ocean to unimaginable horrors.

She lives in the old woman and the one-armed man.

In the small carving burning in my pocket.

She's with me as I stand in his cabin, the broken door tapping lightly against the wall behind me. I drop the axe and stretch out my hand to the small, worn box I've taken from his smashed desk.

A shadow hovers over it, wrapping it lovingly in a miasma that makes me hesitate before I reach for the clasp.

Pain and images sear into my brain. What I've done, who I've killed, the fear I've felt and the fear I've given to others.

I snatch my hand back and fall to my knees, too hurt to scream. My body spasms with the full knowledge of all I've wrought and all I've endured as I fall onto my back.

No wonder he doesn't lock the box. He knows to touch it I would have to face it all.

It's too much. Far too much.

I lie there and tears slip from me as I cradle my hand against my chest.

I lie there until the pain recedes enough for me to breathe again. To feel the tiny, steady beat deep inside myself. A faint pulse of life that isn't tainted. That isn't part of the past and the world we've made.

It belongs here, in this land, the way he does not.

I hear voices shouting and I know the crew has heard the crashing and I have only moments to decide. Moments to choose between a life without pain, and one filled with knowledge and regret and only a tiny spark of hope I carry inside.

It's no contest in the end.

My fingers are sliced to the bone as I reach through my own darkness to touch the clasp. My head swells with agony as I flip the lid back on a scream. But I close bloody palms around the fetid lump inside as Mami burns against my thigh. A good burn that reminds me not all pain is death.

Pain also reminds us we are still here. Still alive. Still fighting what would bury us beneath the violence and the hate and the blood.

All Gods, it seems, like to help those that help themselves.

"You've never loved me," I repeat.

The flames in his eyes dance and I know that expression well. The "you know you don't mean this" curve of his lips.

I mean it as I meant it the day I walked back to the ship, Mami in my hand, and broke into his cabin. I took my battered, shrivelled heart and I left without looking back.

I did it for her. Because she couldn't be me.

I wouldn't let her.

The whole time I knew he would come. He would have to feed, sooner or later.

And she was between us. A thread, ever tightening, leading him to us. So I prayed and I prayed and one day, when the feeding time drew near, I sacrificed the only thing I had left. My only real treasure.

And Mami answered.

She heard and she answered, and she sent her Children.

"We are done." I say to him now.

His head slips sideways and he looks at me as if from one eye. He sucks air between his teeth. "Stop playing, woman. I've had a long journey and there are many lives yet to take."

"You have a longer one ahead of you. Back to the hell you came from."

The air around us tightens. A shadow spreads above. I watch him carefully, wondering if he understands yet, but his eyes are still glowing embers, his smile undefeated. He still thinks he has power, and he does. But not over me. His power flows around me, but it does not touch me. Nothing he has will touch me ever again.

Especially not his teeth.

"You're mine. My treasure," he says, his voice like rum, warm and fiery. "You both belong to me. The time draws near and a wife needs her husband. A girl needs her father."

I laugh. "We have no need of you. *You're* the one with needs. You have no treasure here."

The light dims as a cloud passes over the sun. There is a movement on the river, the sound of something leaping from it, and the fairymaid is behind him, long, dark hair tangled to her waist, the delicate hoof of her one deer leg clattering on the riverbank stones.

He spins and recoils but it's too late. She grins at him and holds up a large, wriggling mass, black as night, insubstantial as smoke.

Finally, finally, his smile fades. He looks smaller in the glare of the fairymaid's inner light, but the truth of him struggles in her slender fingers.

His shadow is winged and torn, light from her fingers renting it in places.

Entirely caught.

The fairymaid, river-daughter to Mami Wata, leaps back into the rushing green waters, and his hands close on air as he snatches after her.

He snarls, upper lip lifted, and I see pink gums...and something else.

For the first time, I smile.

"Mami Wata heard me. She hears her people, even when we are far from her. And she makes us strong."

His eyes are nothing but fire now. His voice hisses like steam from flames. "Strong? What do you know of it? You are food and drink. Meat and wine."

"That's what you wished me to believe. That's not who I am," I say.

He is less solid now. I can see the trees through his royal waistcoat. The sun comes out and the ground behind him welcomes its light, with only the shadow of the trees above to disturb it.

Silvery laughter rises from the swirling river beside us. A dark shape ripples beneath the waves, violent and twisting, caught in its watery binding.

"I am myself. Mami Wata's servant. My daughter's mother. I am my own treasure. And I don't need you. *We* don't need you."

I advance on him as the river roils and he takes a step backward, his eyes the scorching craters of volcanos. I see the moment he knows it's true. The moment he turns his gaze to the water and watches the darkness in it wash away, toward the sea. His roar shakes the ground.

"It waits for you." I say gently. "In the fires you were born to. You have no place in this world anymore."

His broad nostrils flare as he scents me. Scents what's missing – what he expected to find after I stole it back.

What's no longer there.

"Your heart..."

"It was damaged and withered, but Mami accepted it," I say. "A worthy sacrifice for my daughter's future. And your destruction."

The river is placid again and the thing I once loved stumbles and then rights himself. He's a shade now, gray and colourless. I look up and see the first dark edge of a disc touch the sun.

It's time. His time.

And it's too late for him to feed.

He bares rotted teeth.

"My daughter..."

"She is *my* daughter," I say, and my voice is fierce. Fierce as the sea.

"She will grow safe and happy, far from you. She is not yours to feed on. We are not your food. Not your slaves. No one will ever be your slave again."

And like that, it's done. The words are said and cannot be unsaid, will never be unsaid. Joy wells within me, pouring out of every part of me, a rush of sparkling river water that washes away the last fading vestiges of him.

The purple waistcoat melts into purple scales, and golden hoops and buttons curve into yellowed claws. Huge damson wings beat the air. He struggles, trying to escape, to fly free. But he's weak with hunger and the need to feed, and without a shadow – without the dark heart of him – he cannot stay in the mortal realm.

He crumples to the ground and curls in on himself, ash from a fire. The ash takes one breath, two, then collapses in a shower of sparks.

After a while, wind stirs the pile and the ash blows away, toward the sea, dancing embers fading as it goes.

I sit by the river, suddenly too weary to stand, and watch the water flow for what feels like hours.

I meet the dark eyes of the fairymaid as she raises her slick head just above the waterline to stare at me. Her hair drifts around her like seaweed.

I smile. "Thank you."

She rises fully out of the water, and if I still had my heart it would have hurt for the tiny, cooing child she cradles against her bare pointed breasts.

But I no longer have a heart. Or time to mourn it.

She holds my daughter out to me, and I take her, one last time, pressing a kiss to her warm, wet forehead and laughing as chubby hands pull at my braids.

I feel the world slowing around me, even as her baby sounds float on the air like pollen. I look at the fairymaid.

"Will she be loved?"

The nod is slow and serious.

I sigh. "That's all that matters."

I kiss her one more time and whisper my daughter's name in her ear. "Calypso. My heart. Live well."

And after she is gone, I lie with my feet borne up in the warm river as I stare up at the blue, blue sky until the glare hurts my eyes and I close them...just for a moment... to rest.

MICHAEL SWANWICK

Of Finest Scarlet Was Her Gown

Of finest scarlet was her gown;
It rustled when it touched the ground.
Even the Devil, with all her wealth,
Had no such silks to clothe herself.

Su-yin was fifteen when her father was taken away. She awoke from uneasy sleep that night to the sound of tires on the gravel drive and a wash of headlights through her room. From the window she saw a stretch limousine glide to a halt in front of the house. Two broad-shouldered men wearing sunglasses got out to either side. One opened the passenger door. A woman emerged. She wore a dress that covered everything from her neck to her ankles except for a long slit on the side that went all the way up one leg.

A thrill of dark foreboding flew up from her like a wind.

The woman cocked a wrist and one of her bodyguards – Su-yin had seen enough of their kind to know them at sight – handed her a cigarette. The other lit it. Flickering match-light played over the harsh planes of a cruel but beautiful face. In an instant of sick revulsion, Su-yin experienced a triple revelation: first that this woman was not human; then that whatever she might be was far worse than any mere demon; and finally that, given the extreme terror her presence inspired, she could only be the Devil herself.

Quickly, Su-yin pulled on her clothes – jeans, flannel shirt, running shoes – as she had been taught to do if strangers came to the house late at night. But she did not slip out the back door and run through the woods as she was supposed to. Instead, she knelt by the window and watched through the slats of the venetian blinds.

The Devil unhurriedly smoked her cigarette, exhaling through her nostrils. Then she flicked away the butt and nodded. One of her underlings went to the front door and hammered on it with his fist. *Bam! Bam! Bam!* The sound was an assault upon the helpless house. There was a long silence. Then the door opened.

Su-yin's father stepped outside.

The General's bearing was stiff and proud. He listened politely while the bodyguard spoke. Then he gestured the man aside, dismissing him as irrelevant, and turned to confront the dark woman.

She handed him a rose.

For the space of three long breaths, Su-yin's father clutched the flower, black as midnight, staring down at it in horror and disbelief. Then he seemed to crumple. It was as if all the air had gone out of him. His head sagged. Weakly, he half-turned toward the house, lifting a hand in a gesture that as good as said, "At least..."

The Devil snapped her fingers and pointed toward the limousine, where a bodyguard held open a door. She might have been giving orders to a dog.

To Su-yin's shock, her father obeyed.

Doors slammed. The engine growled to life. Heart pounding, Su-yin sprinted downstairs. Snatching the keys from the end table by the door, she ran for the Lexus. She didn't have a learner's permit yet, but the General had taken her to the parking lot at the stadium when no games were in the offing and let her try the car out under his careful supervision. So she knew how to drive. Sort of.

By the time she'd gotten down the driveway and onto Alan-a-Dale Lane, the limousine was almost out of sight. Su-yin drove as fast as she dared, the steering wheel loose in her hands. She could see the limousine's red taillights in the distance and did her best to keep up, wandering off the road and jerking back on again. A truck swerved out of her way, horn blaring. Luckily, there were no cops about. But the limo pulled steadily away from her, dwindling on the miracle mile and then disappearing on Route One.

It was gone.

Su-yin mashed her foot down on the accelerator. The car leaped wildly forward and through a red light. She heard brakes screeching and horns screaming and what might have been an accident, but paid them no mind. All she could think of was her father.

Her father was never a religious man. But when her mother died, he had emptied out the mud room and built a shrine there with candles, a framed photograph of his wife, and some of her favorite things: a carton of Virginia Slims, *Mastering the Art of French Cooking*, a stuffed toy that had somehow survived from her childhood in rural Sichuan. Then he had gone into the little room, closed the door and cried so loudly that Su-yin was terrified. He had seen that fear on her when he emerged, more than an hour later, his face as expressionless as a warrior's bronze mask. Scooping her up, he had lifted her into the air over and over again until she laughed. Then he'd said, "I will always be here for you, little princess. You will always be my daughter, and I will always love you."

Su-yin's hands were white on the wheel and there were tears flowing down her face. It was only then that she realized that she, the General's daughter, was displaying weakness. "Stop that right now," she told herself fiercely. And almost overshot the strip club in whose lot the Devil's stretch was parked.

Su-yin parked the car and composed herself. The club was shabby, windowless, and obviously closed. But where else could they have gone? She went inside. In the foyer a bearded man with a sleeveless shirt that showed biker tattoos said, "You ain't got no business here, girlie. Scram!"

"I have an interview," Su-yin said, making it up as she went along. "An audition, I mean. With the head lady."

"You're talent?" The man stared at her impudently. "Oh, they gonna eat you up." Then he jerked his head. "Enda the hall, down the stairs, straight on to the bottom."

Trying not to show how terrified she was, Su-yin followed his directions.

The hallway smelled of disinfectant, vomit, and stale beer. The handrail down the stairs rattled and some of the treads felt spongy underfoot. A lone incandescent bulb faded farther and farther into the distance behind Su-yin.

Save for the sound of her own feet, the stairway was completely silent.

Flight after flight she descended, the light growing

steadily weaker until she was groping her way in absolute darkness. At some point, because it seemed impossible that the stairway could continue as far down as it did, she began counting landings. At twenty-eight, she bumped into a wall.

By feel, Su-yin found a doorknob. It turned and she stumbled through a doorway into a dim red city. A sun the color of molten bronze shone weakly through its clouds. The air stank of coal smoke, sulfur, and diesel exhaust. Sullen brick buildings, scarred with graffiti, overlooked narrow streets where trash blew in the cold breeze. There was no trace of either her father or the Devil.

Su-yin took a step backward and bumped into the side of a brick building. The door through which she had come had disappeared.

"Where am I?" she asked out loud.

"You're in Hell, of course. Where else would you be?"

Su-yin turned to find herself face to face with a scrawny, flea-bitten, one-eyed disgrace of a tomcat perched atop an overflowing trash can. He grinned toothily. "Spare a few bucks for a fella what's down on his luck?"

"I..." Su-yin seized control of herself. She had to expect things would be different here. "Take me to the Devil, and I'll give you whatever money I have." Then she remembered that she'd left behind her purse. "Actually, I only have a few coins in my pocket – but I'll give you them all."

The cat laughed scornfully. "I can see *you're* going to fit in here really well!" He extended a paw. "I'm Beelzebub. Not the famous one, obviously."

"Su-yin." She shook the paw carefully. Its fur was greasy and matted. "Will you help me?"

"Not for the crap money you're offering." Beelzebub jumped down from the trash can. "But since I got all eternity with nothing better to do, I'll help you out. Not because I like you, understand. Just because it's an offense against local community standards."

Hell was a city like any other city save that there was nothing good to be said about it. Its inhabitants were as rude as Parisians, its streets as filthy as those of Mumbai, its air as tainted as that of Mexico City. Its theaters were closed, its libraries were burned-out shells, and of course there were no churches. Those few shops that weren't shuttered had long lines. The public facilities were far from clean and, without exception, had run out of toilet paper long ago. It didn't take Su-yin long to realize that her father was not going to be easily found. There was no such thing as a City Hall or, indeed, any central authority of any kind. Hell appeared to be an anarchy. Nor was there a wealthy district for the privileged. "It's a socialist's dream world," Beelzebub told her. "Everybody's equally miserable here."

The Devil could be anywhere. And though the cat led her up streets and down, there was not a trace of that Dark Lady to be seen.

In a rundown park little better than a trash dump she came upon a pale-skinned young man sitting cross-legged on a park bench whose back slats were missing. His hands were resting on his knees, palms up, thumbs touching the tips of his forefingers. His head was tilted back. His eyes were closed. "What are you doing?" Su-yin asked him.

"Curiosity? Here?" The young man continued staring sightlessly at the sky. "How... curious." Then he lowered his chin and, opening his eyes, stared at her through a shock of jet-black hair. His eyes were faintest blue. "A pretty girl. Curiouser and curiouser."

Su-yin blushed.

"Watch out for this one, Toots," Beelzebub said. "He'll talk the knickers offa you in no time flat."

"It seems you have a friend. In Hell. Inexplicable.

Tell me what you see."

"See?"

"See," the young man said. "Hell is different for everybody. What you see is pretty much what you deserve."

"Then I guess I don't deserve much." Su-yin described the litter-filled park and the sad buildings that surrounded it as best she could.

"No wasps? No flames? None of those nasty little things you can only see out of the corner of your eye? I begin to wonder if you belong here at all." The young man uncrossed his legs, and sat like a normal boy, all elbows and knees. "In answer to your question, I was meditating, foolish though that may well seem to you. Against all reason, I appear not to have entirely given up hope. But I doubt that you're interested in my story."

"I am, actually." Su-yin sat down on the park bench beside the boy. Unlikely though it was, she couldn't help hoping that he was nice. "What's your name?"

"Rico. When I was alive, I thought I was a pretty hard sort. I cut class, boosted cars, smoked reefer, had sex with girls. Oh, and I died young. That's important. I was shot dead in my very first hold-up. I strutted through the gates of Hell like a rooster, convinced that I was the baddest, wickedest man ever consigned to damnation.

"Oh, was I wrong! So far as I can tell, until you popped up I was the *least* wicked person here. I say that with no pride whatsoever. Because it means that I was damned by the slightest of margins. Patting a dog or smiling at an old woman or dropping a dime in a beggar's hand probably would have been enough to tip the balance. One tiny act of kindness more and I'd be sitting in a penthouse in Heaven today, eating porterhouse steak and drinking Bordeaux wine while pouring Evian water into a Limoges saucer for my pet ocelot. So I thought... maybe if I improved myself that tiny little bit, I'd wake up and find myself somewhere else. See what I mean about hope? I've been doing this for a long, long time, and no results. Still, it's not like I have anything better to do. Now what's your story?"

When Su-yin was done, Rico whistled. "Kindness. Courage. Self-sacrifice. This day grows more inexplicable with every passing moment." Then, "You look hungry. Let me stake you to a meal."

"Don't do it, babe," Beelzebub said. "It's an old jailhouse con. When you first arrive, everything's a gift. But come midnight, Shylock here is going to want his pound of flesh. If you know what I mean."

Rico's face twisted with annoyance. "Okay, now *that* kind of language is more like what I'd expect hereabouts." He turned back to Su-yin. "I wash dishes at the Greasy Spoon. There's an opening there for a waitress, if you want it. The pay's not much, but it comes with three meals a day. Such as they are."

Su-yin realized then that she was likely to be stuck in Hell for a long time. "Well..."

"A hundred a week plus meals and tips, if any," the cook said. He didn't tell Su-yin his name, nor did he ask for hers. "Also, you get to sleep in the storage room. Anybody craps on the floor, you clean it up. I catch you hocking a loogie in the food, you get docked an hour's wages. Got that?"

"Yes, sir."

"Then welcome to the finest fucking restaurant in Hell. Get your ass to work. And get that filthy fucking cat outta here!" The cook grabbed a hot frying pan off the grill and flung it at Beelzebub, who disappeared in a yowl of fur and defiance.

Work Su-yin did, for twelve hours every day, waiting on sullen customers and bussing the counter, scrubbing the floors, unclogging the toilets, and putting out the trash. Serving as a jill-of-all-trades so long as the trade was boring.

In her free time, she scoured the city, searching for her father or the Devil in dark, joyless bars, unventilated parking garages, and basement sweatshops where drab men turned out shoddy furniture and shoes whose laces broke the first time they were tied. Slowly, steadily, she could feel the grayness of the place sinking deeper and deeper into her flesh until it was a constant ache in the marrow of her bones.

The boundaries of Hell ebbed and flowed like the tides, so that the way everything hooked up changed day by day. The city abutted the world Su-yin had come from, but different parts of it on different days. Sometimes she found herself staring yearningly into Los Angeles and other times at the outskirts of Moscow. One day the city abruptly ended in desert – she had no idea which one – and Su-yin found herself contemplating a lone flower whose stalk was the exact same color green as the soda straws back at the Greasy Spoon.

She stared at it for a long time, thinking.

Su-yin showed up early for her next shift and rummaged through the trash, looking for brightly colored packaging. Then she set to work. When she was done, Dolores, a dried husk of a woman who was the other waitress on duty and had yet to say more than four words in a row to Su-yin, stuck her head into the kitchen and said, "You guys gotta see this."

The cook came out of the kitchen and said, "What's that goddamn heap a shit?"

"It's a bouquet of flowers," Su-yin said. "Sort of. I made it out of soda straws and whatnot. The vase used to be a sour pickle jar."

From behind the cook, Rico said. "What's it for?"

"It's just for pretty." She pinched the cook's cheek. "Sort of like Cookie here."

Dolores's mouth fell open. Rubbing the side of his

face, the cook said, "Why the fuck did you do that?"

"No reason. Just felt like it." A customer came in and she brought him a menu. "What'll you have, Sweetie?" For the rest of the day she called the Greasy Spoon's patrons "Hon," and "Sugarpie," and "Darlin'." She had a smile for everyone, and when she mopped the counter she sang. She made little jokes. If there was anything she could do to make the diner a happier place, Su-yin did it. It wasn't easy. But she made the effort.

The next day she did the same. And the day after. And the day after that one too. After a time, the regulars would smile wanly at the sight of her. A couple of them even made unconvincing attempts to flirt with her. One left a tip – it was a slug, of course, but the gesture was good. Smiling, Su-yin tossed it in the air, caught it one-handed, and shoved it in a pocket.

At last, the Devil took the bait.

Su-yin was wiping blood from the dingy Formica countertop when the Dire Lady walked into the diner. Quickly stashing the cleaning rag under the counter, she said, "What can I get you, ma'am?"

The Devil sat and, after a bodyguard lit a fresh cigarette, exhaled a slow, lingering, sensuous serpent of smoke. "Boodles martini, very dry, straight up, with a twist. I want it so cold that it hurts."

"Yes, ma'am." Su-yin turned back toward the kitchen and was not surprised to find that she was in a gleaming – and impeccably clean! – bar. Everything in Hell, apparently, confirmed to its Mistress's wishes. Fortunately, Su-yin had for years made her father's cocktails for him every evening, so she knew what to do. With swift efficiency, she mixed the drink and brought the brim-full glass to the Devil without spilling a drop.

Crimson lips opened moistly. Gin slid down that long, long throat. Perfectly manicured nails plucked the lemon rind from the drink to be nibbled by even white teeth. All against her will, Su-yin admired the elegance of the performance.

The Devil dropped an envelope on the counter. "Read it."

Cautiously, Su-yin shook the document open. It was notarized, but she'd know the General's handwriting anywhere. His phrasing too:

My dearest daughter:

What are you doing? Go home. You can accomplish nothing here.

I used to love you, but there is no love in this place.

Sincerely,
Your Father

Su-yin put the letter down and looked the Devil in the eye. "All this tells me is that I've gotten your attention."

The Devil snorted. "Your attempts at meliorating the pervasive misery of my domain are annoying, yes. But that's all. You think you can defy me? Empires have fallen for less."

"Where is my father?" Su-yin said without trembling.

"He's right behind you."

Su-yin spun around and she was in a hospital room. It smelled of antiseptic and ironed sheets. People walked by unhurriedly in the corridor outside. A television grumbled on the wall. An unseen machine wheezed regularly, a half-beat off of the rhythm of her own breath. Lying in a bed, skin palest white, eyes closed, was her father.

She ran to him and clasped one large, unresponsive hand in both of her own.

Those eyes which in life had always been so cunning and wise opened the merest slit. Dark pupils slid down the curve of eyelids. "Foolish child, why are you doing this?" the General mumbled.

"I'm going to bring you home, Daddy."

"This is my home now. I am here because I deserve

to be here."

"No!"

"You are old enough now to suspect how I made a living. I assure you that I did everything you fear I did, and worse. You cannot save me nor can you undo time."

"I will! I will! I will!" Hot tears of rage and denial coursed down Su-yin's face. "I haven't come this far to be turned away now. I don't know how, but somehow I'll – "

"*Stop that.*" The General was gone and she was back in the bar, transfixed by the Devil's glare. Without any change in how she felt, Su-yin was no longer crying. "What will it take to get you to leave?"

Controlling her emotions as best she could, Su-yin said, "My father."

The Devil threw her martini in Su-yin's face.

The gin was so cold that it stung and for an instant Su-yin feared that it had been magically turned into acid. But she managed not to cry out or to turn away. Fumbling under the bar, she found the cleaning rag and used it to dry off her face.

"I suppose this is what they call love. It looks a lot like pigheadedness." The Devil tapped her nails against the obsidian top of the bar, click, click, *click*. "All right," she said. "I'll deal."

Su-yin waited in silence.

"You are a virgin. Don't think that makes you special here. There are plenty of virgins in Hell. But I'll set you a challenge. Stay a virgin for an entire year and I'll let you take your father away – alive, unharmed, all of that. But if you behave like the slut I'm convinced you are, you agree to simply, meekly, leave."

"I – "

"There are other conditions. You have to go out with anyone who asks you. You'll keep your job here, but I'm giving you the use of a penthouse apartment I maintain as a *pied-à-terre* so you'll have a nice place to bring a boy home to. Don't you dare touch any of my clothes."

"Thank you."

"I'm also giving you a tutor. To teach you, among other things, manners."

Leonid was thin, graceful, acerbic and, Su-yin suspected, gay. He was waiting in the penthouse when she got there. "We will start," he said, "with the fox-trot."

"Can't I just... you know? Kids today mostly just wing it."

"No." Leonid took her in his arms, turned one way, turned the other. Her body naturally followed his. "Your partner controls where you go. If he knows what he's doing, you follow fluidly. Your every movement is easy and graceful as you yield to his movements. The metaphoric content is, I hope, obvious. All the while, your bodies press together. He is constantly aware of your breasts against him, your thighs, your everything. You, in turn, cannot help knowing when he becomes physically aroused."

"I don't think you're very aroused by me," Su-yin said, amused.

"That is not my job. Nor is it yours. You are only to arouse those who ask you out. And I am not going to ask you out."

There was a knock on the door. "Room service," Leonid announced. He let in a deferential servant who swiftly unloaded the contents of a wheeled cart onto a table: linen napkin, silverware, a selection of cheeses on a wood tray, crystal glasses, a carafe of water, a split of champagne.

"I'm not old enough to drink alcohol," Su-yin said.

"Here, you are. One of the many things I am to teach you is how to drink. In moderation, it goes without saying. You must never have more than two glasses in an evening and *never* accept anything you have not seen poured. Drugged drinks are a fact of life."

"Oh," Su-yin said in a small voice.

"I will also teach you some rudimentary self-defense. But only after you have learned how to dance. Dancing is fundamental." Leonid gestured toward the food. "Well? Have at it."

"Aren't you going to have some too?"

"No. I will stand here and critique how you eat."

Her first date was with a man who said his name was Archer. "Just Archer," he said when she asked for his full name. They met in the building's lobby, which looked like it was meant for billionaires, smelled faintly of sour milk, and had Ferrante and Teicher playing on the sound system. He was dressed like a mobster, in a black suit with matching shirt and white tie. He opened his jacket to show her his gun. Then he started to tug out his shirt to show her his tattoos.

"Not now," Su-yin said. "Maybe when we know each other better." Which sounded stupid but was the only thing she could think of to say. She made a mental note to ask Leonid for better responses to such situations.

In the street outside, a cabbie leaned on his horn, long and hard.

"Milady, thy chariot awaits," Archer declaimed. Then he grabbed her arm and yanked her outside. When he helped her into the car, he stroked her bottom.

They went to a restaurant where her date proceeded to order for her, saying, "I've eaten here before and you haven't." Archer chose foods she didn't like, and tried to get her to drink from a flask which, when she refused, he returned to his jacket pocket without sampling. When she had to go to the toilet, he said, "Mind if I come along? I enjoy watching women pee."

Su-yin stayed in the ladies room for as long as she dared. When she returned to the table, Archer had eaten all the veggies off her plate and there were several empty cocktail glasses in front of him. "Say," he said, whipping out his smartphone, "do you want to see some pictures of my mother?"

One glimpse of the screen was enough to make Su-yin whip away her head, reddening. "Not pictures like that."

"Aw, c'mon. We're in Hell. You can get away with anything here."

The meal went on forever. Whenever the waitress came by, Archer leered at her and ordered drinks for the both of them. Then, when his was empty and Su-yin's still untouched, he drank hers as well. In the cab home, he began to cry because when he was alive his father had molested him, and it had screwed up his sex life. Then, when he dropped her off, he grabbed her arms and tried to kiss her. She closed her lips tight and turned away from his mouth, so he licked the side of her face. "At least let me smell your panties," he said.

With a shriek, Su-yin pushed him away and fell backwards out of the cab. She lurched to her feet and, abandoning one of her shoes, ran inside. Behind her Archer shouted, "Come back! You haven't paid the cabbie!"

Inside the Devil's condo, Su-yin's tutor was waiting.

"I won't ask how it went," he said.

"Oh, Leonid, it was awful." He handed her a dressing gown. There was an antique Chinese screen in one corner of the room. Su-yin went behind it and undressed, draping her dress and underwear over the top the way starlets did in old black-and-white movies. "The only good thing to be said about the whole experience is that I was never once in the least bit tempted to have sex with him."

"Don't get cocky. The Devil likes to play games. She'll soften you up with some really awful experiences and then slip in a ringer. A nice dancer, a good listener, a fella who seems to be on your side. That's the one you've got to look out for." Leonid gathered up her clothes. "I'll take these things out to be laundered."

He withdrew then.

Su-yin took a shower to get the smell of Archer and his cigars off her skin. Then she went to bed, praying that she wouldn't have nightmares about him but sure that she would.

Still. One day down and not quite a year to go.

At least three times a week, Su-yin had dates, all of them hideous. One man exposed himself to her, then called her a slut for not sleeping with him. Another got drunk and tried to rip her dress off, right out on the street. A third got her name wrong and, no matter how many times she corrected him, insisted on calling her Ching-chong. He wanted to know if it was "true what they said about Asian girls," and got offended when she told him that whatever they said, she was pretty sure it was wrong. To say nothing of the woman who kept trying to get Su-yin to smell her fingers.

On those nights when she stayed in, Leonid gave her lessons. He showed her the proper way to snort cocaine, the basics of flirtation, the fast way to do up her hair in a French twist. She was taught that a stiletto heel can be driven right through a man's shoe, the social proprieties of makeup, and which of the seven basic perfume categories (Floral, Fern, Chypre, Leather, Woody, Oriental, and Citrus) were appropriate for different situations.

She also learned to play the piano, though the opportunity to do so never arose on a date.

"Why am I learning all this stuff?" Su-yin demanded one evening, while they were playing chess. "It's not like I'm ever going to use it."

"Having skills gives you confidence and having confidence makes you alluring." Leonid slid a bishop forward, putting her queen in check. "That's all."

"I don't want to be alluring." Rather than move her queen, which was protecting her king, Su-yin blocked the attack with a knight.

"Rules of the game, sweetie. Rules of the game." Leonid advanced a pawn, opening a line of attack for his own queen and suddenly the game looked entirely different. "Mate in three. You've got to learn to think at least four moves ahead."

One day, Beelzebub was waiting outside the Greasy Spoon when Su-yin got off work. "Thought I'd warn ya," he said. "Rico's building up his courage to ask you out."

"Is he?" Su-yin said, surprised. "I thought better of him."

"I can see what you're thinking. No, the Devil didn't order him to nail your little virgin tushie. She didn't have to. Setting aside this idiot challenge you got yourself roped into, Rico is young and male. You're young and lovely. You're gonna have your work cut out for you, keeping his hands outa your undies."

Caught by surprise, Su-yin asked, "Am I really lovely?"

"To him, yes. To a cat, not so much."

She laughed and rubbed Beelzebub's head. "That's one of the things I like best about you, Belzie – your unfailing honesty."

"I'm only honest because it's an offense against local community standards."

When she began her shift, Rico came out from the back room, drying his hands on his apron. "Listen," he said. "There's this dance club I know. I was thinking maybe this Friday I could take you there. To dance."

"Oh, Rico." Su-yin sighed. "I'd love to."

So that Saturday they went to the Top of the Town, which was a revolving sky bar with a spectacular view of the river Phlegethon and the delicate blue flames that flickered upon its waters. They danced for a while, and Rico kept stepping on her feet. Then a handsome Algerian named Jean-Luc cut in. He danced beautifully. Which was why Rico punched him out and then hustled Su-yin away to a smoky piano bar for cocktails. There, she took tiny sips from a glass of pinot grigio while Rico got plowed on highballs.

Finally, they took a rusted-out old taxi back to Su-yin's apartment and, true to Beelzebub's prediction, she had to fight to keep Rico's hands out of her dress. When they got out of the cab, she told him she'd had a lovely time and slipped quickly inside, directing the doorman not to let him follow. Behind her, she could hear him throwing up.

Back in her apartment, she kicked off her high heels and, without bothering to undress, threw herself down on the bed. The instant she closed her eyes, she could feel sleep closing about her.

One more day down. Far too many yet to go.

Rico was hung over the next morning, and had a black eye from his encounter with the doorman. So he didn't ask Su-yin out again, which was just as well because she got a call from the Algerian, insisting that they go clubbing.

They went to the Dew Drop Inn, the Hotsy-Totsy Club, the Orchid Lounge, Swank City, the Top Hat, and the Roadhouse and danced to the music of Pat Boone, Doris Day, Barry Manilow, Patti Page, and Wayne Newton. To Su-yin's surprise, Jean-Luc behaved like a perfect gentleman. "When I was alive, I was a jewel thief and a cat burglar," he told her. "A very good one, too. I learned that one has to handle beautiful things with a light touch.

"It would be counterproductive for me to throw myself at you, grasping and snorting," he said. "Though I assure you there is nothing I desire more. I must instead convince *you* to seduce *me*. Which is, notwithstanding the fact that you are unaware of it, something you most dearly desire to do."

"It's not going to happen. My father's soul is at stake."

"That's a problem of course." The Algerian winked roguishly. "I'll just have to be more charming."

"That hardly seems possible," Su-yin said, amused. But she stayed on her guard.

Jean-Luc had a wealth of stories of rooftop robberies and midnight escapes through the squalid alleys of Paris and Algiers. He asked her questions about her life and seemed genuinely interested in what she had to say. He told her that once, when he was wanted, he had hidden in a brothel in Marseille for a month – "the longest month of my life!" – without touching any of its employees. "I was in love, you see, desperately so. Only, when it was safe to come out, Mignette had moved in with a gendarme. She meant to wait for me, but – thirty days? Every woman had her limits."

The Algerian was nice and, under other circumstances, Su-yin didn't see that giving in to him would be entirely wrong. She felt much the same urges he did. So long as she didn't get pregnant or catch a disease, why not?

But she was in a contest with the Devil and it was one she was determined to win.

"This is a feint," Leonid said, during their next foil lesson. "I thrust and you respond with a parry four, knocking my blade outward, or so you expect." He demonstrated in slow motion. "But when you do, I dip my blade under yours and up again on the inside – and lunge." The button of his foil touched Su-yin's jacket, right above her heart.

He stepped back, pulling off his mask. "The whole purpose of the feint – of your Algerian, you understand my metaphor? – is to bring you off guard. To distract you from the real threat."

"Which is?"

"You'll recognize it when it happens. Provided you stay alert."

"Leonid, I never asked you this before, but... why are you doing this? Giving me advice, I mean. I know why you're giving me lessons."

"*Lasciate ogne speranza, voi ch'intrate.* 'Abandon hope, all ye who enter here.' It was very disappointing to discover that Dante's sign didn't exist, and even more so to discover that some faint ghost of hope remains. Your father no more deserves to escape here than I do. But if he did, that would be a kind of revenge upon Miss Spite, and I would derive some thin, sour satisfaction from that." Leonid shrugged. "That's all."

"Heads up again," Beelzebub said. "Young Lochinvar's hot for a second serving." And before Su-yin could respond, he was gone.

Sure enough, Rico asked her out again. "Just over to my apartment. To hang out. Nothing fancy. I won't try anything, I promise."

"I'll go if you want," Su-yin said. "But last time was such a disaster. Why repeat it?"

"Because being with you makes me feel better," Rico said. "Not happy, of course, that's not possible here. But less miserable. Sometimes I think that if only I could make you happy then I'd be happy too, almost. Just a little bit."

So she went.

Rico's apartment was every bit as squalid as she'd expected: filthy dishes clogging the sink, unwashed clothes kicked into the corners. But he'd made a sort of coffee table out of a crate and a Parcheesi board from a discarded pizza box. "I got the idea from you," he said. "From your fake flowers. The dice are made from that tasteless white root that Cookie uses in his stew. Turnip, maybe? Parsnip? The pips are stale peppercorns."

After so many dates with older men, Rico's youth – his callowness – was painfully obvious. He talked too much about himself. He knew nothing about what passed in Hell for current events. When Su-yin mentioned the race for the meaningless office of Persecutor General, he didn't even know who was running, much less which of the candidates had already bought the election. He gloated whenever the dice favored him.

Still, Rico didn't try to grope her, and played the game with real enthusiasm, and on those rare times when Su-yin managed to turn the conversation around to topics of interest to her, he listened to what she had to say with genuine interest. So it could have been worse.

When it was finally late enough that Su-yin figured she could call it a night without hurting Rico's feelings, she asked to be taken home. They walked back to her apartment building and when they got there, Rico said, "Tonight was really nice. I mean, it was almost pleasant. Really. It was easily the least awful time I've had since dying."

Su-yin blocked his clumsy attempt to kiss her. Then, she planted a swift peck on his cheek and fled inside.

"We should do this again sometime!" Rico shouted after her.

When she got back to the apartment, Su-yin cried

for hours. For the first time, her life here really did feel like Hell.

So it went. A blind date who took her not to a restaurant but to an orgy where old men stood about naked, waiting for young women to service them. Which they did, unenthusiastically and in a variety of ways that Su-yin could not have imagined six months earlier. She stayed for as long as she could stand to watch and then demanded to be taken home. Followed by a truly delightful evening with Jean-Luc. Then a man who liked to tear off his own scabs and eat them. A woman who said she wouldn't be a lesbian if it weren't for Su-yin and demanded to know how she planned to make it up to her. A Lord of the Inner Circles who was offended she hadn't heard of him. A creature of uncertain gender who suggested things that Su-yin didn't think she understood and certainly didn't want to do. Jean-Luc again, and a yacht party at which they played games where the losers were thrown into the acidic waters of the Acheron. Another sad evening with Rico, where they played pinochle with cards he had made from discarded paper plates, and he shared every regret he had from an innocently misspent youth.

All too slowly, the months passed. Sometimes the dates were so awful that Su-yin threw up afterward. Other times, they were not so bad. Always, she managed to be cheerful while she worked, whether she felt like it or not. Sticking it to the Devil was how she thought of it. Though, whether out of spite or a heavy workload, that Fearsome Lady never showed her face.

On the next to last evening of the competition, the Algerian told Su-yin to dress formal and then drove her out of town to a trash dump to shoot rats. Su-yin knew how to shoot because her father had insisted on it, and of course the Devil's penthouse had an indoor firing range, so she'd kept in practice. Still, it was a bit of a letdown. "I feel silly being here dressed like this," she said.

"Don't." Jean-Luc was carrying a matched pair of Anschutz bolt action rimfires. He handed her one. "The contrast only makes you look all the more elegant."

Su-yin checked the sight, made sure the rifle had a full clip, and thumbed the safety off. "How do we do this?"

"*Mes frères!*" Two men stepped out of darkness. Each carried a gasoline can. "Michel and Thierry will be our beaters tonight." He gestured toward a mound of garbage. "Let's start with that one."

The beaters trudged over to the mound and began sloshing gasoline on it.

"How this is done is as follows: When the garbage is set afire, it will drive out the rats living in tunnels within. They emerge with their fur aflame, so they are easy to spot. But they will be running as fast as they can, so they will not be easy to shoot. That's what makes it sporting. I'll target those that break right, you take the others. The winner is whoever pots the most rats. Ready?"

Su-yin raised her rifle. "I guess."

"Excellent." He raised his voice. "Light the fire!"

It should have been grotesque. It should have been disgusting. But against all expectations, it wasn't. Hell's rats were filthy creatures, even more loathsome than their terrestrial counterparts, so shooting them didn't make Su-yin feel bad at all. Plus, they were difficult enough to hit that there was genuine satisfaction when she did get one. By her third kill, Su-yin was laughing with every shot.

"To your left!" her beater cried as more rats shot, burning, from the trash fire. "Three!"

Su-yin led a flaming rodent with her rifle, squeezed

the trigger, and watched it flip over in the air. She made a slap shot at the second and missed, while the third got clean away. Another rat tried to escape and she got it in one. Then she was out of ammunition. She held out her hand and Thierry slapped a fresh clip into it.

"I pegged four," the Algerian said. "You?"

"Five. So far."

"I'm impressed." The Algerian's face glistened in the light of the trash fire, but he held himself with perfect aplomb. He might have been modeling his suit for a fashion shoot. "I think this mound's about played out. Time to light up a second one."

By the time they were done, Su-yin was sweaty and bedraggled and her dress reeked so of burning garbage she doubted it could be salvaged. But she was also ahead by a dozen rats. Michel and Thierry took their rifles and the Algerian led Su-yin back to his Maserati.

As he drove, the Algerian placed his hand on Su-yin's thigh and squeezed. She supposed she should have told him not to, but tonight had been so much fun – the only time she'd actually enjoyed herself since coming to Hell – that she felt she owed him at least that much. Anyway, it felt good.

At the door to her apartment building, the Algerian took Su-yin into his arms and said, "This is your last chance to invite me up to your room."

"Oh, Jean-Luc, you know I'd like to."

"Then do. It's that simple."

"I can't."

The Algerian released her, lit a cigarette, took a long drag, exhaled. "I swore I would wait until you beckoned me. I thought I had that much pride. But as it turns out, your self-control is stronger than mine. So it is I who must beg. Please. I know you are not... experienced. That doesn't matter. I can give you the first night every young woman deserves: passionate, romantic, lingering. Allow me to introduce you to the pleasures of being an adult in a manner you will cherish forever."

Su-yin found herself responding to his words more than she would have expected. Worse, when she tried to conjure up her father's image to help strengthen her reserve, she couldn't. After all this time, she was beginning, it seemed, to forget the General. This was a terrifying thought. But she could not deny it.

The Algerian's eyes twinkled cynically. The cigarette dangling from one corner of his mouth made him look every inch a scoundrel. The kind of scoundrel that women like. "By now we have spent enough time together," Su-yin said, "for you to know that when I say no I mean it."

"Oh, well. Alas." Jean-Luc shrugged. "Would you mind if I stubbed my cigarette out on the palm of your hand?"

"What? No!"

"*Quel dommage*." Taking her hand as if to kiss it, the Algerian stubbed out his cigarette on its back.

Back at the apartment, Leonid rubbed salve on her burn. "Tomorrow you'll wear gloves, of course."

"I can't believe Jean-Luc did that to me. I thought he was nice! And all the while..."

"He showed his true colors. He's gone. Forget him. Tomorrow is your final date. You can be sure that the Devil has something special in mind."

"Who will it be?"

"I don't know. Nobody tells me anything. One gets used to it. But your date will pick you up in the lobby at seven. Be on your guard. Remember everything I taught you. Whoever he is, he'll be almost irresistible. Resist him. Don't forget that your victory is my victory too. In a small, petty, and unworthy way."

The next night – her final one in Hell – Su-yin came home from work to find Leonid looking pale and fearful. "It was Her Nibs," he explained. "She came by and she was *not* in a pleasant mood." He nodded toward the bedroom. "She laid out a dress for you to wear tonight."

Draped across the bed was a silk gown of deepest scarlet. The skirt was long and had a slit up one side. Su-yin could see at a glance that she was not supposed to wear any underwear with it. The silk flowed like water; its thread count had to be astronomical. When she put it on, it fit her so elegantly that she felt three inches taller.

It made her feel wanton.

It took some time to get her makeup right. But when Su-yin slipped on her heels and, blushing, emerged at last into the living room, Leonid's astonishment made it all worthwhile. "I begin to understand," he said, "what heterosexual men see in you creatures."

Then he was fussing over her hair, pinning it up, *tsk*ing over imperfections that only he could see, speaking rapidly all the while. "Tonight's not going to be easy. The Devil has her wiles. Don't let yourself be drawn off guard. Think four moves ahead – five, if you can manage it. Watch the alcohol. Don't do drugs of any sort. There's no place to hide a weapon in that dress, but your do is held together with a hairpin that's as good a dagger in a pinch. You could kill a man with it, but I really think you should avoid doing that if at all possible. It would spoil your coif. Is this a split end? Don't think that you can get into a heavy petting session and pull out of it before it's too late. That's the oldest self-delusion in the book. Remember, Miss Venom will be watching. Don't do anything that would make her happy."

At last, he stepped back and said, "It'll do."

There was a triple mirror in one corner of the room. Su-yin stood before it, stunned, for one long minute.

Then, slowly, she spun about in order to see herself from every angle. She was perfect. She wished she could look like this forever. She knew she would remember this moment for the rest of her life.

Then the concierge called up to say that her date had arrived. Su-yin promised to be right down.

"Be on your guard!" Leonid called after her as she stepped into the elevator.

"I will!" she cried. "Don't worry!"

As the doors closed, she heard him say, "We don't know who you've been set up with, but we know he'll be dangerously hard to resist."

It was Rico.

He wore a baby blue tuxedo, which he explained was a rental. He also brought along a corsage, which he clumsily pinned to her gown. "How can you afford all this?" Su-yin asked, when the limousine pulled up.

"I've been saving up all year. No big deal. It's not as if there's much of anything else to spend it on."

They went to the Cavern, a boutique club with flashing lights, distressing art on the walls, and live nude dancers in iron cages hung from the ceiling over the bar. They looked a hundred times sexier than Su-yin would ever be but after his first glance Rico never looked at them again. All his attention was on her.

The music was hot and desperate when they entered and the club was thronged with sweaty bodies moving frantically. But when they stepped onto the dance floor, the tempo changed, so that they had no choice but to slow dance, holding each other close.

"You've been practicing!" Su-yin exclaimed. Rico was nowhere near as good as the Algerian, of course. But he didn't step on her feet even once. And though she could tell he was aroused – how not? her dress covered everything and hid nothing – he did not let it influence how he behaved toward her.

"Well, I didn't want tonight to be a fiasco like the last time. You know?"

By twos and threes, the other dancers drifted back to their tables, until finally there was nobody but just the two of them on the floor, holding onto each other and watched by hundreds of envious eyes. Above them, the women in their cages rubbed themselves against the bars, moaning with desire. At the bar, ice cubes rattled and drinks were poured. The band played slow number after slow number until, wearied, Su-yin suggested they take a breather.

When Rico broke free of her eyes, he seemed baffled to realize they had been dancing all alone. But he led Su-yin to a table, where she ordered a moonflower, a cocktail made from champagne, elderflower liqueur, and a peeled litchi, and Rico asked for a cola.

Once they were seated, the music grew raucous again, and the clubbers filled the dance floor to its capacity and beyond.

"So this is your last night, huh?" Rico said when their drinks had come.

"I guess."

"What are you going to do when you get back?"

"I hadn't given it any thought. Go back to school, I guess. A lot depends on what my father wants." It was, Su-yin realized with surprise, going to be difficult to go back to being a dutiful daughter after a year in which she'd been free to do whatever she wanted. She imagined the General would be grateful for having been saved from eternal damnation. But she didn't for an instant think that meant he would be any more permissive toward her. Certainly, he wouldn't let her go to clubs like this. The General had expected her to refrain from dating until she was in college – and only then because he knew he couldn't be there to watch over her.

Unexpectedly, Su-yin felt a twinge of regret for the freedoms she would be losing when she returned home.

She stood. "Let's go outside. I need some fresh air. Less stale air, I mean."

Out on the street, they wandered aimlessly down crumbling sidewalks and past shuttered buildings ugly with graffiti. Half the streetlights were out. When Rico tried to put his arm around her waist, Su-yin moved away from him. She didn't think so small a gesture would do any harm. But this late in the game she wasn't taking any chances.

They came to the waterfront and stopped. There, by the oily black waters of the Acheron, Rico found a discarded shopping cart, which they turned on its side and used for a bench. "I'll miss you," he said. "But it was kind of a miracle you were here in the first place, wasn't it? You don't feel the miseries or see the abominations the rest of us do. Just being in your presence I can imagine a little bit what it must be like to be you. Glorious."

Su-yin didn't feel the least bit glorious. But she refrained from saying so. She leaned lightly against Rico, cherishing his solidity, hoping the warmth of her body would provide him some small comfort. "Let's not talk about that. Tell me something else instead."

"Okay." After a brief silence, Rico said, "I grew up in Baltimore. People think that big cities are divorced from nature but that's not true. There are butterflies in the spring and in autumn the trees turn bright gold and red. Sometimes in the winter it snows so hard that all the traffic stops. The streets are covered in sheets of purest white and the silence... the silence is... I can't do this."

"What?"

"I can't do this to you. I'm sorry."

Rico stood and turned away from Su-yin, drawing her up in his wake. Carefully, she said, "What are you talking about?"

"The Devil came to see me today."

"Oh," Su-yin said.

"I'd never seen her before. But she walks in the door and you know who she is, don't you? She told me that if I could score with you tonight, she'd let me out of this place. You can't imagine how it felt, hearing that. She said that we'd leave the club and wind up here. That I should talk about my childhood, crap like that. That the words would just come to me. But this is not what I want. Well, I do want it. But not like this."

Rico looked so forlorn that Su-yin started to take him into her arms to comfort him. He was such a sweet boy, she thought, such an innocent. It came to her in that moment that she had a choice. She could free her father from Hell or she could free Rico. Either way, she'd feel guilty about leaving one of them behind. Either way, it would be an epic accomplishment. And if she were to choose Rico...

"You prick! You bastard!" Su-yin pushed Rico away from her and then punched him in the chest as hard as she could. "This is part of the script, isn't it?" All her emotions were in a jumble. She didn't know whether to laugh or to barf. "Well, you can just go – "

"Daughter."

Su-yin whirled, and there was the General, looming over her like a thunderhead. Her heart soared at the sight of him, even as she took an involuntary step back from his frown. She wanted to hug him, but even when he was alive that was an impertinence he would not allow in such a mood.

"Take a good long look at yourself, young lady. Out unescorted, at night, with this hooligan. Using bad language. Dressed like a prostitute. Living in... this place. Is this the life you imagine I had planned for you?"

"I – "

"I left you well provided for. Then I came here to be punished for doing things I should not have done. This is not only the way things are, it is the way they should be." The General wavered in Su-yin's sight like a candle flame, her eyes were so full of tears. "Do not speak! I am going to tell you what to do and you are to obey me without question. Do you understand?"

"I... yes."

"I have experience being in positions where there are no good choices. All you can do is negotiate the best deal you can. Have sex with this inappropriate young man. Then go home and never do anything shameful like that again. Many good women have such incidents in their past. Even your mother did things she later regretted." The General turned to Rico. "You."

"Sir?

"Give my daughter your hand."

He did so.

"Go into the nearest apartment building. The lobby will be clean and the doorman will give you the key to a decent room. There you will do what you must. There will be a condom on the nightstand – use it. Afterward, my daughter will lead you out of Hell. You can show your gratitude by never trying to see her again."

Rico nodded assent and turned to go.

But when he did, Su-yin did not follow. Pulling her hand free of his, she said to her father, "How do you know all this? About the room, the condom, the nightstand?"

"Don't ask foolish questions. Just do as you're told."

An icy rage surged up within Su-yin. "You're in league with the Devil, both of you. Maybe Rico doesn't know it, but you certainly do. Good cop, bad cop. One of you weak, the other harsh." When her father's face went hard as granite, he looked like a gaunt version of Frankenstein's monster. How could she not have seen this before? "After all I've gone through for you!"

Rico reached out pleadingly toward Su-yin. But the General shoved him aside. Then, unthinkably, he raised up a hand to slap her.

Su-yin screamed and flinched away. Before the slap could land, she kicked off her heels and ran. Barefoot, she sped down the street, away from the both of them, as fast as she could go.

Four moves ahead, she thought wildly. Don't let yourself be drawn off guard. The hell with Rico and, for that matter, the hell with her father too. She wasn't going to be fooled as easily as *that*.

Back at the penthouse, Leonid was waiting. "Well?" he said anxiously.

All the way up in the elevator, Su-yin had been a bundle of hysteria and misery, equally mixed. Now, however...

In trembling disbelief, she said, "I passed the test."

They broke out the Cristal and, laughing, drank down glass after glass. Leonid put on some music and they stumblingly danced the tango. Then they collided with the couch and tumbled down atop it and somehow they were kissing. Clothing got pushed this way and that way and then Leonid had his hands under her dress and she was fumbling with his zipper. It was wrong and she knew it, she'd never even thought of Leonid in that way, and yet somehow she couldn't seem to stop herself.

They did it right there on the couch.

It wasn't that great.

When they were done, Leonid gathered up his scattered clothes, dressed, and said, "It's almost midnight. I suggest you be out of Hell by morning."

Shocked, Su-yin said, "You... That was *planned*! All year you pretended to be my friend, when you knew from the start that you were going to... going to... do that."

"Believe it or not, I did you a huge favor," Leonid

said. "The Devil would never have let you win. If you had held out against me, she would have arranged for you to be very brutally gang-raped. The only reason that didn't happen as soon as you cut a deal with her was that she wanted to teach you a lesson. Let's be honest here: You never had a chance. The Devil likes to play games. But all her games are rigged."

He adjusted his cravat, bowed, and left.

Su-yin had been told to leave Hell and she would. But she hadn't been told how to go about it. So she went to see Rico.

His face brightened when he saw her in the doorway of his sad little apartment, then dimmed again when she told him the reason she had come. "Any direction you take will lead you away from here," he said. There was a hurt look in the back of his eyes, but he said nothing of what he must have been thinking. "You could just walk out."

"Like heck I could. I lost the challenge. I lost my father. I lost a year of my life. I am not going to spend a single minute more than I have to in this place. I want to be out of here just as fast as I can manage."

"I lost all that too," Rico mumbled, "and more."

Su-yin pretended she hadn't heard him. "What did you say?"

"I said yeah, I can help you."

On a shadowy street just off the clubbing sector, Su-yin stopped in front of a Lincoln Continental. She liked how it looked. Also, she wanted something big. "This one," she said. It took Rico only seconds to break into the Lincoln and hot-wire the ignition. "How about that?" he said. "I guess the old skills never go away."

"Open up the trunk for me, would you? I have something I want to put in the back," Su-yin said. When he had done so, she bent briefly inside. "Oh, no!" she cried. "I dropped my brooch, the one my mother left me when she died, and I can't reach it. Rico, you're tall..."

Rico leaned far into the trunk, groping in its dark recesses. "I don't see anything."

"It's way in the back. It bounced there." Su-yin waited until Rico was stretched as far as he could go and grabbed his ankles. With all her strength, she lifted him off the ground and toppled him over into the trunk. Then she slammed it shut.

A muffled voice said, "Hey!"

Su-yin climbed into the front of the car. As she did, a black streak of fur leaped over her and into the passenger seat. "You're not leaving without me," Beelzebub said.

"Of course not." Su-yin put the car into gear and started slowly down the road, ignoring the hammering from the trunk. "When we get home, I'm going to wash you and brush you and take a flea comb to your fur, though. Then I'll buy you a pint of cream."

"Make it a quart of scotch and you got a deal."

Su-yin shifted gears into second and then third. She sideswiped a parked Volkswagen van and, tires screeching, accidentally ran a red light. Luckily, there wasn't much traffic hereabouts at this time of night.

"Whoah!" Beelzebub cried. "Has anybody ever told you that you're the absolute worst driver in the universe?"

"You're the first." They were coming to the city limits now. Beyond lay what Su-yin was pretty sure was the Meadowlands. As they crossed into New Jersey, she floored the accelerator, sending two oncoming cars veering off the road to avoid collision. Then she pulled the Lincoln back into its lane and they were barreling down the road, a full moon bouncing in the sky overhead, only slightly out of control. She noted with satisfaction that Rico was still shouting at her from the trunk. Apparently, hot-wiring the car had been just enough to bring his karma into the positive digits. "I'm not doing too badly, though. Considering."

She had lost her father and she didn't think the pain of that would ever go away, not totally. But at least she had a boyfriend now. She wasn't quite sure just what one *did* with one, other than going dancing and having sex. But she'd find out soon enough, she supposed.

Su-yin rolled down the window to let the wonderful stink of marshes and rotting garbage into the car, reveling in the hot summer night, the way the wind batted her hair about, and the neon lights of Hell fading slowly behind her in the rearview mirror.

ANDY DUNCAN

A Diorama of the Infernal Regions or The Devil's Ninth Question

My name is Pearleen Sunday, though I was always called Pearl, and this is the story of how I met the widow of Flatland House and her 473 dead friends and sang a duet with the Devil's son-in-law and earned a wizard's anger by setting that wizard free.

At the time I did these things, I was neither child nor woman, neither hay nor grass. I was like a cat with the door disease. She scratches to be let in or scratches to be let out, but when you open the door she only stands halfway and cocks her head and thinks deep cat thoughts till you could drown her. Had I been on either side of the door that summer, things might have turned out differently, but I could not decide, and so the door stood open to cold winds and marvels.

Devil's Ways

I grew up in Chattanooga in Professor Van Der Ast's Mammoth Cosmopolitan Musee and Pavilion of Science and Art. Musee is the French word for museum, and cosmopolitan means citified, and Professor Van Der Ast was born Hasil Bowersox in Rising Fawn, Georgia. Whether his were the quality Bowersoxes, who pronounce "Bower" to rhyme with "lower," or the common Bowersoxes, who pronounce "Bower" to rhyme with "scour," I cannot say, for Professor Van Der Ast never answered to either. The rest of the name of Professor Van Der Ast's Mammoth Cosmopolitan Musee and Pavilion of Science and Art is self-explanatory, although the nature of science and art is subject to debate, and it was not a pavilion but a three-story brickfront, and I would not call it mammoth either, though it did hold a right smart of things.

You would not find the museum if you looked today. It sat in the shadow of the downtown end of the new Walnut Street Bridge across the Tennessee River. Years before, General Sherman had built a bridge there that did not last any time before God washed it away, but He seemed to be tolerating the new one for now.

I was told my parents left me in a hatbox in the alley between the museum and the tobacco warehouse. Two Fiji cannibals on their smoke break took pity and took me inside to the Professor, who made me a paying attraction before I was two years of age. The sign, I was told, read "Transparent Human Head! All Live and On the Inside!" What was inside was me, sucking a sugar tit with a bright lamp behind my head so my little brain and blood vessels could be seen. Every word on the sign was true.

A young girl like myself with no mother, father or schooling could do worse in those days than work in an educational museum, which offered many career opportunities even for girls with no tattoos or beards and all their limbs. Jobs for girls at Professor Van Der Ast's included Neptuna the Living Mermaid, who combed her hair and switched her tail in a pool all day, and the Invisible Girl, who hid behind a sheet and spoke fortunes into a trumpet, and Zalumma Agra the Circassian Princess, Purest Example of the White Race, who when snatched from the slave traders of Constantinople had left behind most of her clothes, though not enough to shut us down. Our Purest Example of the White Race in summer 1895 was my friend Sally Ann Rummage of Mobile, Alabama, whose mother had been a slave, though not in Constantinople. Sally Ann was ashamed of the museum and wrote her parents that she had become a teacher, which I suppose she had.

I had none of those jobs that summer because I was in that in-between age, and the Circassian Princess in particular was no in-between sort of job. No, I was so out of sorts with myself and the world that Professor Van Der Ast cast me entirely from the sight of the paying public, behind our Diorama of the Infernal Regions.

Now a diorama in those days was only a painting, but a painting so immense that no one ever would see it all at once. It was painted on a long strip of canvas 10 feet high, and to see it, you rolled it out of a great spool, like a bolt of cloth in a dressmaker's shop for giants, and as it rolled out of the first spool it rolled back up in a second spool about twenty feet away. In between the spools the customers stood shoulder to shoulder and admired the sights that trundled past.

The spools were turned by an engine, but someone in the back had to keep the engine running and make sure the canvas threaded smooth, without snagging and tearing – for your town may have had a fine new Hell, but Chattanooga's was as ragged and patched as a family Bible. That someone in the back was me. I also had to work the effects. As the diorama moved past, and as Professor Van Der Ast stood on the public side and narrated the spiel, I opened and closed a bank of lanterns that beamed light through parts of the canvas – to make the flames of Hell flicker, and bats wheel through the air, and imps and satyrs wink in and out of existence like my evil thoughts as I sweated and strained like a fireman in a furnace-room. Every day in the spotty mirror over my wash-stand upstairs, I rubbed my arms and shoulders and wondered what man would ever want a woman with muscles, and what man she might want in return.

Ours was the only diorama I ever saw, but Professor Van Der Ast said that one famous diorama in New York City was a view of the riverbank along the entire length of the Mississippi, from Minnesota to New Orleans. Park Avenue swells in boater hats could lounge in air-cooled comfort and watch it all slide past: eagle-haunted bluffs, woodlands a-creep with Indians, spindly piers that stopped at the overalled butts of barefoot younguns, brawling river towns that bled filth for miles downstream. Professor Van Der Ast himself had been no farther north than Cleveland, Tennessee, but he described New York's Mississippi just as well as he described Chattanooga's Infernal Regions. You felt like you were there.

"Observe, my friends, from your safe vantage point this side of the veil, the ghastly wonders of the Infernal as they pass before you. I say, *as they pass before you!*" (The machinery was old and froze up sometimes.) "First on this ancient scroll, bequeathed us by the Chaldean martyrs, witness the sulfurous vapors of Lake Avernus, over which no sane bird will fly. Here is Briareus with his hundred arms, laboring to drag a chain the width of a stout man's waist, and at the end of that mighty leash snaps the hound Cerberus with his fifty heads, each of his fifty necks a-coil with snakes. Here is the stern ferryman who turns away all wretches who die without Christian burial. Next are the weeping lovers wringing their hands in groves of myrtle, never to be reunited with their soulmates. Madame, my handkerchief. Your pity does you honor. Next is the whip of scorpions that flays those who believed their sins concealed in life. Here is the nine-acre giant Tityus, chained at the bottom of the abyssal gulf. Here are sufferers chin-deep in water they are doomed never to drink, while others are doomed to bail the water with sieves."

A weeping schoolmarm might ask: "But what about the realms of the blessed? the Elysian fields? the laurel groves?"

"For such consolations, madam, one must consult canvases other than mine. And here we have the writhing Pandaemonium of pleasure, where all noble and spiritual aims are forgotten in the base fog of sensation and lust. Next is the great – "

"Hey, buddy, could we have a little more light on that there Pandaemonium of pleasure?"

"This is the family show, friend, come back at ten. Here is the great wine-press in which hundreds of the damned are crushed together until they burst. Here are the filthy, verminous infants of ingratitude, which spit venom even as they are hoisted with tongs over the fire. Note, ladies and gentlemen, that throughout this dreadful panorama, the plants in view are all thorny and rank, the creatures all fanged and poisonous, the very stones misshapen and worthless, the men and women all sick, feeble, wracked and forgotten, their only music Hell's Unutterable Lament! Where all suffer horrid torments not for one minute, not for one day, not for one age, not for two ages, not for a hundred ages, not for ten thousand millions of ages, but forever and ever without end, and never to be delivered! Mind your step at the door, next show 2:30, gratuities welcome."

That was Professor Van Der Ast's side of the canvas, the public side. I told no one what I saw on my side: the patches and the stains, the backward paintings, the different tricks played by the light. I could see pictures, too, but only half-glimpsed, like those in clouds and treetops in leafy summertime. The pictures on my side were not horrible. I saw a man wrestling a lightning rod in a storm; and a great river catfish that sang to the crew in the gondola of a low-flying balloon; and a bespectacled woman pushing a single wheel down the road; and a ballroom full of dancing ghosts; and a man with a hand of iron who beckoned me with hinged fingers; and a farmer who waved goodbye to his happy family on the porch before vanishing and then, reappearing, waved hello to them again; and an angry face looking out of a boot; and a giant woman with a mustache throwing a man over the side of a riverboat; and a smiling man going over Niagara Falls in a barrel while around him bobbed a hundred hoodoo bottles, each with a rolled-up message for Marie Laveaux; and a hound dog with a pistol who was robbing a train; and a one-eyed man who lived in a gator hole; and a beggar presenting a peepshow to the Queen of Sheba; and a gorilla in a boater hat sitting in a deck chair watching a diorama of the

Mississippi scroll past; and a thousand other wonders to behold. My Infernal Regions were a lot more interesting than Professor Van Der Ast's, and sometimes they lighted up and moved without my having to do a thing.

My only other knowledge of magic at the time was thanks to Wendell Farethewell, the Wizard of the Blue Ridge, a magician from Yandro Mountain, North Carolina, who performed at Professor Van Der Ast's for three weeks each summer. I never had the chance to see his act because, as the Professor liked to remind us, we were being paid to entertain and not to be entertained, but I was told that at the climax he caught in his teeth a bullet fired through a crystal pitcher of lemonade, and I believe it was so because sometimes when a pinhead was not available, the Professor asked me to go on stage after the show and mop up the lemonade and pick up the sharp splinters of glass.

The tricks I saw the wizard Farethewell perform were done after hours, when all the residents of the museum went to the basement for drinks and cold-meat sandwiches and more drinks. I squirmed my way into the front of the crowd around a wobbly table made of splinters and watched as he pulled the Queen of Hearts out of the air and walked coins across his knuckles and floated dollar bills. "Just like the government," he always said when he floated a dollar bill, and we always laughed. He showed us fifty-seven ways to shuffle a deck of cards and seventeen of the ways to draw an ace off the top whenever one was needed, even five times in a row. "Do this in a gambling hall," he said, "and you'll get yourself shot. Do it among you good people, and it's just a pleasant diversion, something to make Little Britches smile."

That was what Farethewell called me, Little

Britches. He was the only one who called me that. Big Fred, who played our What-Is-It?, tried it once, and I busted his nose.

If the night wore on and Farethewell drank too much, he got moody and talked about the war, and about his friend, an older man he never named. "The 26th North Carolina mustered up in Raleigh, and I couldn't sleep that first night, without no mountains around to hold me, so I mashed my face into my bed-roll and cried. I ain't ashamed of it, neither. The others laughed or told me to hush, but this man, he said, 'Boy, you want to see a trick?' Now, what boy don't want to see a trick? And after he's seen it, what boy don't want to know how it's done?" As he talked he stared into space, but his hands kept doing tricks, as if they were independent of the rest of him. "At New Bern he taught me the back palm, the finger palm, the thumb palm; at the Wilderness the Hindu Shuffle and the Stodart egg; at Spotsylvania the Biseaute flourish, the Miser's Dream, the Torn and Restored. I learned the Scotch and Soda and the Gin and Tonic before I drank either one; and all through the war, every day, I worked on the Three Major Vanishes: take, put and pinch." As he said that, three coins disappeared from his hand, one by one. "So that was our war. It kept my mind off things, and maybe kept his mind off things, too. He had the tuberculosis pretty bad, toward the end. The last thing he taught me was the bullet catch, in the stockade at Appomattox, just before he died. I got one of his boots. The rest, they burned. When they turned out his pockets, it was just coins and cards and flash paper. It didn't look like magic no more. It just looked . . . It looked like trash. The magic went when he went, except the little he left to me."

Someone asked, "What'd you learn at Gettysburg?" and Farethewell replied:

"What I learned at Gettysburg, I will teach no man. But one day, living or dead, I will hold the Devil to account for what I learned."

Then he began doing tricks with a knife, and I went upstairs to bed.

My in-between summer came to an end after the last viewing of a Saturday night. As I cranked the diorama back into place, I heard the Professor talking to someone, a customer? Then the other voice got louder: "You ain't nothing but an old woman. She'll do just fine, you watch."

I could hear no more over the winding spool, and I did not want to stop it for fear of being caught eavesdropping. Then the Professor and the wizard Farethewell were behind the diorama with me.

"Shut off that engine, Little Britches. You can do that later. Right now, you got to help me." He had something in his hand, a tangle that glittered in the lamplight. He thrust it at me. "Go on, take it. Showtime was five minutes ago."

"What are you talking about?" It was a little sparkly dress with feathers, and a hat, and slippers with heels. I looked at Farethewell, who was drinking from a flask, and at the Professor, who was stroking his silver beard.

"Pearl, please mind Mr. Farethewell, that's a good girl. Just run along and put that on, and meet us in the theater, backstage." I held the costume up to the light: what there was of the light, and what there was of the costume. "Sukie can't help Mr. Farethewell with the ten o'clock show. She's sick."

"Dead drunk, you mean," Farethewell roared, and

lifted his flask. The Professor snatched it away. Something spattered my cheek and burned.

"Get as drunk as you like at eleven," the Professor said. "Pearl, it'll be easy. All you have to do is wave to the crowd, climb into the box and lie there. Mr. Farethewell will do the rest."

"The blades won't come nowhere near you, Little Britches. The box is rigged, and besides, you ain't no bigger'n nothing. You won't even have to twist."

"But," I said.

"Pearl," said the Professor, like there were fifteen R's in my name. So I ran upstairs.

"What's wrong with you?" Sally Ann cried when I burst in.

I told her while she helped me out of my coveralls and my blue denims and into the turkey suit. "What in the world are they thinking?" Sally Ann said. "Hold still, Pearl, if I don't cinch this you'll walk plumb out of it."

"My legs are cold!" I yelled.

The hat was nothing I would have called a hat. In a rainstorm it would have been no cover at all. I finally snuggled it down over my hair and got the ostrich plume out of my face. Sally Ann was looking at me funny.

"Oh, my," she said.

"What?"

"Nothing. Come on, let's go. I want to see this. Clothes do make a difference, don't they?"

"Not to me," I said, and would have fallen down the stairs if she hadn't grabbed me. "Who can walk in any such shoes as this?"

There's no dark like the dark backstage in a theater, but Sally Ann managed to guide me through all the ropes and sandbags without disaster. I carried the shoes. Just inside the backdrop curtain, the Professor made a hurry-up motion. I hopped one-legged to get the shoes back on and peered through the slit in the curtain, but was blinded by the lamps shining onto the stage.

Farethewell was yelling to make himself heard over what sounded like a theater full of drunken men. "And now, my lovely assistant will demonstrate that no cutlass ever forged can cut her, that she can dodge the blade of any cavalryman, whether he be a veteran of the Grand Army of the Republic – "

The crowd booed and hissed.

" – or whether he fought for Tennessee under the great Nathan Bedford Forrest!"

The crowd whooped and stomped its approval.

"Here she is," muttered the Professor, as he held the curtain open.

I blinked in the light, still blinded. Farethewell's big callused hand grabbed mine and led me forward. "Ladies and gentlemen, I give you Aphrodite, the Pearl of the Cumberland!"

I stood frozen.

The crowd continued to roar.

Lying on a table in front of us was a long box like a coffin, open at the top. A pile of swords lay beside it.

"Lie down in the box, honey," Farethewell murmured. He wore a long blue robe and a pointed hat, and his face was slick with sweat.

I walked to the box like a puppet and looked down at the dirty pillow, the tatty blanket inside.

"And if you don't believe me when I tell you how amazingly nimble Aphrodite is, why when I am done shoving cutlasses into the box, those of you willing to pay an additional fifty cents can line up here, on the stage, and look down into the box and see for yourself that this young woman has suffered no injury whatsoever, save perhaps to her costume."

The crowd screamed with laughter. Blinking back tears, I leaned over the box, stepped out of the shoes: first left, then right. I looked up and into the face of a fat man in the front row. He winked.

In my head I heard the Professor say: "This is the family show, friend, come back at ten."

I turned and ran.

The noise of the crowd pushed me through the curtains, past Sally Ann and the Professor. In the sudden darkness I tripped over a sandbag, fell and skinned my knees, then stood and flailed my way to the door and into the corridor beyond.

"Pearl! Come back!"

My cheeks burned with shame and anger at myself and the crowd and Farethewell and the Professor and Sally Ann and those stupid, stupid shoes; I vowed as I ran barefoot like a monkey through the back corridors that I would never wear their like again. I ran as fast as I could – not upstairs, not to the room I slept in, but to the one place in the museum I felt was mine.

I slammed the door behind me and stood, panting, behind the Diorama of the Infernal Regions.

Someone, probably the Professor, had done part of my job for me, and shut down all the lamps. It was the job I liked least, snuffing the lights one by one like candles on a cake. But the Professor had not finished rolling up the canvas. It was backstage dark, but up there on the canvas, at eye level, was a little patch of light, flickering.

I'm sure that when I went missing, my friends thought I had run away, but they were wrong. I was running *away* from nothing. I was running *to* something, though I did not know what it was. Running to *what* is the rest of my story – is all my story, I reckon.

I walked right up to the flickering spot on my side of the canvas. The tip of my nose was an inch from the paint. When I breathed in, I smelled sawdust and walnuts. When I breathed out, the bright patch brightened just a little. If you blow gently on a flame, it does not go out, but flares up; that's how the canvas was. I almost could see a room through the canvas, a paneled room. Behind me, a woman's voice called my name, but in front of me, I almost heard music, organ music.

I closed my eyes and focused not on the canvas, but on the room beyond.

I stepped forward.

Have you ever stepped through a cobweb? That's how I stepped out of Professor Van Der Ast's Mammoth Cosmopolitan Musee and Pavilion of Science and Art and into a place without a ticket booth, into my own canvas, my own Infernal Regions.

Not a funeral, a ball. The organist was playing a waltz.

I opened my eyes.

I was in a ballroom full of ghosts.

I reached behind to feel the canvas, to feel anything familiar and certain. Instead I felt a cold hard surface: a magnificent stained-glass window that ran the length of the wall, depicting mermaids and magicians and a girl at the lever of an infernal engine. Window and room spun around me. My knees buckled, and I sank onto a beautifully inlaid wooden floor.

The room wasn't spinning, but the dancers were. Fifty couples whirled through the room, the silver chandeliers and mahogany paneling and gold-leaf wallpaper visible through their transparent bodies. I never had seen such a beautiful room. The dancers were old and young, richly and poorly dressed, white and black and Indian. Some wore wigs and knee breeches, others buckskins and fur caps, others evening gowns or tailcoats. They didn't look like show people. All moved faster than their actual steps. No feet quite touched the floor. The dancers were waltzing in the air.

Against the far wall was a pump organ, and sitting at the bench with her back to me was a tiny gray-haired lady, shoulders swaying with the force of her fingers on the keys, her feet on the pedals. I tried to see the sheet music through her but could not. She was no ghost; she was substantial. I looked at my hand and saw through it the interlocking diamond pattern of the floor. That's when I screamed.

The music stopped.

The dancing stopped.

The old lady spun on her bench and stared at me.

Everyone stared at me.

Then the dancers gasped and stepped – no, floated – backward in the air, away from me. There was movement beside me. I looked up to see a skinny girl in a feathered costume step out of the stained-glass window. I screamed again, and she jumped and screamed, too.

She was me, and she also was becoming transparent.

"Five minutes break, please, everyone," trilled a little-old-lady voice. "When we return, we'll do the Virginia Reel."

The second Pearl had slumped onto the floor beside me. A third Pearl stepped out of the stained glass just as the old lady reached us. She wore an elaborate black mourning-dress with the veil thrown back to reveal chubby, ruddy cheeks and big gray eyes. "There, there," she said. "This won't do at all. The first rule of psychic transport is to maintain integrity, to hold oneself together." A fourth Pearl stepped from the glass as the old lady seized my hand and the second Pearl's hand and brought them together, palm to palm. It was like pressing my hand into butter; my hand began to sink into hers, and hers into mine. We both screamed and tried to pull back, but the old lady held our wrists in a grip like iron.

"Best to close your eyes, dear," the old lady said.

My eyes immediately shut tight not of my own doing but as if some unseen hand had yanked them down like windowshades. The old lady's grip tightened, and I feared my wrist would break. My whole body got warmer, from the wrist onward, and I began to feel better – not just calmer, but somehow fuller, more complete.

Finally the old lady released my wrist and said, "You can open your eyes now, dear."

I did, and it was my own doing this time. I stared at my hands, with their lines and calluses and gnawed-to-the-quick nails, and they were so familiar and so *solid* that I started to cry.

The ballroom was empty but for me – *one* of me – and the old lady kneeling beside me, and a single ghost bobbing just behind her, a little ferret-faced mustached man in a bowler hat and a checked waistcoat that might have been colorful once, but now was gray checked with gray.

"Beautifully done," said the floater. "You have the hands of a surgeon."

"The hands are the least of it, Mr. Dellafave, but you are too kind. Goodness, child, you gave me a fright. Six of you stranded in the glass. Good thing I was here to set things right. But I forget my manners. My name is Sarah Pardee Winchester, widow of the late William Wirt Winchester, and this is my friend Mr. Dellafave." She eyed my costume, reached over and tugged on my ostrich plume. "Too young to be a showgirl," she said, "almost."

I shuddered and wiped my nose with the back of my wonderful old-friend hand and asked: "Am I ... Are you ... Please, is this Heaven or Hell?"

The old lady and the bowler-hatted man both laughed. His laugh sounded like steam escaping, but hers was throaty and loud, like a much younger, much larger woman.

"Opinions differ," the old lady said. "We think of it simply as California."

She called the place Llanada Villa, which she said was Spanish for "Flatland House." I had never lived in a house before the widow took me in, so you might call Flatland House my introduction to the whole principle of houses. And what an introduction it was! No house I've seen since has been a patch on it.

There was the size, to start with. The house covered six acres. Counting the rooms that had been walled off and made unreachable except by ghosts, but not counting the rooms that had been demolished or merged into larger spaces, the house had a hundred and fifty rooms, mostly bedrooms, give or take a dozen. "I've slept in only seventy or eighty of them myself," the widow told me, "but that's enough to get the general idea."

Still the place was not finished. Workmen were always in the process of adding rooms, balconies, porches, turrets, whole wings; or in the process of dismantling or renovating what they had built just the month before. The construction had moved far away from the front of the house, where the widow mostly lived, but the distant sounds of saws and hammers and the men's voices calling to one another – "Steady! Steady! Move it just a hair to the right, please, Bill" – could be heard day and night. They worked in shifts around the clock. Once a week the foremen took off their hats and gathered in the carriage entrance for payday. The widow towed from the house a child's wagon full of heavy sacks, each full of enough gold pieces to pay each foreman's workers the equivalent of three dollars a day. The foremen were all beefy men, but even they strained to heft the bags and tote them away. They never complained, though.

"Aren't you afraid?" I asked the widow, that first payday.

"Of what, dear?"

"Of one of those men breaking into the house, and robbing you."

"Oh, Pearl, you are a caution! You don't need to worry about robbers, oh, no. Not in *this* house."

I suppose intruders would have gotten quickly lost, for many parts of the house simply did not make sense. Staircases led to ceilings and stopped. Doorways opened onto brick walls, or onto nothing, not even a balcony, just the outside air. Secret passageways no taller than the widow crisscrossed the house, so that she could pop in and out of sight without warning, as if she herself were a ghost. The widow told me the front door had never been opened, never even unlocked, since its hinges were hung.

I found the outside of the house even more confusing. If I walked around any corner, I found arched windows, recessed balconies, turrets and witch's caps and cupolas with red tile roofs, and miles of gingerbread trim. If I walked around the next corner, I found the same thing, only more of it. Many houses, I'm told, have only four corners to walk around, but Flatland House had dozens. Looking away from the house was no help, because no matter what direction I looked, I saw the same high cypress hedge, and beyond that, rolling hills of apricot, plum and walnut trees stretching to the horizon. I never made it all the way around the place, but would give up and go back inside, and where I went inside always seemed to be the breakfast-room, with the widow knitting in the wicker chair just where I left her. She always asked, "Did you have a good trip, dear?"

In all those hundred and fifty rooms was not a single mirror. Which suited me just fine.

I did get lonely sometimes. Most of the ghosts had little to say – to the living, anyway – beyond "Lovely day, isn't it?" The few indoor servants seemed afraid of me, and none stayed in the house past sundown. The workmen I was forbidden to speak to at all.

"Do you never have any visitors," I asked the widow, "other than the workmen, and the ghosts, and the servants, and me?"

"Goodness, that's enough, wouldn't you say? I know there are 473 ghosts, not counting the cats, and Lord only knows how many workmen coming and going. And don't ever think of yourself as a visitor, Pearl dear. Consider this your home, for as long as you wish to stay."

The only ghost willing to spend time with me, other than the cats, was Mr. Dellafave. Three weeks into my stay at Flatland House, during a stroll around the monkey-puzzle tree, I asked him:

"Mr. Dellafave, what did you do before . . ."

His face had the look of someone expecting his feelings to be hurt but game not to let on.

". . . before you came here," I finished.

"Ah," he said, smiling. "I worked for a bank, in Sacramento. I was a figure man. I added, mostly, and subtracted twice a week, and, on red-letter days, multiplied. Long division was wholly out of my jurisdiction, that was another floor altogether – but make no mistake, I could have done it. I was ready to serve. Had the third floor been swept away by fire or flood, the long division would have proceeded without interruption, for I'd had the training. But the crisis, like most crises, never came. I arrived at the bank every morning at eight. I went across the street to the saloon every day at noon for two eggs and a pickle and a sarsaparilla and the afternoon papers. I left the bank every day at five, and got back to the boarding house for supper at six. Oh, I was a clockwork, I was.

'You can set your watch by Dellafave,' that's what they said at the bank and the saloon and the boarding house and, well, those are the only places they said it, really, because those are the only places where anyone took any notice of me at all. Certainly that streetcar driver did not. He would have rung his bell if he had; it's in their manual. That was a sloppy business all around, frankly, a harsh thing to say but there it is. I know the time had to have been 12:47 precisely, because I walked out of the saloon at 12:46, and the streetcar was not due to pass until 12:49. I was on schedule, but the streetcar was not. I looked up, and there it was, and I flung up my arms – as if that would have helped, flinging up my arms. When I lowered them, I was standing in what I now know as Mrs. Winchester's potting shed. I was never an especially spiritual man, Pearl dear, but I considered myself fairly well-versed on all the major theories of the afterlife . . . none of which quite prepared me for Mrs. Winchester's potting shed. I didn't even bring my newspaper."

"But why – "

He held up a hand, like a serene police officer at an intersection. "I have no idea, Pearl, why I came here. None of us does. And I don't mean to imply that we're unhappy, for it is a pleasant place, and Mrs. Winchester is quite good to us, but our leaving here seems rather out of the question. If I were to pass through that cypress hedge over there, I would find myself entering the grounds through the hedge on the other side. It's the same front to back, or even up and down."

"I guess Mrs. Winchester is the magnet, and you and the others are . . ."

"The filings, yes. The tacks pulled from the carpet. I stand in the tower sometimes – if you can call it standing – and I look over all these rooftops and chimneys, all connected to the same house, and I'm forced to admit that this is more room than I allowed myself in life. If the boarding house were the front door of

Llanada Villa, the bank would be at the carriage entrance, and the saloon would be at the third sun porch, the one that's been walled in and gets no sun. Which is such a small fraction of the house, really. And yet the whole house feels such a small part of the Earth, and I find myself wishing that I had ventured a bit farther, when I could."

We walked together in silence – well, I walked, anyway – while I reflected that the owner of the house seemed quite unable to leave it herself. And what about me? Could I leave Flatland House, and were I to leave it, where would I go? Professor Van Der Ast's seemed much farther away than a single continent.

"You'd best get inside, Pearl. The breeze from the bay is quite damp today."

I moved my face toward Mr. Dellafave's cheek, and when he began to blur, I figured I was close enough, and kissed the air.

"Shucks," he said, and dissipated entirely.

I felt no bay breeze, but as I ran back to the house I clutched my shawl more tightly anyway.

The next day, the earthquake struck.

The chandeliers swayed. The organ sighed and moaned. The crystal chittered in the cabinets. One nail worked its way free and rolled across the thrumming floorboards. A rumble welled up, not from below the house, but from above and around the house, as if the sound were pressing in from all sides. The ghosts were in a mad whirl, coursing through the house like a current of smoke overhead, blended and featureless but for the occasional startled face. I lurched along the walls, trying to keep my balance as I sought the exit nearest me, the front door. Once I fell and yelped as my palms touched the hot parquet.

Plaster sifted into my eyes as I stumbled through the entrance hall. I knew my mistake when I saw that massive front door, surely locked, the key long since thrown away or hidden in a far scullery drawer of this lunatic house. If the entire edifice were to shake down and crush me, this slab of swirling dark oak would be the last thing standing, a memorial to Pearl.

The grandfather clock toppled and fell just behind me, with the crash of a hundred heavy bells. I flung myself at the door and wrenched the knob. It turned easily, as if oiled every day, and I pulled the door open with no trouble at all. Suddenly all was silent and still. A robin sang in the crepe myrtle as the door opened on a lovely spring day. A tall black man in a charcoal tailcoat stood on the porch, top hat in hand, and smiled down at me.

"Good morning," he said. "I was beginning to fear that no one was at home. I hope my knock didn't bring you too dreadfully far. I know this house is harder to cross than the Oklahoma Territory."

"Your knock?" I was too flabbergasted to be polite. "All that was your knock?"

He laughed as he stepped inside, so softly that it was just an open-mouthed smile and a hint of a cough. "That? Oh, my, no. That was just my reputation preceding me. Tell me, pray, might the mistress of the house be at home?"

"Where else would I be, Wheatstraw?" asked the widow, suddenly at my elbow and every hair in place.

"Hello, Winchester," the visitor said.

They looked at each other without moving or speaking. I heard behind me a heaving sound, and a muffled clang. I turned just as the grandfather clock resettled itself in the corner.

Then the widow and the visitor laughed and embraced. She kicked up one foot behind. Her head did not reach his chin.

"Pearl," the widow said, "this is Mr. Petey Wheatstraw."

"Pet-ER," he corrected, with a little bow.

"Mr. Wheatstraw," the widow continued, "is a

rogue. My goodness," she added, as if something had just occurred to her. "How did you get in?"

We all looked at the front door. It was closed again, its bolts thrown, its hinges caked with rust. No force short of dynamite could have opened it.

The man Wheatstraw nodded toward me.

"Well, I'll be," the widow said. "She makes as free with my house as a termite, this one does. Well, you haven't come to see me, anyway, you old good-for-nothing," she said, swatting him as she bustled past. "It's a half-hour early, but you might as well join us for tea."

Wheatstraw offered me an arm and winked. This was far too fresh for my taste, but I was too shaken by the not-quite-earthquake to care. As I took hold of his arm (oak-strong beneath the finery), I felt my muscles complain, as if I had done hard work. I looked over my shoulder at the seized-up door as Wheatstraw swept me down the hallway.

"I heard you were here," Wheatstraw said.

"How?"

"Oh, you're a loud one, Miss Big Feet, clomp clomp clomp." He winked again. "Or is that just your reputation I heard?"

Something was wrong with the corridor, something I couldn't quite put my finger on. Then I realized that it was empty. Everything in the house was back to normal – paintings returned to their nails, plaster returned to the walls – except the ghosts, which were nowhere to be seen. I was so used to them flitting past me and over me and through me, even gliding through my bedroom wall and then retreating with apologies, like someone who didn't realize the train compartment was occupied, that their presence hardly bothered me at all. Their absence gave me a shiver.

"They'll be back after I'm gone," Wheatstraw said.

I laughed. "You telling me you scared off the haints? I mean, are you saying that Mrs. Winchester's, uh, guests don't like you?"

"I'm sure they have nothing against me personally. How could they? Once you get to know me, I'm really a fine fellow, full of learning and grace and wit, a decent dancer, a welcome partner at whist. I never snort when I laugh or drag my shirtsleeves in the soup. No, it must be my business affiliation. The company I represent. The Old Concern. My father-in-law's firm, actually, and my inheriting is out of the question. But these days we all must work for somebody, mustn't we?"

I thought of Sally Ann the Circassian Princess, and of Farethewell's hand on mine. "True enough," I said.

Wheatstraw set down his teacup and saucer with a clatter and said, "Well, enough chitchat. It's question time."

"Oh, Petey," the widow said. "Must you? We were having such a nice visit. Surely that can wait till later."

"I am in no hurry whatsoever, Winchester, but my father-in-law is another story. You might say that impatience rather defines my father-in-law. It is the cause of his, uh, present career. Pearl, please pay close attention."

I said nothing, having just shoved another chocolate cookie lengthwise into my mouth. I never quite realized that I was always a little hungry at Professor Van Der Ast's, until I came to Flatland House.

Wheatstraw rummaged in the inside pocket of his jacket and produced an atomizer. He opened his mouth and sprayed the back of his throat. "La la la la la," he said. "La la la la laaaaa. Pitch-perfect, as ever. Winchester?" He offered her the atomizer. "Don't, then. Now: Pearl."

He began to sing, in a lovely baritone:

Oh, you must answer my questions nine
Sing ninety-nine and ninety
Or you're not God's, you're one of mine
And you are the weaver's bonny.

"Now, Pearl, when I say, 'one of mine,' please understand that I speak not for myself but for the firm that I represent."

"And when you say 'God,'" I said, speaking carefully, "you speak of the firm that you do *not* represent."

"In a clamshell, yes. Now, if you're quite done interrupting – "

"I didn't interrupt!" I interrupted. "You interrupted yourself."

He slapped the table. "The idea! As if a speaker could interrupt himself. Why, you might as well say that a river could ford itself, or a fence jump itself."

"Or a bore bore himself," the widow said.

"You're not helping," Wheatstraw said.

"And I'm not the weaver's bonny," I said, becoming peevish now, "whatever a weaver's bonny is."

"Well," Wheatstraw said, "a weaver is a maker of cloth, such as aprons are made with, and gags, and a bonny is a beauty, a lovely creature, a precious thing."

"I don't know any weavers," I said, "except my friend Sally Ann taught me to sew a button. And I'm not beautiful, or lovely, or precious."

"Granted, that does seem a stretch at the moment," Wheatstraw said. "But we mustn't always take things so literally. When you say, 'I'm a silly goose,' you don't mean you expect to be plucked and roasted, and when you say, 'I'm fit to be tied,' you aren't asking to be roped and trussed, and when you say, 'Well, I'm damned,' you don't mean . . ."

His voice trailed off. A chill crept into the room. The sunlight through the bay window dimmed, as if a cloud were passing.

". . . anything, really," Wheatstraw continued, and he smiled as the sun came out. "So, for purposes of this song, *if no other*, who are you?"

I folded my arms and forced my shoulders as far as I could into the padding of the loveseat and glared at Wheatstraw, determined to frown down his oh-so-satisfied smile.

"I'm the weaver's bonny," I mumbled.

Am not, I thought.

"Fine and dandy," Wheatstraw said. "Now, where was I? I'll have to go back to Genesis, as Meemaw would say." He cleared his throat.

Oh you must answer my questions nine
Sing ninety-nine and ninety
Or you're not God's, you're one of mine
And you are the weaver's bonny.

Ninety-nine and ninety *what*? I wondered, but I kept my mouth shut.

What is whiter than the milk?
Sing ninety-nine and ninety
And what is softer than the silk?
Oh you are the weaver's bonny
What is higher than a tree?
Sing ninety-nine and ninety
And what is deeper than the sea?
Oh you are the weaver's bonny
What is louder than a horn?
Sing ninety-nine and ninety

And what is sharper than a thorn?
Oh you are the weaver's bonny
What's more innocent than a lamb?
Sing ninety-nine and ninety
And what is meaner than womankind?
Oh you are the weaver's bonny

It was a short song, but it seemed to last a long time; as I sat there determined to resist, to be defiant and unamused, I realized I wasn't so much listening to it as being surrounded by it, filled by it, submerged in it. I was both sleepy and alert, and the pattern in the parquet floor was full of faces, and the loveseat pushed back and kneaded my shoulders, and the laces of my high-topped shoes led into the darkness like tracks in the Lookout Mountain tunnel. I could not vouch for Wheatstraw being a decent dancer as he claimed (though I suspected *decent* was hardly the word), but the man sure could sing. And somewhere in the second hour of the song (surely, I think now upon telling this, some lines were repeated, or extended, or elaborated upon), Wheatstraw's voice was joined by a woman's, his voice and hers twined together like fine rope. That voice was the widow Winchester's: *And you are the weaver's bonny.*

I sucked air and sat up as if startled from a dream, but felt less alert than a second before. The song was over. The widow pretended to gather up the tea things, and Wheatstraw pretended to study his fingernails.

"That part about womankind is insulting," the widow said.

"I didn't write it," he said. "The *folk* wrote it."

"Menfolk," she said.

"Eight," I said, and only after I said it did I realize

why I had said it.

"Hm?" Wheatstraw asked, without looking up.

The widow held a tipped teacup, looking at nothing, as a thread of tea like a spider's descended to the saucer.

"Eight," I repeated. "Milk, silk, two; tree, sea, four; horn, thorn, six; lamb, kind, eight." I sang, rather than spoke, in surprise at my voice: "*Oh, you must answer my questions nine* . . . It ain't questions nine, it's questions eight. What's the ninth question?"

Wheatstraw looked at the widow, and the widow looked at Wheatstraw. "Maybe that's it," Wheatstraw murmured. "'What's the ninth question,' maybe that's the ninth question."

"No," I said.

"Why no?" Wheatstraw cooed.

"Because," I said. "Because that would be stupid."

Wheatstraw laughed and slapped his thigh with his hat. The widow slammed two plates together.

"Indeed it would be," she snapped. "Petey, take these plates. Take them, I say. Do a lick of work for once in your lazy son-in-law of a life."

"So what's the ninth question?" I asked again.

"That's for you to tell us," Wheatstraw said.

"To tell *you*, you mean," the widow said, driving him from the room beneath a stack of dishes. "Don't drag *me* into this."

"Oh, excuse me, Lady Astor, whose house is it? The girl's a wizard, Sarah, and you can't stow a wizard in the china-cupboard like a play-pretty, like one of your ghosts, like Mr. Dellafave in there," he shouted as he passed a china-cupboard. Its door trembled, and someone inside squeaked.

"You know the rules," Wheatstraw continued as we all entered the kitchen in a clump. He dumped the dishes into the sink with a crash and whirled to face us. I tried to hide behind the widow, though she was a foot shorter. Wheatstraw pointed at her like he wanted to poke a hole in the air. His gentleman's fingernail was now long and ragged, with something crusted beneath, and his eyes were red as a drunkard's. "Just look at her," he said. "Just stand near her, for pity's sake! She's stoked with magic like a furnace with coal, and the wide world is full of matches. She's in a different world now, and she has got to learn." He turned to me. "Tea party's over, my dear. From now on, it's test after test, and you have your first assignment, your first nine questions."

"Eight," I said.

He threw back his head and roared like a bull. I clapped my hands over my ears and shrieked. Our dresses billowed as if in a strong wind. The cords stood out on Wheatstraw's neck. His hot breath filled the room. Then he closed his mouth, and the roar was gone. "All righty then," he said. "Eight it is. You owe the Old Concern eight answers – and one question." He jammed his hat two-handed onto his head down to his eyebrows, then sprang into the sink. He crouched there, winked, and vanished down the drain with a gurgle. His hat dropped to the porcelain and wobbled in place until it, too, was snatched into the depths. Wheatstraw's voice chuckled through the pipes, and ghosts flowed keening from the faucet.

"Showoff," the widow said. She squeezed my arm. "He's a liar, too. Absolutely terrible at whist."

"When he said I had to answer those questions, was that a lie, too?"

"Ah, no, that part was true enough."

"And the part about me being . . . a wizard?"

The widow smiled. "Truest of all," she said.

The Devil's Ninth Question

"All wizards have much the same talents," said the widow, as she washed the unbroken dishes and I dried them, "just as all carpenters, all painters, all landscapers do. But each wizard also has a specialty, some talent she is especially good at. Some work at the craft for decades before realizing what their specialty is. Some realize what it was only in hindsight, only on their deathbeds, if they ever realize it at all. But other wizards have their talents handed to them, almost from birth, the way we all are granted the earth and the sky.

"I myself was no taller than a turnip when I realized that many of the little friends I played with every day, in the attic and beneath the grape arbor and in the bottom of the garden, were children that others could not see, and I realized, too, that my parents did not like for me to speak of them, to say, 'Oh, Papa, how funny! Little Merry just passed through your waistcoat, as you were stirring your tea.' How cross he became that day."

She wrung dry a dishcloth in her tiny fists. I blew soap bubbles from my palm into the face of a sleeping tabby as it floated past. The bubbles bobbed through the cat, or was it the other way around? The widow had been scrubbing dishes with pumice, so the bubbles were reddish in color and seemed more substantial than the wholly transparent cat. Then the bubbles vanished, and the tabby remained.

The widow continued: "And so I began keeping my talent secret, and once you start keeping your talents secret, why, you're well along the path of the wizard."

"My talents are a secret even from me," I said.

"There now, you see how wrong you can be?" said the widow. She popped my shoulder with the dishtowel. "You play with dead cats. You converse with all my boarders. You unbind the front door and then bind it again without half trying. You come here from Tennessee in a single step, as if the world were a map you could fold. My goodness, that's a step even Paul Bunyan couldn't take, and Paul is a big, big man." After a moment's reverie, she shook her head and with a great splash yanked free the plug. "Well, that's done!" she cried over the rush of the emptying sink. "May it all go down Wheatstraw's gullet." She stood on tiptoe and kissed my cheek. Her kiss was quick, dry and powdery, like the dab of a cotton swab. "Never you fret, child," she said, taking my arm and leading me down the steps into the garden. "You've got talent to burn, as Mr. Winchester would have said. And now that you've begun to focus, well, you'll tumble across a specialty or three very soon, I daresay."

"Mr. Wheatstraw said I'm in a different world now."

The widow snorted. "Different world, indeed! You can't change worlds like garters, my dear. This is the same world you were born into, the same world you are stuck with, all the days of your life. Never forget that. But the older you get, and the more traveling you do, why, the more of this world you inevitably will see – and inevitably be *able* to see, I daresay."

"Because I walked through the diorama, you mean?"

"That was a powerful bit of traveling, indeed it was. Doubtless it broadened your mind a bit. Who knows? A few weeks ago you might have been as ignorant of the spirit world as my carpenters, might have looked right through Mr. Dellafave without even seeing him, much less being able to converse with him. And what a shame that would have been," she said, not sounding quite convinced.

I considered telling her that Mr. Dellafave was in love with her, but decided she knew that already. Instead, I finally dared to ask a question.

"Mrs. Winchester. In all these years since Mr. Winchester died, has he ever, well . . . visited?"

"Ah, that's sweet of you to ask, child," said the

widow, with a sniff and a toss of her head. "No, not yet, though early on I looked for him and listened for him, by day and by night. Especially by night. I confess I even hired a medium or two to conduct a séance – for those were all the rage, a few years ago." She waved absently as we passed a headless brakeman, who raised his lantern to her. "A phantom herd of buffalo might have stampeded through the parlor without those frauds noticing. And the mess! We mopped up ectoplasm for days." She leaned against the trunk of an English yew and stared, not unhappily, into the sky. "I finally concluded that Mr. Winchester – like my Mama and Papa, and my old nurse, and my little dog, Zip, that I had when we were first wed, and my poor child Annie – that I will be reunited with none of them until I'm as insubstantial as that lady in the pond over there."

In silence, we watched the woman as she rose from the water, stood a few moments on the surface, then sank out of sight amid the lily pads, her face unreadable. Her dress was from an earlier time. Where had all her lovers got to, I wondered, and what did she remember of them?

"I'll tell you the puzzle that worries me," the widow Winchester abruptly said, "and it's not Mr. Winchester, and it's not where all the dogs go. What worries me is that in all these years of receiving the dear departed in my home, I have met not one – not one – who was, in life, a wizard."

"Sarah!" the man yelled. "Sarah!"

The widow and I ran to the bay window in the parlor. I knew that voice.

A two-horse wagon had pulled up in front of the house, and a big man in a black suit and black hat was climbing out of it. It was a warm fall day, but his hat and shoulders were dusted with snow, and ice clung to the spokes of the wheels. The wagon was faded blue and covered with painted stars and crescent moons. The side read:

WIZARD OF THE BLUE RIDGE
MAGICIAN OF THE OLD SOUTH
PURVEYOR OF MAGIC AND MIRTH

He removed his hat and called again: "Sarah! I got him! I finally got him!"

It was Mr. Farethewell.

By the time we reached the front door – which the widow opened with a wave of her hand – a horse and rider had galloped up. It was Petey Wheatstraw, dressed like a fox hunter in red coat, white breeches and high boots.

"Winchester, do something!" he yelled as he dismounted. "Farethewell's gone crazy."

"Crazy, nothing," Farethewell said. "He's trapped like a bug in a jar."

"Who is?" the widow asked.

"Old Scratch himself!" Farethewell replied. "Here's your Devil."

He went to the back of the wagon and began dragging out something heavy, something we couldn't yet see.

The widow looked to Wheatstraw. "Is this true?"

He threw up his hands. "Who knows? No one's seen the Old Man in days."

Farethewell dragged the whatever-it-was a little closer to the end of the wagon, and an old boot thumped to the gravel. I stepped closer, out of the shadow of the porch.

"Well, hello, Little Britches," said Farethewell. "Sarah told me you were here. So you decided to pull some magic after all?" He pulled a flask from his jacket, looked at it, then laughed and flung it across the yard. It landed in the rosebushes with a clank.

"She told you?" I cried. I got behind a pillar. Just the sight of Farethewell made me feel flushed and angry. "You *know* each other?"

"Well, he *is* a wizard," Wheatstraw said.

Farethewell stood there, hands on hips, and looked pleased with himself. The widow peered into the wagon.

"Where is he? Is that his boot?"

Farethewell snatched her up and hugged her and spun her around. "That ain't his boot. That's him! He's in the boot! Come look, Little Britches!"

"Don't you call me that," I yelled, but I stepped off the porch anyway. Farethewell took hold of the boot with both rough hands and walked backward, hunched over, dragging the boot toward the house as if he dragged a big man's corpse. The boot tore a rut in the gravel.

"Couldn't be," Wheatstraw said.

"It is!" Farethewell said.

"Blasphemy," the widow said.

"Bad for business, anyway," Wheatstraw said.

Farethewell let go of the boot and stepped back, gasping, rubbing the small of his back with his hands. "I run him down in the Sierras," he said. "He'd a got away from me, if he had just let go of that chicken. Seven days and seven nights we fought up and down them slopes. The avalanches made all the papers. I've had this boot since Appomattox. It's my teacher's boot, hexed with his magic and with his blood. On our eighth day of wrestling, I got this jammed down over the Devil's head, and just kept on jamming till he was all inside, and now the Devil will pay!"

We all gathered around the boot.

"It's empty," the widow said.

Wheatstraw cackled. "Sure is. Farethewell, you are crazier than a moonstruck rat."

I did not laugh. Peering out through the laces of the boot was a face. The two blue eyes got wider when they saw me. The face moved back a little, so that I could see more of it.

It was Farethewell in the boot.

I looked over my shoulder. Yes, big Farethewell stood behind me, grinning. But the tiny man in the boot was Farethewell also, wearing a robe and pointed hat, as I last had seen him at Professor Van Der Ast's.

The little Farethewell hugged himself as if he were cold and began silently to cry.

"What's the matter, child?" the widow asked. I shrugged off her little spindly hand of comfort. It was like twitching free of a spider.

"What you see in there?" Wheatstraw asked.

"Tell them, Little Britches!"

"Don't take on so, dear. What could you possibly see? This has nothing to do with you."

"Maybe it does," said Farethewell. "Who you see in there, girl? What's this varmint to you?"

"What's his name this time?" Wheatstraw asked. "The Old Man answers to more names than the Sears and Roebuck catalog."

I didn't answer. Little Farethewell was backing up, pressing himself flat against the heel of that old floppy boot. I stepped forward to see him better, and he shook so, the whole boot trembled.

"He's scared," I said, more loud and fierce than I meant to sound, for in fact this scared me worse than anything – not that I was faced with a second Farethewell the size of a kewpie you could win with a ball toss, but that I was more fearsome to him than his larger self was. What kind of booger did he take me for? This scared me but made me mad, too. I snarled and made my fingers into claws like Boola the Panther Boy and lunged.

"Yah!"

Little Farethewell twitched so hard the boot fell over. The sole was so worn you could see through it nearly, and a gummy spot at the toe treasured a cigarette butt and a tangle of hair.

"He's ours," big Farethewell hissed into my ear. "Whatever face he's showing you, girl, whoever he once was to you, he is ours now and no mistake. All the way here, off the slopes and down the river and through the groves, it was all I could do to keep him booted and not kicking the boards out of the wagon, but now you got him broken like a pony. And a girl loves a pony. He's mine and yours together now."

"Don't listen," the widow said.

"Sarah. You forgetting what we got in there? You forgetting Gettysburg, Cold Harbor, Petersburg? The tuberculosis that carried off your William, the marasmus that stole Annie from the cradle? Don't you care what this *thing* has done to the world, what it still could do? Ain't you learned nothing?"

"Some things ain't fit to be learned," the widow said, "and some wizards breathing God's free air are cooped up worse than this creature is. Petey, tell him. You've seen worse than Cold Harbor, worse any of us."

Wheatstraw did not answer at once. He did not seem to be listening. He was in the act of dusting a metal bench with his handkerchief. He slowly refolded the handkerchief, then flicked off one last spot of dust and sighed and settled himself on the bench, perched on the edge as if delicacy alone could keep his breeches away from the iron. The moment he sat, a transparent cat jumped onto his lap and settled itself. Wheatstraw scratched between its ears as it sank out of sight, purring, until Wheatstraw was scratching only his leg.

"What I see," Wheatstraw finally said, "is that whatever half-dead thing you dragged in, Farethewell, it ain't yours anymore. It's Pearl's."

"Pearl's!" said Farethewell and the widow, together.

"Pearl's," Wheatstraw repeated. "Otherwise she couldn't see it, could she? So it's hers to do with as she will. And there ain't no need in y'all looking like you just sucked down the same oyster. Folks making up their own minds – why, that's the basic principle of the Old Concern, the foundation of our industry. And besides," he added, as he leaned back and tipped his felt hat over his eyes and crossed his legs at the ankles, "she's done made it up anyhow."

When he said that, I realized that I had.

"No," Farethewell said.

I picked up the boot. It was no heavier for me than a dead foot. The thought made me shiver.

"Wheatstraw," said Farethewell. "What have you done to me, you wretch? I can't move."

"It ain't my doing."

"Nor mine," said the widow.

"Pearl. Listen to me."

I held up the boot and looked at it, eye to eyelet. The trembling shape no longer looked much like Farethewell – more like a bad memory of him, or a bad likeness of him, or just a stain on a canvas that put you in mind of him, if you squinted just right. To whatever it was, I said, "Go home."

Then I swung the boot three times over my head and let it fly.

"Noooo!" Farethewell yelled.

The boot sailed over the fence and past the point where it ought to have fallen back to earth and kept on going, a tumbling black dot against the pale sky like a star in reverse, until what I thought was the boot was just a floater darting across my eye. I blinked it away, and the boot was gone.

Mr. Farethewell stared into the sky, his jaw working. A tear slid down his cheek. He began to moan.

"Whoo! Don't reckon we need wait supper on him tonight," Wheatstraw said.

"I knew it," the widow said. She snapped her fingers in Wheatstraw's face. "I knew it the moment she and her fetches stepped out of the ballroom window. Her arrival was foretold by the spirits."

"Foretold by the spirits, my eye," Wheatstraw said. "She's a wizard, not the 3:50 to Los Angeles."

Farethewell's moan became a howl.

I suddenly felt dizzy and sick and my breath was gone, like something had hit me in the gut. I tried to run, without quite knowing why, but Farethewell already had lunged across the distance between us. He seized my shoulders, shook me like a rag, howled into my face.

"I'm sorry!" I cried. "I had to do it. I had to!"

He hit me then, and I fell to the grass, sobbing. I waited for him to hit me again, to kill me. Instead the widow and Wheatstraw were kneeling beside me, stroking my hair and murmuring words I did not understand. Farethewell was walking jerkily across the yard, like a scarecrow would walk. He fell to his knees in the rosebushes and scrabbled in the dirt for his flask, the thorns tearing his face.

I stayed in bed a few days, snug beneath layers of goosedown. The widow left the room only to fetch and carry for me. Mr. Dellafave settled into a corner of the ceiling and never left the room at all.

When she felt I was able, the widow showed me the note Mr. Farethewell had left.

I never should have hit you, Little Britches, and I am sorry for it, but you never should have got between me and the Devil. Many women and children in Virginia got between the armies and died. Hear me. Farethewell.

"His fist didn't hurt you," the widow said.

"I know," I said. "Doing what I did with the boot, that's what hurt me. I need to find out what I did, and how to do it right. Mrs. Winchester?"

"Yes, child."

"When I am better, I believe I shall take a trip."

"Where, child?"

"All over," I said. "It was Mr. Dellafave's idea, in a way. I need to see some of the other things in the diorama, and I need to meet some other wizards. As many as I can. I have a lot to learn from all of them."

She pulled a handkerchief out of her sleeve and daubed her eyes. "I can't go with you," she said.

"But I'll always come back," I said. "And you mustn't worry about me. I won't be alone."

I considered walking back through the ballroom window, but I had been there before. I ran my finger over the pebbled face of the stained-glass girl to say goodbye.

When I walked out the front gate of Flatland

House, toting an overstuffed carpetbag, I half-expected to find myself walking in at the back, like Mr. Dellafave. But no, there were the orchards, and the lane leading over the hill to San Jose, and Petey Wheatstraw sitting cross-legged on a tall stump like a Hindu fakir.

I waved. He waved, and jumped down. He was dressed like a vagabond, in rough cloth breeches and a coarse shirt, and his belongings were tied up in a kerchief on the end of a stick.

"You're a sight," I said.

"In the future," he replied, "they'll call it *slumming*. Which way?"

"That way, to the top of the hill, and then sideways."

We set off.

"Also, Mr. Wheatstraw, I have some answers for you."

"Are you prepared to sing them? Anything worth saying is worth singing."

"I am."

"You're so agreeable this morning. It can't last." He sang:

Oh you must answer my questions nine
Sing ninety-nine and ninety
Or you're not God's, you're one of mine
And you are the weaver's bonny

I sang back:

Snow is whiter than the milk
Sing ninety-nine and ninety
And down is softer than the silk
And I am the weaver's bonny.

Heaven's higher than a tree
Sing ninety-nine and ninety
And Hell is deeper than the sea
And I am the weaver's bonny
Thunder's louder than a horn
Sing ninety-nine and ninety
And death is sharper than a thorn
And I am the weaver's bonny
A babe's more innocent than a lamb
Sing ninety-nine and ninety
And the Devil is meaner than womankind

–"And MAN kind too," I said, interrupting myself–

And I am the weaver's bonny.

Wheatstraw gave me a half-mocking salute and sang:

You have answered my questions nine
Sing ninety-nine and ninety
And you are God's, you're none of mine
And you are the weaver's bonny.

Then I asked him the ninth question, and he agreed that it was the right question to ask, so right that he did not know the answer, and together we reached the top of the hill and walked sideways, right off the edge of the world.

Just this year I made it back to Chattanooga. The town was so changed I hardly recognized it, except for the bend in the river and the tracks through the tunnel and Lookout Mountain over everything.

The Devil's Ninth Question

The new bridge is still hanging on, though it's no longer new and carries no proper traffic anymore, just visitors who stroll along it and admire the view and take photographs. Can you call them photographs anymore? They need no plates and no paper, and you hardly have to stand still any time to make one.

At the end of my visit I spent a good hour on the bridge, looking at the river and at the people, and enjoying walking my home city on older, stronger legs and seeing it with better eyes and feeling more myself than I had as a girl – though I'm still not as old-looking as you'd expect, thanks to my travels and the talents I've picked up along the way.

How you'd *expect* me to look at my age, I reckon, is *dead*, but I am not that, not by a long shot.

I wondered how many of these young-old people creeping along with the help of canes, and candy-faced children ripping and roaring past me, and men and women rushing along in short pants, my goodness, their stuck-out elbows going up and down like pistons – how many of them dreamed of the world that I knew. But what had I known myself of the invisible country all around, before I passed into the Infernal Regions?

Up ahead, sitting on one of the benches along the bridge, was a girl who put me in mind of my old Chattanooga friend Sally Ann Rummage, with her red hair and her long neck and her high forehead like a thinker. Probably about sixteen, this girl was, though it's hard to tell; they stay younger so much longer now, thank goodness. She didn't look very happy to be sixteen, or to be anything. A boy was standing over her, with one big foot on the bench like he was planting a flag, and he was pointing his finger in her face like Petey Wheatstraw was known to do, and his other hand was twisting her pretty brown jacket and twisting her shoulder, too, inside it, and she looked cried-out and miserable. He was telling her about herself, or presuming to, and when he glanced my way – no more seeing me than he would a post or a bird or a food wrapper blowing past – I saw that he was Farethewell. He was high-cheeked and eighteen and muscled, where Farethewell was old and jowly, and had a sharp nose unlike Farethewell, and had nothing of Farethewell's shape or face or complexion, but I recognized him just the same. I would recognize Farethewell anywhere.

I stood behind him, looking at her, until she looked up and met my gaze. This is a good trick, and one that even non-wizards can accomplish.

The boy said to me something foul that I will not lower myself to repeat, and I said, "Hush," and he hushed. Of all the talents I've learned since I left Flatland House, that may be the handiest.

The girl frowned, puzzled, her arms crossed tight to hold herself in like a girl I once knew in a California parlor long ago. I smiled at her and put in her head the Devil's ninth question:

Who am I?

And while I was in there, in a thousand places, I strewed an answer like mustard seeds: *I am the weaver's bonny.*

Then I walked on down the bridge. The sun was low, the breeze was sharp, and a mist was forming at the river bend, a mist only I could see. The mist thickened and began to swirl. The surface of the water roiled. In the center of the oncoming cloud, twin smokestacks cleaved the water, then the wheelhouse, then the upper deck. The entire riverboat surfaced, water sluicing down the bulkheads, paddlewheel churning. I could read the boat's bright red markings. It was the *Sultana*, which blew up in 1865 just north of Memphis, at the islands called the Hen and Chickens, with the loss of 1,700 men. And my, did she look grand!

At the head of the steps to the riverfront, I looked back – for wizards always look back. Have I not been looking back since I began this story, and have you not been looking back with me, to learn the ways of a wizard? I saw the girl striding away from the boy, head held high. He just stood there, like one of Professor Van Der Ast's blockheads with a railroad spike up his nose. The girl whirled once, to shout something at him. The wind snatched away all but one word: " – ever!" Then she kept on walking. The mustard was beginning to sprout. I laughed as loudly as the widow Winchester, and I ran down the slick steps to the river, as giddy as a girl of ninety-nine and ninety.

CURTIS C. CHEN

One Of Our Angels Is Missing

The Devil has a twin brother named Stanley. Satan-Ley, the Fifth and final Aspect of the Devil, made in Lucifer's image. It had been Lou's cruel joke to leave his twin with nothing but a title for a name.

Stan lived by himself, on top of a mountain deep in the south side of Hell, and he was surprised to get a visitor all the way from the Capitoline. Miika, a female Draconis, landed on his balcony and knocked on the sliding glass door to be let in.

She brought unsettling news about Stan's brother.

"Lou got *summoned*?" Stan put the tea tray on his coffee table and sat down across from his guest. "I thought that summoning stuff didn't work no more."

"It's not supposed to." Miika said, folding her leathery wings behind her back and settling down on his settee.

Stan looked at her curiously. He had never met one

of the Serpent Guard before, and he wondered if Miika's scales covered all her… bits under her armor. "Ain't that why me and the four stooges live where we do? To form a protective conflagration or somethin'?" The Five Aspects of the Devil, Stan and the four others, were always connected to each other by invisible lines of force – *ley* lines forming a pentagram, the protective sigil covering Hell. That was why each Aspect resided in a separate, distant domain of the underworld. By maintaining this arcane configuration, Lucifer's kingdom was shielded from heavenly interference. Or so it was supposed to be.

"Indeed," Miika said. Her eyes kept changing color, which made it hard for Stan to read her expression. "You haven't been reading any holy books, have you? Keeping pet birds? Rearranging the furniture?"

"Course not," Stan said, mildly offended. "I know the rules. Never break the circle, never speak The Name – "

"I'll need to cast some runes," Miika said. "Just to make certain. You understand. You're the last of the Five, and I need to rule everything out."

"Yeah, you do what you gotta do. Make yourself at home." The timer on the table dinged. "Tea's ready. You take milk and sugar?"

"Just one slice of lemon, please." Miika started unpacking her runes, a mixture of polished stones and bone fragments.

"Lemon," Stan grumbled. "Coming right up."

He walked back into the kitchen and opened the icebox. He always kept some firstfruit on hand for when Yevgenia visited, which wasn't often these days, now that she was in the Tartars, but having the little round lumps on hand reminded Stan of her, and that was nice too.

He picked up a firstfruit, whispered to it, and watched it shape itself into a fresh yellow citrus. His nose wrinkled at the scent. He sliced it up, arranged the pieces on a lime green plate, and brought that back into the parlor.

Miika looked up from where she knelt on the carpet, studying the runes she'd cast. Her eyes seemed brighter than before.

"What have you done?" she said in a deep, rumbling voice.

Stan looked down at the plate of lemon slices. "Are they too thin?"

Miika stood and unfurled her leathery wings as Stan approached. "Where are the other four Aspects?" She clapped her hands together. A whirlwind of lightning blazed into being around Stan, constricting him in spiky blue-white spirals.

"What the – " Stan frowned at Miika. "What are you doing?"

"I have my orders," Miika said. "You will accompany me back to the Capitoline."

"I ain't goin' nowhere with you, lady." Stan snapped his fingers, and an invisible hand slapped Miika sideways through the plate glass door and over the edge of the balcony.

The lightning around Stan sputtered and fizzled out.

He walked onto the balcony and looked down over the railing. Miika was flying away, like a giant bat in a hurry.

"There goes my afternoon," Stan muttered. He grabbed his jacket and started the long walk down the mountain.

It takes a solid half hour for a human-sized person to walk from Stan's apartment on the peak down to the lobby at ground level. The staircase spirals around the bulk of the mountain, a tunnel bored through rock with small windows at irregular intervals. As Stan proceeded down the steps, feeling his weight increase and smelling more and more of the sulfurous odors from the nearby fire-pits, he smiled. He had forgotten how nice it was on the ground. He took a moment to enjoy the rancid air before going into the lobby.

Ronnie, the watchman, was not sitting behind his desk. He stood between Stan and the exit, holding his long wooden guard-staff in one hand.

"Good afternoon, Mister Stanley." Ronnie's other hand reached into his vest pocket. "Everything all right?"

"Long story," Stan said. "I'm just going for a walk. Be back soon."

Ronnie shook his head. "I'm sorry, Mister Stanley, I can't let you do that."

Stan took a step toward the exit. Ronnie tipped his staff forward, and the beast-head carved into the knot of wood at its end quivered. Stan thought about taking another step, then thought better of it.

"So I'm a prisoner here?" Stan said.

"Of course not, Mister Stanley." Ronnie pulled his staff back. "I just think, with whatever's going on with your brother, it'd be safer for you to stay here. Indoors. Protected."

"I don't need protection."

"That's what your brother thought. And where is he now?"

Stan glared. Ronnie fidgeted with something in his pocket. That was kind of odd. Stan shrugged off his jacket.

"Okay," he said. "Thanks for watchin' out for me, Ronnie."

"It's what I'm here for, Mister Stanley."

"Could you maybe make a phone call for me?" Stan asked. He wasn't allowed to keep any communication devices in his home, a restriction he normally appreciated. Staying away from the heart of Hell made for a more relaxing existence.

Ronnie hesitated for a split second before answering. "Wish I could, Mister Stanley. Whatever's happening out there also knocked out my telephone. Repair demon's on the way. I'll let you know as soon as it's fixed."

Stan nodded. "Oh, yeah, I do have a couple'a maintenance things. My icebox is on the fritz again, and that glass door on my balcony got, uh, damaged."

Ronnie frowned. "Broken glass? You're not hurt, are you, Mister Stanley?"

"Nah, I'm fine. It, uh, broke from the inside out."

Ronnie chuckled. "Part of that 'long story' you mentioned?"

"Yeah."

"No problem." Ronnie turned away, toward his desk. "Let me just write those up – "

Stan threw his jacket over the top of the guard-staff, covering the beast-head, then bashed his fist into the base of Ronnie's skull. The watchman crumpled to the ground, and Stan followed him down to make sure he was out cold.

Satisfied that Ronnie wouldn't cause any more trouble, Stan retrieved his jacket, kicked the staff away, and pulled Ronnie's hand out of his vest pocket. Between his fingers was a small, silver coin stamped with runes on one side and a stylized bird on the other.

"Well, shit," Stan said. Only one group in Hell used silver doves as currency, and they shouldn't have been anywhere near Stan's mountain.

He pocketed the coin and started toward the exit. Halfway there, he had another thought and went back to Ronnie's desk. Stan lifted the telephone handset to his ear and heard a steady dial tone.

"Right," Stan muttered, and dialed the only number he knew. He heard three rings before someone picked up.

"I speak for the Morning Star," said a sultry female voice.

"This is Stanley. Lemme talk to whoever's in charge over there."

"I'm sorry, sir," the voice said. "The Prince of Lies is not available at this time. May I take a message?"

"I know *he's* not available," Stan said. "You know who I am, right? The Fifth Aspect? I wanna talk to *your* boss. Now."

"If you have a complaint, sir, I can transfer you to our customer service department."

"No," Stan said, enunciating carefully, "I want to talk to your *supervisor*, you idiotic homunculus."

"Thank you, sir," the voice said. "Please hold for customer service."

"No, wait, don't – "

The line clicked, and an instrumental, slow-jazz version of "Highway to Hell" filled Stan's ear and began eroding his will to live.

"Aw, fuck this," he said.

He slammed down the phone and walked outside.

Some may think of the underworld as chaotic and undisciplined, but it is in fact quite orderly. It must be, in order to serve each of its resident populations appropriately. There are the demons, and there are the dead; and among the dead there are the newly deceased, who need proper initiation into their eternal torment, and the longtime residents, whose experiences need to be re-calibrated from time to time to ensure maximum efficacy.

And then there are the angels.

The Fallen live in Tartarus. It is not a prison. It is a land of the exiled, those who must be kept separate but cannot be punished. No one knows the precise details of the arrangement between The Devil and The Name for housing those who periodically fall from Heaven's grace, but Lucifer himself was once an angel, and it is difficult to deny one's heritage.

On the other hand, everyone in Hell knows of the Tartars, those who guard the angels' cage. No one goes in or out of Tartarus without their knowledge and permission, and the consequences for flouting their authority are severe. But Stan wasn't worried when he approached the main guard house at Tartarus.

He asked for Yevgenia by name. There were more guards on duty than usual, and it took them a while to disengage from their duties and call Yevgenia to the gate. Stan passed the time in the waiting room by thumbing through a four-month-old issue of *In Touch Weekly*.

"Stanley!" Yevgenia hissed from the doorway. She wore full battle armor and clutched her helmet under one arm. Her face glistened with sweat, as if she'd been running around. Stan thought she looked beautiful. "What in the blue-sky are you doing here? You shouldn't be off the mountain!"

"Nice to see you, too, Evie," Stan said. He dropped the magazine and stood. "We prob'ly shouldn't talk here."

"*You* shouldn't be *outside*." Yevgenia grabbed Stan's arm and put on her helmet. "I'm taking you home."

"I need to show you something first."

Yevgenia squinted at him. "Keep it in your pants, Stanley. Wait until we're somewhere more private."

"Sheesh, Evie, get your mind out of the gutter." Stan pulled the silver coin out of his pocket. "You know what this is?"

"Judas Priest, Stanley!" Yevgenia closed her fist around the coin, then looked around nervously. "Where did you get this?"

"Yeah, it's a funny story," Stan said. "I took it off Ronnie. You know Ronnie, my doorman? He didn't want me to go outside neither. He also lied to me about the phones bein' dead. What's goin' on, Evie?"

"It's bad," Yevgenia said. "You know your brother disappeared."

"Yeah, he got summoned, I've heard."

Yevgenia shook her head. "No. We don't know what happened, but it was definitely *not* a summoning. Your brother presided over morning rituals as usual, but his ten o'clock appointment walked into an empty office. No residue, no afterglow. It wasn't The Name."

Stan blinked. "No way. Who in any world could kidnap Lou? Ain't nobody around here got that kind of power. It's impossible."

"'Impossible' is a strong word," Yevgenia said. "Somebody bribed your doorman with a *columba argenta*. And one of our angels is missing."

"What, like escaped?"

Yevgenia grumbled and tucked the coin away inside her armor. "Let's go talk to Ronnie before any other birds try to fly the coop."

"Water and ice, Stanley," Yevgenia said, "what did

you do to him?"

"I only banged him up a little bit," Stan said. "Gimme your smelling salts."

They were in the lobby of Stan's mountain, kneeling on either side of the unconscious Ronnie, whom they'd propped up against the marble wall behind his desk. Yevgenia adjusted her armor, pulled a vial off her equipment belt, and handed it to Stan. He popped the cork and held the tiny bottle under Ronnie's nose.

"Wha – !" Ronnie yelped. He looked from Stan to Yevgenia and back again. "Oh no."

"Heya, Ronnie," Stan said. "You remember Evie?"

"Of c-course," Ronnie said. "Good to see you again, Miss Yevgenia."

"I wish I could say the same, Ronnie." Yevgenia held up the silver dove coin. "Who gave you this?"

Ronnie shook his head. "I can't say."

Stan put a hand around Ronnie's throat. "You know Evie's a Tartar, right, Ronnie? She's authorized to use lethal force at her digression."

"Discretion," Evie said.

"Yeah, that too," Stan said. "Evie can take down an *angel* if she needs to, Ronnie. But she don't need you to be in one piece to question you. We can just remove your head, bring that back to one'a her dungeons, and continue this conversation there."

"Please, Mister Stanley," Ronnie rasped. "I would tell you if I could. They – *they* did this to me, when they gave me that coin. It wasn't a payoff. It was cursed. *I can't say.*"

Stan relaxed his grip and looked at Yevgenia. "You buyin' this?"

Yevgenia studied the coin. "It's possible. An angel could have done something to the silver that I can't detect."

Stan turned back to Ronnie. "Okay, so you can't say exactly who it was. Was it an angel? Yes or no."

Ronnie struggled briefly. "I c-can't. I'm so sorry, Mister Stanley."

"Wait." Yevgenia leaned forward. "You said 'they.' Was there more than one?"

Ronnie's eyes widened, and he nodded.

"How many?" Yevgenia asked.

Ronnie gurgled, then held up one hand, fingers splayed.

"Five?" Yevgenia said. "There were five of them?"

Ronnie nodded again, dropped his hand, and gasped for breath.

"Okay, just rest there for a minute." Yevgenia patted Ronnie's shoulder and gestured to Stan. She stood up and walked around the desk. Stan followed her.

"This is bad," she said, tapping two fingers on her sword hilt.

"Yeah, I thought you said only one angel was missing," Stan said. "Maybe you guys missed the other four?"

Yevgenia gave him a peeved look. "Anyone in Tartarus so much as flutters a wing, and alarm bells go off. We knew about the missing bird immediately. The cage is in full lockdown. All the other Fallen have been accounted for."

"Then your escapee is workin' with people on the outside," Stan said.

"Yeah," Yevgenia said. "That's bad."

"So tell me about this missing – "

The lobby doors burst inward in a shower of wood splinters and stone shards. Yevgenia threw her arms around Stan and hurled him to the ground, landing on top of him. Stan might have enjoyed it, except for all the heavy armor and the fact that a horde of armed Draconis, led by Miika, stormed into the lobby and surrounded them.

"By the authority of The Wicked One," Miika said, her eyes glowing red, "the Serpent Guard now takes you both into custody. You will cooperate, or we will bind you. I do not care which. Choose."

Yevgenia rolled off Stan into a kneeling position, but kept a hand on his chest. "We'll cooperate," she said, shooting him a warning look. "No binding."

Stan grumbled as the Draconis dragged him to his feet and led the way out.

"Tell me again why we cooperated?" Stan muttered.

"Shh." Yevgenia held up a hand and closed her eyes.

They stood in a cold, empty stone chamber. Stan didn't hear anything except water dripping in the corner and the rumbling of a brimstone furnace nearby. They were both naked and each confined to a small circular area by pentagrams which the Draconis had scrawled into the ground. Stan tried to look on the bright side by admiring Yevgenia's body, but it was difficult to get turned on right now.

"What are you listenin' for?" Stan asked.

Yevgenia opened her eyes and shook her head. "I was trying to determine whether I could breach this," she said, pointing at her pentagram. "No such luck. Those Draconis are well trained."

Stan grunted. "We coulda taken 'em."

"Thirteen dragons in full riot gear? Not worth the risk," Yevgenia said. "We're safer here in the Capitoline. Whoever's behind this coup attempt needs you and the four other Aspects to subdue The Dark Lord. However they have him trapped now, it won't last for long. And when they eventually come looking for you, we'll have the entire Serpent Guard to protect us."

"Unless they're in on it, too."

"Don't be ridiculous," Yevgenia said. "The Draconis are The Adversary's most loyal servants. Them turning on him would be–"

"Impossible?" Stan said. "Like Lou being abducted right out of his office was *impossible*?"

Yevgenia grimaced. "I was going to say 'unthinkable.'"

"Yeah, well, I'm thinking about it right now," Stan said. "I'm thinking real hard."

The heavy lock on the dungeon door clanged, and then the door itself creaked open. Miika and three other Draconis walked into the room, their hands resting on the longswords slung at their sides.

An angel followed them in.

"Fuck," Yevgenia said. "That's our missing bird."

Stan had never seen an angel up close. He was more brilliant and awesome than Stan could have imagined. It wasn't just the lustrous aura, or the alabaster wings, or the inscrutable and radiant face. There was something about the way the angel moved – *glided* – across the floor, the way his limbs undulated in harmony with each other, a coordinated and endless dance of perfect motion that turned Stan's stomach.

Fuckin' A, is this what everything's like in Heaven? Stan tried to imagine an entire world full of unnatural beings like this one – or even just one city. *Judas, how does Evie walk around Tartarus all freakin' day without losin' her lunch?*

Behind the angel, the other four Aspects of the Devil filed into the room. The Snake, slithering with endless golden-green coils; a pillar of thick, dark Smoke that reached from floor to ceiling; a miniature yellow star of roiling Fire; and the Beast, a grotesque, swarthy bulk of matted fur.

"Double fuck," Yevgenia muttered.

"Aw, crap." Stan glared at Miika. "You lied to me. You knew where the Aspects were all along. You just wanted to make sure I was still in the dark."

The Draconis did not respond.

The Snake slithered over to the edge of Stan's pentagram and raised its head to Stan's eye level, flashing its fangs.

"Hey, Snakey," Stan said. "Who's your pale-faced friend?"

The angel spoke in a voice that hurt Stan's ears. "*I AM WEDRIEL.*"

"Ow," Stan said. "You wanna dial back the divinity there, fella? Don't forget where you are."

"I apologize," Wedriel said in a less magnificent tone. "But I'm afraid you'll have to get used to my voice. We're making some changes around here."

Stan ignored him and stared at the other Aspects. "And you chumps are okay with this?"

The Aspects did not respond. They simply hovered there, silent and stationary.

This was bad. Each Aspect was supposed to stay on its own mountaintop, like Stan, anchoring one point of the protective star which shielded the central regions of the nether world – and Lucifer himself – from excessive scrutiny by The Name and his minions. Putting them all in one place…

The Snake bobbed its head and flicked its tongue at Stan.

"I've helped your four brothers here realize there's more to life than waiting on Lucifer's whim," Wedriel said. "I'm sure you understand how they feel."

"Don't listen to him, Stan!" Yevgenia called. "Remember what you – "

Miika waved a hand, and Stan could no longer hear Yevgenia. He saw her mouth moving, and her arms beating against the invisible barrier of the pentagram, but no sound escaped her circle.

"Stanley." Wedriel spread his hands, palms up in supplication. "Aren't you tired of living up on that mountain all alone? Wouldn't you like more freedom, more power?"

"I'd like some more clothing is what I'd like," Stan said.

Wedriel's laugh made Stan feel sick, even though not quite enough to actually throw up. Too bad. Puking on an angel would totally have been worth it.

"Join your brothers on my side," Wedriel said. "You may wear any costume you desire."

"These assholes ain't my brothers," Stan said. "I'm the final Aspect. I only got one brother, and he's gonna kick your ass from here to Purgatory when he escapes whatever weaksauce binding you managed to engineer."

"This will be easier if you agree," Wedriel said, "but your cooperation is not required."

"Why you wanna do this anyway?" Stan asked. "If you don't like it in Tartarus, you got plenty of other places you can go. Don't blame Lou for your problems with The Name."

Wedriel scoffed. "I don't blame anyone for my Fall. I was fated to end up here. I know that now. It is my destiny to rule in Hell, and to rule better than its current overlord."

Stan rolled his eyes. "Oh boy, we got a live one here."

"Show some respect!" Miika charged forward, her sword half-drawn. "Lord Wedriel will lead us to victory over our oppressors!"

Stan frowned. "Seriously? You're playing *this* old song again?"

"The war with Heaven is coming," Wedriel said. "It is inevitable. How many angels have fallen since the dawn? Enough to fill a city. Enough to form an army, each of us with reason to hate those above. But Lucifer has ignored this fact, has failed to prepare Hell for the great conflict. What has he done for the last several centuries? *Nothing.* No soldiers have been trained, no siege engines constructed, no spies deployed. Your brother is a bureaucrat, not a leader."

"And *you're* going to lead Hell into battle?"

Wedriel gestured at the Aspects and the Draconis. "I seem to be doing pretty well so far."

Stan looked around the chamber, at the challenging stares of Miika and her fellow guards, at the blank facades of the other Aspects, at Yevgenia.

She was holding one hand up to the barrier, palm forward, all five fingers splayed. Her mouth moved. She might have been saying: *You are five. Five are as one.*

Her fingers closed into a fist.

Stan nodded at Yevgenia, then turned back to Wedriel.

"Okay, sure," Stan said. "You're obviously a smart bird, I'll give you that. You got out of Tartarus, you talked these four morons into helping you kidnap Lou, you convinced the dragons to back your play. Props for all that."

"You can be smart, too, Stanley," Wedriel said. "Do the smart thing here."

Stan laughed and shook his head. "Nah. Come on, I'm not smart. I'm a dummy. I know it. And I'm okay with that.

"Lou's always telling me I ain't smart enough to really be evil. You gotta be smart to be bad, he says, 'cause being good means you just follow the rules. No thinking required, no free will necessary. Being bad means you make up your own rules, and that takes brains I don't have.

"Well, maybe I don't have brains, but I know what's what. And I know this hostile takeover won't help anybody. It'll just make things worse."

"I am disappointed," Wedriel said. "But very well, we'll do it the hard way – "

"Shut up," Stan said. "I'm not talking to you. I'm talking to these maroons." He pointed at the other Aspects and the Draconis. "I'm giving 'em one last chance to *not* get their shit fucked up when Lou returns. 'Cause he ain't the forgivin' type. And he don't like it when people break the rules."

Wedriel turned to Miika. "Bring him and the other Aspects up to the altar. I can't free my fellow Fallen from Tartarus until the force lines of the Satan-Ley are dismantled."

"Yes, my Lord," Miika said, sheathing her sword. She waved to another Draconis, and the two of them moved toward Stan.

"We got rules for a reason," Stan said. "These ain't rules that somebody made up just for laughs. They didn't get handed down to us on crappy stone tablets. *Lou* wrote these rules, negotiated forever to get 'em just right, because he knew *we* all had to *live* down here. This is our *home*. And you don't shit where you sleep."

Miika gestured, marking sigils in the air beside him. Stan felt the pentagram barrier dissipating. Before he could move, Miika and the other Draconis grabbed his arms and manhandled him forward.

"All done?" Wedriel asked. "Ready to go now?"

"You may be smart, but you don't know the rules," Stan said. "Never speak The Name. Never break the circle. And never put all Five Aspects in the same fucking room."

Stan closed his eyes, made a fist, and uttered an

unholy phrase.

The other reason the Five Aspects of the Devil are kept separated by great distances, on isolated mountaintops on opposite sides of Hell, is because their combined power rivals that of the Prince of Darkness himself. And when the distance between the Five is small enough, Stanley can combine and control all of them.

Yevgenia averted her gaze before Stan incanted the blast which killed Wedriel. The Draconis were not so fortunate. They collapsed into quivering, gibbering heaps on the cold stone floor. The entire chamber shook, vibrating with the shock of a divine destruction.

It was all over in less than a second. Stan pulled away from the other Aspects, releasing his control. The Fire and The Smoke wavered for a moment, then flitted out through the open door. The Beast ran in circles for a while, urinated in the corner and defecated near one of the fallen Draconis before following them.

The Snake moved over to Stan, who sat on the floor catching his breath, and nuzzled the back of Stan's hand with the top of its scaly head.

"Go home, Snakey," Stan said.

The Snake bobbed once, then slithered out of the chamber.

Stan struggled to his feet and limped over to where Yevgenia was still trapped. She said something he couldn't hear and pointed behind him.

He turned and saw his brother leaning against the wall, smiling as only The Devil can.

"When did you get here?" Stan asked.

"Oh, a minute ago," Lucifer said. "I was just admiring our ass. It's quite fantastic, if I do say so myself, and I don't often get a chance to really appreciate it."

"I'm not even going to dignify that," Stan said. "Help me get Evie out."

"Of course, of course." Lucifer followed Stan toward the pentagram. "By the way, that was a lovely speech you gave to what's-his-name about following the rules. Beautiful and heartfelt. Would you mind repeating it in public sometime? I've been thinking about starting up my podcast again. You could be my first guest."

"Nobody listens to your stupid podcast." Stan slammed a fist against the invisible barrier. "Let her out."

Lucifer waved a hand, and the barrier around Yevgenia disappeared with a soft *whoosh*.

"Thanks," Stan said. "We're going to go find some clothes now."

"Oh, don't rush off," Lucifer said. "We see each other so rarely. I've got some time before my next meeting. Stay and chat. Or, you know, we don't even have to talk." He winked at Yevgenia. "If you kids wanted to get into a three-way kind of situation here, I'm totally open to that. What do you say, Evie? Double your pleasure, double your fun?"

"No," Yevgenia said firmly. "Thank you. Sir."

Lucifer glared and stepped closer to her. "You do know who I am, right?"

"Yes."

"And you're going to say 'no' to me?" Lucifer's eyes were dark, bottomless pools.

"Sir – "

"Aw, I'm just fucking with you!" Lucifer laughed and clapped both Stan and Yevgenia on the back. "Stan knows I'm cool, don't you, Stan?"

"I'm sorry my brother is such an asshole," Stan said

to Yevgenia.

"Anyway, nice to finally meet you, Evie," Lucifer said. "And Stan. I meant what I said. You're not dumb. Give yourself a little credit. You *could* make all kinds of trouble for me. You follow the rules because you know it's better for everyone."

"I just want to go home," Stan said.

"Exactly," Lucifer said. "Go home, have a few stiff drinks, then bend your girlfriend over the couch and –"

"Again," Stan said to Yevgenia, "I'm sorry my brother is so obnoxious."

"All right, all right, I can take a hint!" Lucifer stomped over to the now-catatonic Draconis and shook his head. "I've got a lot of cleaning up to do anyway." He snapped his fingers and disappeared.

Yevgenia turned to Stan. "You okay?"

He nodded. "I'll be fine. Just need some rest, I think."

She stroked his shoulder. "You did good today, baby."

Stan shook his head. "Well."

"What?"

"I did *well*," Stan said. "This is Hell. We don't do good here."

Yevgenia chuckled, kissed his cheek, and walked him out.

DARRELL SCHWEITZER

The Hag

Long, long ago, when I was a young man and newly made a knight, my cousin the Duke Orlando was to be married, and on the day before the wedding a great hunt was held to procure fresh meat for the feast. I was there. I sat up with the others the night before that, drinking and boasting about the great beasts we would slay, and when the hour grew late I retired with them. On the morrow a trumpet blast awoke us and we breakfasted, and while the party was being made ready, the Duke took me out a few steps beyond the gate of his castle and pointed over the fields, which rolled green and crop-filled over hill after hill, to the place where they stopped and a deep forest began.

'Those woods," said my host, "are entirely uninhabited. Once you leave the open ground and enter into them you are as far gone from civilization as if you walk the bottom of the sea. The trees swallow you up."

"Why does no one live there? Can the land not be cleared?"

At this my cousin laughed. "Most generous, courteous, brave, and noble Sir Julian, if we stand here talking all day we shall not be back from the hunt before sundown!"

"If no one lives there, why do you fear the woods after dark?" I called after him, but he did not hear me. He was already shouting orders to the keepers of his hounds.

It was a wild ride that day. The dogs caught a scent early and let out a collective yelp of delighted bloodlust, then were released from their leashes and let run. We followed them with a thunder of hooves down dusty roads, over fences and hedges. We brushed through fields of ripened grain. We scattered the peasants before us and laughed to see them scramble. Then we came to the edge of all human domains that my cousin had shown me, and plunged beyond that edge into the unknown, into the forest of dubious repute, led by the howling pack. At once two careless riders, two overplumed dandies whose names I had never taken care to learn, were swept from their mounts by overhanging branches. We left them behind. The horns of the huntsmen echoed through the leafy abyss like the cries of Neptune and his giants beneath the green sea, both to let men know where their fellows were and to frighten I the quarry ahead of us, whatever it was.

I glimpsed a shape once, during that glorious, reckless, and | seemingly unending run. It was little more than a patch darker than the surrounding' brush, and moving, before my eyes for an instant and then gone. All the rest of the day we galloped, horns blasting, the prey unseen, running, running, running before us. No one saw more than I had.

Horses fell behind in exhaustion. Mine was covered with foamy white lather. Gradually the hoofbeats and the sounds of the horns diminished and remained always at my rear, until I realized that I was in the lead. My steed that had carried me to my first battles and back was hardier than all the rest, and the killing would be mine, I looked over my shoulder and saw only one rider near me, the Duke.

"Ho!" he cried. "You and I shall have the quarry!"

But at that instant, as if to belie him, his horse stumbled – over a root I think – and sent him catapulting over the pommel of his saddle and onto the ground. I heard the shriek of the animal and the Duke's trailing curse, and I looked back again and saw them thus. I reined and turned about to see if he was injured, but he got to his feet and waved me on.

"Keep going you fool! Keep going! The prize is yours now if you don't let it get away!"

So I continued after the bounds, my horse laboring. I knew the animal could not go much farther before it dropped. The chase would soon be over, one way or the other. All I could hope was that the beast I would be facing alone would be tired also. It would have to be, if it were an earthly creature at all.

Then the cries of the dogs changed, becoming snarls of anger and howls of pain. They were fighting with something. The underbrush ahead of me rattled, as if Titans were wrestling in it.

I passed one of Duke Orlando's best bloodhounds, disemboweled on the ground, yet still alive and snapping. And another, and a third this way, and a fourth. The shape, the patch I had seen, showed in the greenery again and crashed away. Finally in a clearing, the thing I pursued turned to face me and fight, and I saw what had driven the canines to such frenzy. It was a huge wild boar, the biggest I had ever seen, as large as a pony and more massive, with blood-smeared tusks like curving swords, and red eyes all aflame.

I lowered by spear, shouted with all the strength left in me, and charged. The boar remained frozen almost to the last minute, glaring at me, until my lance tip was no more than a hand's breadth from it. Then it darted off to one side and disappeared again into the forest. I went on a ways before I could stop, turn, and follow, and in the process my lance caught among branches and snapped. The force was almost enough to unseat me. When I had recovered myself I saw that I was alone and out of the clearing, the trees towering over me again, their ancient trunks like rows of Olympian legs. Darkness was already gathering where the leaves were the thickest to mark the beginnings of the end of the day.

The shadows deepened. I bent low against the overhanging boughs and vines, galloping still in the direction the beast had fled, maintaining a pretense of pursuit. I wondered how I would conquer my enemy with only my sword left to me. Yes, I thought of the boar as my foe – it had defeated all the others and I alone was left to give it battle and snatch the victory. I had not seen another hunter for hours. If I failed this day's effort would be wasted, and the Duke's wedding the following morning would be without new-slain meat.

But my efforts, too, came to naught. There were no more hounds to lead the way. Either all had been slain, or they too had given up the chase. Once or twice I heard the boar itself trampling ahead of me, receding, the sounds of the trampled underbrush growing fainter and fainter, until I could hear nothing and unavoidably came to realize that defeat was mine. When there could no longer be any doubt of this, I reined my already staggering steed. The poor creature could not have gone more than a few more steps anyway.

I dismounted and sat on the trunk of a fallen tree, only then feeling the full weight of my weariness. I could hardly bring myself to stand again to relieve myself. I had been in the saddle from dawn till dusk, riding hard. The excitement of the hunt had given me extra strength, but now it had deserted me. I sat down again, soaked in already stinking sweat. I took off my helmet and wiped the grime from my brow. My hair was plastered down. I felt just then that the unfortunate Orlando would not only have to do without a roast boar for his wedding, but he would have to find someone else to fill my seat. I was in no condition to go anywhere.

A brook rippled nearby. Stiffly I rose once more, and the blood rushed from my head and I felt faint, but when I had recovered my balance I led my horse by the bridle to the water's edge. We both drank deeply. I sat still in the cool of the evening and watched the night birds circle above me as the stars came out.

It was while I sat there by the edge of the stream, the twilight giving way to a night that yielded to another twilight when the swollen harvest moon rose, that I noticed something not part of the natural forest. It lay on the opposite shore and downstream a ways. It was too low and too wide, too square-shaped to have grown where it stood. I rose wearily and waded a distance for a better look. It was a building, a hunting hall long abandoned and fallen into ruin. No light came from its empty windows. There were no sounds from within.

I brought my horse over to the place and tethered it to a half-grown oak. I would spend the night here. I could never find my way back to my cousin's castle in the darkness, and I knew it. I didn't even know how far into the forest I had gone, and the path hunt had turned several times. I wasn't even sure of the direction.

The front door hung ajar, but would not move. For generations now vines had grown over it, making it theirs, holding it in place where hinges no doubt would have failed. Sideways I slipped into the hall, rustling the leaves of the vines, and I looked upon the place where long ago some lord, perhaps even a pagan chieftain swearing mighty oaths to his strangely named gods, had feasted with his huntsmen. Still there were overturned benches strewn about. The dirt floor beneath my feet was soft and damp. In the center of the room, in what had once been a firepit, straggling weeds grew beneath an opening in the roof. Off to the sides, hidden from direct light, pale toadstools flourished.

I went back outside and gathered up some dry twigs and leaves, then returned, set them down in a heap at the edge of the pit, and striking flint to steel lit a fire to keep cold and the wolves away for the rest of the night.

Then I lay down on the spongy ground and tried to sleep.

I did not rest long. Perhaps an hour passed, perhaps a few minutes, while mosquitoes whined in my ears and I tried to ignore them. Then I heard my horse outside stirring uneasily. I sat up, hand on sword hilt. Moonlight streamed through the opening in the roof, and through the half overgrown windows, illuminating patches and bands on the floor, including the spot where I was sitting. I kicked out the fire, retreated into darkness, slid my sword out of my scabbard, and waited.

My horse neighed, then stamped, then shrieked with terror. Suddenly all the forest was alive with the cries of night-owls and goblins, and then, as if the sounds had been to announce something that had just arrived, all was silent once more, save tor the frantic horse that tugged at the tether rope, then broke loose and galloped off. All this took place in the space of a few seconds. By the time I could run to the window to see what the matter was, my mount was gone and I knew what had frightened it.

Thousands of serpents had surrounded the house like a coiling, living sea.

They oozed in over the windowsills, through the vine-held door like a liquid mass, yet with intelligence and a single purpose. I crossed myself helplessly in holy terror. Instinctively I drew back from them. It was all I could do to keep myself from screaming, from moving quickly and insanely, from doing anything that would draw their attention to me. I returned to my corner in the shadows and stood with my back to the wall, as far away from the windows as I could be. I was rigid as a stone man. If they came over to me, a single motion would betray me. I stared wide-eyed as they amassed in the center of the room where I had been lying. They circled the ashes of my fire and passed under and through them heedless of any remaining heat, looking for something that wasn't there. I had not been noticed. It was impossible, but none had ventured within three cubits of my feet. Once satisfied, or disappointed in their search, these creatures left the hall, again at once, as if a single mind directed them, and they slipped out the way they had come. They drained away like water over the doorstep, and through unseen cracks and holes at the bases of the walls.

When all were gone I had only one thought – to quit this haunted place. I had no horse now, but I knew my feet would carry me far and fast.

But again the branches of the trees echoed with screeching, and again something was announced and something arrived. This time rats came, an army of them storming the unmanned defenses of the hall, their eyes glowing in the moonlight like the pinpricks of a billion tiny torches. They too poured over the windowsill. They scratched down the walls and rattled the vines as they flowed over the door. They came to the center of the room as their predecessors had, circled, probed my dead fire, and left, never noticing me where I stood.

And again before I could escape a third invasion was heralded. This time it was of wolves, strangely silent; a sea of their eyes, muzzles, and tails filling the entire room. They crowded against me but still, incredibly, showed no awareness of me. They pawed the ashes, sniffed, and departed. Next came hawks, bursting through the chimney hole and the windows until the air was filled with their voices and whirring wings. Then they were gone, leaving only a few drifting feathers to assure me of their reality, and it was then that I thought I understood. These things were preludes, coming as rain and hail come before a cyclone.

The cyclone came immediately thereafter, in this form: the front door of the hall exploded into splinters, the vines rent aside, and in burst a battering ram of flesh, the very same titanic beast I had pursued all the day, the boar with its teeth like swords. It too ran into the center of the room as if expectant, stopped, and prodded the ashes with its hooves, but unlike the others it did not go away. It turned directly, knowingly, to where I stood. Digging its feet into the ground and snorting as a bull does, it made ready to charge.

I had some fantastic idea of killing the thing for Duke Orlando's feast. Some spirit of madness whispered to me that this was possible, that the hunt would not be fruitless after all, but my rational mind knew that the animal before me was not mortal. It was a thing beyond nature, sent by God or the Devil for a purpose, and that purpose was more profound than filling the stomachs of a hundred lords and ladies.

I lowered my sword, knowing it useless. Then I addressed the beast, saying, "What are you truly and why are you sent?"

The boar backed away, grunted, and began to change. Its form collapsed like a punctured water bag. I felt at that instant as if mighty forces were contending all around me, tides pushing against supernatural tides, crushing me between them. I was a puppet as I approached the melting mass. I watched as it grew darker, as its hide became shiny, and hairless, as it flowed and sank down into a pool of shapeless muck, and I jumped back in amazement when it expanded and rose again in a new form.

It was now a unicorn with a deadly, lance-long horn, with a pale body and ugly red eyes.

And again a falling, a shifting, a change yielding a small dragon, golden scaled and hissing blue flames. And again – a black, two-headed bird taller than a man, called by the pagans a roc; this melting into a scarlet cat the size of an elephant, with claws like long razors.

At last it settled and became an old woman with bent back, shoulders twisted out of shape, and a head that rested oddly on a short neck. The face was hideous, pockmarked with scars, covered with boils, and wrinkled like badly tanned hide.

She laughed with a voice that wasn't even remotely human. It was – what? – the creaking of rusty hinges, the chatterings of all the rats in the billion sewers of the universe, the snapping of dry bones.

"Well, well, a noble knight is to be my guest."

"Your – your guest?"

She twitched her mouth from side to side, picked her nose and sneezed, then pointed a shrunken finger at me and laughed again.

"Yes, to pay for my hospitality with favors. To wait on me and mine – "

With that a wave of revulsion and unthinking terror. "No!" I cried, and I raised my sword to strike.

For a third time she laughed.

"You cannot harm me. I who have lived so long will not be put to rest so easily. Sheathe your weapon, Sir Knight. Know that I can snatch your soul out of you before the blow falls."

I put my blade away, pretending I was planning, waiting for a better opportunity.

"Listen to me," she said. "I brought you here for a reason. All you have gone through this day has been my doing. I beguiled the hunters and separated you from them. I brought you here to do the deed I have in mind. I shall ask a great favor – "

"A favor? How can you – ?"

"Quiet! Listen! Many years ago, many centuries past, my fathers built this hall and lived in it. Here they boasted and made merry and planned their feuds, and some of them died. Others were born here and the gods smiled on them, for they were a proud, fierce, mighty race, pleasing to the ones above. But then the new god came and drove out the old, and the priests came. Most of the folk listened to the new word and abandoned this place, but my parents did not. They stayed and clung to the old ways and worship, until a curse was put on them by the priests of the new god and they died. And the curse continued even to me. Look on my face and you are sick. You turn from me in disgust. This is my true face, and this the body into which I was born. Such are the gifts of the savior Christ. Such are the products of his mercy. This was the burden he sent me to bear, and to finish the fine picture he threw the paint pot in my face. No man would ever touch me; no man, no matter how desperate, would have me."

"Lady, this is a tale filled with woe, but what can I – ?"

"Listen and you shall learn! Can it be any wonder that in the end I called on the Dark One and took him into my bed? He gave me powers and many forms, but he bound me to him."

"Why are you telling me this? Am I a priest that you have called me all this way for a confession?"

"Not a priest," she answered, "but a servant even while you are a guest. Many knights have I met here, and all have prepared a meal for me. You shall do the same."

"A meal? But there is no food here. I have nothing."

"Your horse. Go outside and bring it here, then slay it. It fled but I have recalled it. Do not try to mount and escape. The shapes you have seen can bring down any prey, and man, most easily. I will be satisfied, by courtesy or by force."

Many courteous knights had she met in this hall. What had become of them? I doubted very much that they all walked away, minus their mounts. There was something more than that. Every minute the trap into which I had stepped closed tighter and tighter.

I did as I was commanded. Outside, my steed was waiting untethered, as the hag had foretold, and I led the weary, trusting animal into the hall. It was easy now that the door had been smashed. And when I was again before her, treacherously, I carried out the rest of my mission. I slew my mount with my sword. Killing a horse is a messy business even when done with a single stroke to the heart. The dying creature fell, thrashed about, whinnied, and spat blood and foam from its mouth. I stood back from the flying hooves and waited until it expired, then drew back even more in horror and revulsion when the old lady put her mouth to the wound, and began to suck.

Her eyes were wide with delight. She choked once, spitting blood down her chin and neck, and then continued, clinging to the animal like an obscene leech, impossibly draining all the substance from it. As I watched, the ribs began to protrude and the skin stretched tight over legs, shoulders, neck, and skull. At a glance it would have seemed that famine took the horse's life, not the sword. It was an empty husk.

I wanted dearly to pass my sword through the heart of the crone, but there was no chance to surprise her. Even as she crawled over her feast she remained aware of my every motion. If I even shifted weight from one leg to the other she would glance up, her face communicating a wordless warning, as if she could anticipate my thoughts.

At last when she was done she stood up and smiled, slobbering flesh and gore. She was the same as she had been before, her form not changed at all. It was not as I had expected. I'd assumed she was drawing some special power from the life of my poor steed which would enable her to make a special transformation.

As it turned out I was halfway right.

"Now take your clothes off," she said, "and spread them on the ground here that we may lie on them."

I knew right then what I should have done, what my vows of chivalry demanded of me. I should have charged with my sword aloft, in the faint hope that the witch could be killed by the downstroke of my dead arm. I should have died then a martyr to my God and to all mankind and cast my soul into the arms of some angel who would bear it softly heavenward. I should have, but I didn't, for I knew deep within me that my death would be for nothing. The monster could not be slain, and whether I died or lived she would remain as she was. The only matter at stake was my life, and then more than ever before I wanted to live. I told myself that the blue of a clear sky, the flowers of a sun-blest field, the laughter of children, the love of a beautiful maiden; all could wash away the stain of what I was about to do. I weighed these in one hand against the boar, the dragon, the wolves, and the darkness of the unknown forest in the other, and need I say which I found more desirable? All my oaths, all my vows of knighthood fled from me and were gone, impossible, unworkable, ridiculous.

Beneath her garments, she was rotten like a week-old corpse with huge, livid veins like clotted rivers spread over her. Her flesh was soft, too soft, and sticky. The stench was unbearable. I gave myself up to her and all my senses deserted me.

An eternity of terrible dreams I awoke, naked on

the floor of the ruined hall, atop a heap of my own garments. It was still night. The moon was low but its light was still bright, the almost horizontal beams filtering through the forest beyond the western windows.

Beside me lay another, and when I saw her I thought I still dreamed. It was not the putrid hag at all, not the Devil's whore, but a lovely, perfectly formed young woman. Her flesh was pale and utterly flawless, her features beyond the power of the most skilled artists to portray. Her soft yellow hair flowed down over her breasts like a river of silk.

She awoke and saw me, and seemed disoriented for a time. Then she spoke directly, clearly. Her voice was musical. She was almost singing. She hugged her own naked shoulders and smiled rapturously at the feeling.

"I think you understand many things about me now," she said.

"About you? I have never seen you before. How did you come to this terrible place?"

"I am the same who was here before. Behold, I am in the form I have wished for always. It is part of the curse upon me that I can tell no one of my plight unless I am in this shape. I have been in it many times before, but always in the presence of the Dark One who gave me the power to change. This is the rest of my tale:

"When I called him to me in the agony of my desperation he told me that he could make me fair, but only by his touch. So he touched me and took my body to his and I was fair, and all that night I gratefully praised the name of Satan. But then, on the morrow, when I went into the village and said to the men there, 'Am I not beautiful?' they mocked me. They spat on me and with a hail of stones drove me back into the wood. I was not beautiful at all. The spell had worn off. The next night when my winged lover came I cursed him and he laughed, 'If you can get another to take you as I have done, as you are without knowing what you shall be, then you shall have this beauty unfading forever, even when you come into the flames of my kingdom. But after you have accomplished this I will try once more to take you, and if I succeed you shall be then as you always were, and our tryst will continue each night until I tire of it. Thus the one who transforms you must meet me that same night. He must be your champion.'"

I jumped up, grabbing my clothes, dressing as I stood.

"Nay! Am I mad? I'll not do it!"

She wept and pleaded with me, and overwhelmed my reason. I knew that this could easily be just another guise she was in, that the story could be a fabrication, and underneath the lovely face lurked the hag. It seemed likely that she could change into this form as the occasion demanded, the same way she would become a dragon or a boar. She called me now as a siren calls – no, as a beetle does when it hides in the depths of a flower and springs out to devour the bees that come to suck the honey. But, as I said, she overwhelmed me and I could not turn away. Her beauty, her seemingly renewed innocence, which I could not bear to see spoiled, defeated me more surely than any foe.

"Are you a knight?" she sobbed. "Is this chivalrous game you play a lie?"

"Lady, I confess that it probably is. At times I have been certain. I want to live as much as anyone else. I'm not willing to lay down myself for another."

"But you have had something of a life already, and I haven't. I was cheated at birth. Let me live my first life now. Make all the noble things you swore mean something, as they never have before. Help me...."

In the end I consented.

"What must I do?"

"When he comes either fight him or do all he asks. Nothing more can I tell you. I must go now, before he arrives."

She pulled on the soiled rags the crone had worn – still I could think of them only as two, never one and the same – and they seemed no longer ugly, but comical, as the famed Helen would be wearing a rough sack. I wanted to laugh.

As she started toward the door I said. "Wait." I fell to my knees, outwardly in jest, but inwardly in all earnest. "Fair lady, I pray you give me your hand once before you depart."

And startled, she did, and I kissed it as one kisses the hand of a queen. Then she knelt down and kissed me on the mouth and embraced me, and the horror of all that had gone before was forgotten.

I waited the rest of the night through, alone, ready for another battle with no hope of victory, yet with a purpose in my defeat. It was a beautiful, tranquil thing, infrequently lanced through with worries. How far has she gone now? Can she find the path out of the forest? I would guard the hall for her and keep her adversary at bay as long as I could, granting her more seconds of precious time. I felt triumphant, as a father feels when the midwife tells him that his child has been brought safely into the world. I had created this woman, given her shape and flesh. Now I would be her champion, as brave as any in romance, so that she might live and be fulfilled.

So I waited, and just before dawn the enemy came. I heard first the flapping of heavy wings, then a thump, then clattering like a stallion running across the roof, and I drew my sword and waited for him to appear in the ruined doorway.

His feet were cloven hooves, but above the ankles he was a man, naked and splendidly muscled, with skin not dark brown like an African's but shiny black, the color of hard coal. From his shoulders stretched graceful feathered wings, the wings of a huge black swan.

The most beautiful of the fallen angels stood before me and smiled, understanding all that had happened.

"She has done well," he said, "and I am pleased. Her purpose is served and I release her. Now you. Sir Julian, are mine, but I shall not take you now. You will come to me in your own way and at your own time, but still you will come. For now I command you, live, wander, and see all the strange world in my name."

Then the sun came up and he was gone, and the world was revealed to me by the light, a world that was for me new, strange, and terribly different from the one I had known the day before.

IMOGEN HOWSON

Frayed Tapestry

The first time it happened was almost a year after he'd married her. They were giving a drinks party, and the spacious top-floor apartment was filled with sleek, beautiful people in immaculately cut trousers, or little black dresses and the discreet glint of gold jewelry.

Candy had been busy since the first guests arrived. Clym liked her to keep the canapés coming and make sure he was supplied with ice for the drinks. With that, as well as welcoming new guests and trying to make sure she remembered everybody's names, she'd scarcely sipped her own glass of wine.

So, afterwards, although she tried to blame the alcohol, she knew she couldn't.

She was in the kitchen, cutting up more lemons for the gin and tonics. She had a gleaming steel bowl of them, glossy polished yellow next to the duller green globes of limes, and a neat little serrated knife to slice them into perfect rounds. But then, of course, she had everything. She'd seen it reflected in her guests' eyes. Her, this nineteen-year-old, already with a beautiful apartment, a handsome, adoring, powerful husband...

The knife slipped. It shouldn't have – she was holding it carefully; its edge had already bitten into the yellow rind, sending the sharp fragrance up to her nose. But it did: slipped downward sharply and sliced into the side of her left thumb.

The pain was instant and shocking. She gasped, dropping the knife, and clamped her right hand over her left. Such a small cut – it shouldn't hurt so much. But after a second she realized the pain came from the lemon juice seeping, acidic, into the wound.

"Oh, you *stupid...*" With her uninjured hand, she twisted the tap on the sink next to her. It stuck a moment and, the pain unendurable; she put her thumb in her mouth to soothe it.

Water poured into the sink so hard it splashed up against the matt black tiles above the taps, spattering the worktop. She thrust her thumb under the water, swallowing against the tears coming to her eyes.

And it happened. All at once her hand was submerged in a rush of water so cold it instantly numbed the pain. Her other hand was grasping not the tap but the rough bark of a twisted, moss-covered tree branch. Her bare toes clung to damp, gritty stone and cold air struck her skin, raising goose bumps on her bare arms.

And it was familiar. She knew where she was, knew if she turned away from the waterfall she'd see the cliff rising to the sky, and knew the tree was an oak, ancient and craggy, home to thousands of tiny creatures. She'd stood here before, feet cold on the stone, stood here with –

"Candy? Are you in the kitchen?"

She jumped, lost her grip on the branch, grabbed for another handhold, feet slipping on the wet – On the wet kitchen floor.

"*Candy!*" Arms came around her. For a moment she didn't recognize them, didn't know who was holding her. "What are you doing?"

Clym's voice. *Oh, of course* – Clym's hands. She stood in his arms, her thumb streaking watery blood all over his shirt, the front of her dress drenched.

He reached past her and turned off the tap. "What happened? What did you do?" His voice roughened with bewilderment and exasperation. "You've got the tap on so that it's splashing all over the floor – no wonder you slipped." Then his voice went cold and suddenly his hands seemed cold too, sending ice into her bones. "Where are your shoes?"

She looked down, her breath already coming short at that tone in his voice. "I don't – I was *wearing* them." But sure enough, there were her feet, bare and brown against the white tiles, their toenails neat and straight, shiny with pale gold nail polish.

"Sit down."

He moved her backwards and she sat on one of the kitchen stools. From the sitting room behind him came the jumble of conversation, laughter, the click of high heels as someone stepped out onto the balcony, the ripple of the low music she'd spent an hour selecting. Clym reached over her head and pulled the first aid box off its shelf. "Give me your hand." He wiped the cut with a disinfectant wipe, not roughly, but not bothering to be gentle either, and then stretched a plaster over it.

She sat motionless, still feeling that bite of cold in his fingers as he touched her. He always had cold hands. Sometimes she teased him about it – but only in bed. She'd learned early on not to seem to make fun of him anywhere else – and never, ever in front of other people.

He pressed the plaster down to seal it firmly over the cut. Pain jabbed through her thumb. "You know I don't like you not wearing shoes. Especially on this floor. If you'd been wearing them you wouldn't have slipped."

Well, that was ridiculous. The shoes she'd put on for the party were dainty, strappy things with smooth soles – plenty more slippery than bare feet. And where were they, anyway? If she'd taken them off in the kitchen wouldn't they be around here somewhere?

"*Candy*."

Her attention jerked back to him. He was looking down at her, his eyes very dark. "Go and dry your dress and put some shoes on. No – not that way." This as she got off the stool and took a step towards the sitting room. "Do you think I want our guests to see you like that?"

This time the anger came clear through his voice. She turned and went through the little corridor at the other end of the kitchen – narrow and lined with shelves, it was normally only used as a store cupboard – then into the entrance hall, and from there into their bedroom.

She rubbed her dress and feet with a towel, found some other shoes. Grit and a dusting of earth came off on the towel. She shook it into the bath, rinsed it away, and stuffed the towel into the laundry bag. Hopefully he wouldn't ask her to find the missing shoes. The grit on her feet had only confirmed what she already, really, knew. Wherever she'd left her shoes, it wasn't in the apartment.

The next morning she woke with a headache and lay still, eyes shut against the sunlight that turned red as it came through the curtains. Clym liked red. To her, though, it seemed the wrong color for curtains. Curtains should be pale gold, leaf green, letting through dappled light that moved like sunspots on water…

She felt her thoughts pause. Where had that image – huge trees filtering the sunlight, a wide milk-calm lake – come from? Nowhere in the city, where she'd lived her whole life –

And at that she paused again, stuttered as if she'd met a break in the track of her thoughts. *My whole life? But where was I before I married Clym?*

"Wake up, baby."

She eased her eyes open. Clym stood, a shadow against the sunlit curtains, holding a tray. She moved to prop herself up on her elbows, trying to clear her mind of the weird jumble of thoughts that made no sense.

"I don't think I should have had those other glasses of wine," she said. "I feel like death."

Clym laughed, setting the tray down on the bedside table. "Baby doll, a few glasses of wine won't have done you any harm. Like I said, you needed it after cutting your thumb so badly. Now, you need a good breakfast, that's all. Sit up."

She wriggled up to lean against the bank of huge, marshmallow-soft pillows. Clym passed her a mug of tea – gentle, pale brown, with plenty of milk. The scent of honey drifted up with the steam and she breathed it in.

"Oh, that's heaven. Thank you."

"Here." He moved the tray over onto her duvet-covered lap. "Chilled melon slices. And – you need protein – scrambled eggs on toast."

He sat on the bed next to her, moving carefully so as not to tip the tray. She bit into the melon slice and cold, sweet juice filled her mouth. Its fragrance seemed to travel up through the roof of her mouth into her head, clearing it of the ache, smoothing the jagged tracks of her thoughts.

Clym had cut the thick slices of white toast into fingers, golden with a shimmer of butter. He leaned forward to put one into her mouth and it crunched deliciously between her teeth.

"Last night," she said. "I don't know why I took my shoes off. Are you still angry?"

"No, baby. I know you didn't mean to worry me. Just" – he leaned forward, brushed a kiss over her nose – "be more careful next time, okay?"

"Okay." She smiled at him, feeling warm, relaxed, floating on the pillows as if they were clouds. She reached for the fork and his hand came down on hers, stopping her. She blinked at him. "Hey, I need protein, remember?"

He laughed. "I'll feed you, sweetheart. Here, open wide."

She really wanted to feed herself. She was hungry now, and he was clumsy, and buttery crumbs and bits of egg got spilled on the crimson satin duvet cover. But it was worth it, to know he wasn't angry with her, that he'd forgiven her. And while he was with her, laughing, spooning eggs into her mouth, leaning over to kiss her, then eventually putting the tray on the floor so he could join her under the duvet, she knew her thoughts were safe. While he was here her thoughts wouldn't go jagged, they wouldn't hiccup and pause and shoot strange familiar images into her head. They'd be safe, and so would she.

Clym went to work six days a week and she didn't yet know many of their neighbors, but she had plenty to do. It was only a short walk to the avenues of shops, and Clym had accounts at all of them. It was fun to try on slinky little outfits, then, if she especially liked one, walk out dressed head to toe in all new clothes.

This time, she found a chiffon dress in different shades of green, beech-leaf to moss, fastened with a gold belt that hugged her rib cage, just under her breasts. Pulling the dress on over her head, she imagined she smelled cut grass, the drifting sweetness of honeysuckle.

They knew her here; she told them she'd take it, asked them to send her clothes home, and stepped out of the shop, lifting her face to the warmth of the sunlight.

And stopped. It was – it *was* sunlight, but what had she been expecting? She looked up into the arc of indigo sky, from which the sun shone, golden-red and familiar – and wrong. In her head was an image of something different, something brighter, cleaner...*higher*, although that was ridiculous.

She shook her head as if to clear it. She needed to buy new shoes. She looked down at herself, and her shoulders slumped a little. This was exactly the sort of dress that didn't even *look* good with shoes. Which was probably, really, why she'd bought it. She *missed* going barefoot.

Well, you should have thought about that before you married him, she told herself severely, beginning to walk again. *If you marry a man who thinks bare feet look slutty, then you know very well what you're getting into.*

Except – *had* she known?

Her feet stuttered on the pavement. The sun – the odd, wrong-colored sun – blazed down at her. She felt sick, a little dizzy.

She was just passing the cool, dim doorway of a coffee shop. She turned in to it, and sat at a small round table. Its metal surface was patterned with irregular diamond shapes that seemed to run into each other, making the surface look as if it were warped. She spread her fingers on it, and of course it was perfectly flat. Her heart was pounding horribly, down next to her stomach so she felt nausea pulse through her.

She couldn't remember. She couldn't remember deciding to marry him. She couldn't remember meeting him. She couldn't remember her *wedding* day. *What sort of freak can't remember her wedding day?*

"Can I get you anything?"

She looked up at the thin, dark-haired waitress and answered automatically. "Latte, please."

"Anything else?"

"No, thank you."

The waitress disappeared behind the counter. Candy pressed her hands hard on the table, watching the skin around her nails whiten. This was insane. What was wrong with her? For the past year she'd lived this idyllic life. She'd been wonderfully, dreamily happy. Clym adored her, all his friends treated her like a queen, and she had everything she could want. Then one slip of a knife, and she no longer even recognized her own *mind.* How could it have done that? How could it have affected her so much?

Her hand stilled. Slowly, she turned it over so she could see the ugly mark on her thumb, the flesh around it bruising as it healed. It hadn't happened when she cut herself. It had happened when she'd put her thumb in her mouth, when she'd tasted her blood.

Not that that made any more sense. But somehow, in those echoes in the back of her mind, she knew blood was important. It had...meaning, significance beyond the obvious. If she could just remember properly, pull the memories forward to look at, maybe something would start to make sense.

A saucer clinked gently on the table.

"One latte."

"Thank you." She stirred in sugar, picked the cup up and sipped, the foam soft on her upper lip. Her heartbeat slowed and the tightness in her chest eased. She shut her eyes for a moment and sipped again.

She was so silly. Sitting here, heart pounding, letting all sorts of thoughts into her head. She was hungry, that's all. She'd have lunch, and then she'd be much more able to work out why her imagination was suddenly getting the better of her like this.

She ordered a hot-smoked salmon salad and a freshly squeezed orange juice, and sat drinking her coffee, letting the warm sweetness travel down through her, easing her into relaxation, until the food arrived.

The salmon broke into thick flakes under her fork,

and the curly lettuce and slices of translucent green cucumber tasted of olive oil, lemon juice and black pepper. It came with a split ciabatta roll, dusty with flour, and a pat of butter, golden and oily from being next to the warm roll.

The orange juice glowed in its tall frosted glass, thick with specks of orange pulp, sweet and sharp. She sipped the last of it as she used the ciabatta crust to mop up the remnants of the salad dressing, and although she knew something had been bothering her, she could no longer remember what it was. So she signed the bill – she was so lucky, Clym had accounts everywhere – and went out again into the sunshine to buy the sexiest shoes she could find.

The sunlight was lovely today, and after buying her shoes she decided to walk home through the meadows. They called them meadows, but it was a park really, with wide paths. The flowers grew neatly in flowerbeds as well as straggling, skimmed-milk white, amongst the faded green of the dry grass in the fields stretching down to the river.

Across the river was where Clym worked. But she didn't let her feet drift towards it. "I have to deal with people who aren't very nice, baby," he'd said, months ago, when they were first married. "So when I'm at work I'm not very nice, either. If you saw me there" – and he'd laughed, rubbing the tip of his nose on her forehead – "maybe you wouldn't like me any more."

"Oh, *Clym*," she'd said, laughing with him, but partly shocked that he'd ever think such a thing, "as if that would make any difference!"

Still, the subject had dropped, and somehow she hadn't liked to raise it again.

But all the same it was nice to sit in the long, prickly-soft grass, letting the sun warm her hair, knowing she wasn't far away from him. And that maybe, if she sat here long enough, and if he decided to walk home this way, she might meet him and they could walk home together.

In the distance, she caught sight of other visitors. There were so many coming back and forth, strolling down the paths and wandering through the tall grass, that it was odd that, in all the times she'd visited the meadows, she'd never come close enough to speak to any of them. Nor, in almost a year, had she ever seen the same face twice.

Idly, she plucked a few of the flowers' thin stems. Their petals were soft – she could hardly feel them where they touched her skin – but their leaves were long and tough, coming to spiky points. She'd thought she could take them home, arrange them in a vase, but looking at them now, she realized they'd fade to invisibility against the blacks and reds of the apartment. And even as she held them, they drooped, their petals melting into nothing, leaves shriveling, the stalks drying, twisting into something like hair between her fingers that, released, floated away over the nodding grasses.

She hadn't thought they'd die so quickly. She pushed her fingertips down into the earth, wondering what their roots were like, that, once severed from them, they died so fast.

Except there was no earth. She dug her nails into the ground, looking down, bewildered, and met nothing but the faded, springy stuff she sat on, that she'd thought was the tangled lower stems of the grasses, the growth of new plants, a layer of dry soil that would crumble under her fingernails... It wasn't. It was fibres, woven tightly together, a tapestry of ochre, sand-color and faded brownish-green. Completely convincing until you touched it.

Candy snatched her hand back. No, she wasn't going to do this. Her world was perfect, *perfect*. She wasn't going to go prying and poking beneath the surface. She wasn't going to try and think back, try and remember how or when things had changed. She wasn't going to ask questions. She wasn't going to let the panic come back in.

She got to her feet, brushing broken bits of the flowers off her skirt. She wouldn't wait for Clym after all. She'd go home, have a shower, and put wine to chill. Then later, he'd come home and she'd let his hands and his mouth blot out the day, take her down into dark oblivion with him.

She gathered up her bags. Dust from the dead flowers clung to her dress, a thin pale sheen like the skin of a soap bubble. She shook her skirt, hoping it wouldn't stain...but of course it wouldn't. She was thinking of pollen. The asphodel didn't pollinate, they were just *there*. That's why they had no smell, why there were no insects, no bees, in the long grass. The meadows didn't grow, or change – that wasn't what they were there for –

"*Stop it*," she said aloud, and her own voice made her jump. "Go home. Go *home*."

She walked home fast, her heels clicking on the pavement, the skin between her shoulder blades damp with sweat. She was feeling dizzy again, as if her eyes couldn't focus properly, as if the world were too small, then too large. At the corner of her eye things moved, shimmered – in the *heat haze*, that was all.

Her key slipped in her fingers as she put it into the lock, and the door swung open onto the dim hallway. Cool, definite lines, the black marble floor cold and solid under her feet. She pushed the door shut behind her, and let her eyes fall closed for a moment, breathing in the chill of the air, the scent of polish.

"Mrs Rich, are you all right?"

Candy's eyes snapped open. "Oh, Mari – I'd forgotten it was your day! I'm fine, just hot. I'll just get a drink and get out of your way."

Frayed Tapestry

The maid, pale as narcissi in her black top and trousers, moved back against the wall as Candy went into the kitchen. Candy took a glass from the cupboard and ran water, making sure it was cold. Mari made her uncomfortable. She looked so thin, tired – it seemed wrong that she was here to do Candy's housework, to clean Candy's bathroom, and all Candy did was shop and have showers and prepare delicious little meals for when Clym came home.

She turned the tap off, hitched her bags onto her wrist, and turned to go back through the hall to her bedroom. "I'll just be in my room, Mari. You carry on." The discomfort, the edge of unreasonable guilt, made her direct a smile – slightly too wide – at the maid as she opened her bedroom door. Mari was already turning away. The hem of her trouser leg drew up over one white, bony ankle, and Candy froze.

Mari wore chains.

A metal band circled her ankle. Heavy, rough edged, splotched with rust: it was no ornament. The chain snaked down from it, then over the floor and out through the door. *How did I not see it when I came in? How did I never see it before?*

"Mari – " She stopped as the maid looked back towards her. Fear weighed her tongue, made her throat go cold. Mari had been the maid for the apartment before Candy came here, when it was just Clym's. Clym knew about this.

She swallowed. "Mari, don't worry about the kitchen. I'm going to go in there and cook and I'll just make a mess anyway."

The maid's eyes widened. Before they'd just been tired, dull. But now fear came into them as it had into Candy's voice. Too late, the thought came: *She's not here for me. It doesn't matter if I excuse her. It's Clym. It's what he wants. It's what he says.*

"I'm sorry," she said. "Take no notice of me. I know you need to clean the kitchen."

Mari ducked her head – "Yes, Mrs Rich" – and

turned away again. The chain slithered along the floor after her and, as she disappeared into the kitchen, Candy realized one last thing that struck cold not just into her throat but all the way through her, numbing her fingers, making her legs feel as if they didn't belong to her. The spots on the ankle cuff weren't rust. They were blood.

It seemed ridiculous, now, to think she'd been afraid just of her world changing, of finding out things weren't quite how she'd thought. Standing in her bedroom, icy fingers clasped together, Candy knew it wasn't just that things weren't quite right. Things were terribly wrong.

She turned her hands over and stared down at the ragged cut on her thumb. If all this had started to happen when she tasted her own blood, she could make it happen again. Would it be worse, next time? Already the skin of her beautiful world was unraveling, coming apart, showing things underneath that she'd never wanted to see – if she revealed even more, what would it be like?

She scratched at the healing wound with her fingernail, and it twinged, a precursor of pain. She could make it bleed again – but her stomach clenched and, again, her head swam with dizziness. She was scared, scared of the pain and scared of what she'd discover.

But wait. That first time, the sudden flash of oak tree, crashing waterfall, the scent of cold damp leaves – that hadn't been frightening. Okay, so it had opened her up to all this other stuff, the scary bones protruding through her world, but that moment, that feeling of stepping out of her life into something wonderful – and wonderfully familiar – that had been a good thing.

And you're not really a coward.

She blinked. The thought had come from nowhere, words whispered through a space in the world. She stood here, shivering, dressed like an expensive doll in clothes her husband let her choose, ashamed to look her own maid in the eye – just as the world wasn't the way she'd thought it, maybe this wasn't who she really was, either.

She clenched her jaw and marched across the room to the en-suite bathroom. Catching a glimpse of herself in the mirror as she went past, she didn't recognize her own reflection and checked, disoriented for a moment.

Clym's razor lay by the side of the sink, its reflection like a smudge of shadow in the shining white porcelain. She shut and locked the door, then picked up the razor and flipped the head so she could remove its sliver of blade. She wouldn't think about it, she wouldn't look. She turned her head away, biting her lip, and drew the blade across the back of her arm. It stung, sharp and brief, and she looked down – expecting to see nothing but the faintest scratch – to find she'd cut deeper than she'd realized and blood was oozing in a fat crimson line an inch long across her skin.

It was automatic to suck the wound, and the blood was in her mouth before she'd made the conscious decision to do so. But then her stomach heaved – what was she *doing?* – and she had to fight against the impulse to spit it out, had to force herself to swallow it.

She swallowed, and the world changed.

Trees stood all around her – oak trees and silver birches, their leaves a rustling whisper in the air –

but not close enough to prevent the sunlight streaming down onto the knee-high grass in which she stood. Real grass, tall and living, spiky with seed-heads, scent rising from the crushed stalks under her bare feet. Midges rose around her, tiny specks of life, a bee blundered past her leg, and somewhere, invisible, grasshoppers chirped.

Oh. She found herself crying, without meaning to, almost without realizing. She knew this place. It was like a bereavement, to stand here and not know why she recognized it, not know why it felt like home in a way the apartment – oh, the apartment had *never* felt like this.

It was the memories that made this place precious, memories she couldn't remember, and yet she knew they were there.

Was it Clym who'd taken them, stolen her memories and left her with nothing but blankness, like looking into mist so thick it made you feel you'd gone blind? But why? And *how?*

She swallowed again, the taste of the blood a metallic layer in her mouth, overlaying the traces of salmon and orange juice – *the food.* That was how he was doing it, using the food he gave her, drugging it. Or no, that didn't seem quite right, it didn't seem like a drug, and it wasn't just the food he gave her. She remembered how she'd gone into the coffee shop, panicking, needle-sharp aware of something being wrong, and how the first sip of coffee, thick with sugar and foamed milk, had smoothed down all the edges of fear, pushed her back into dreamy forgetfulness.

She drew in a long breath, trying to think, and breathed in the scent of grass and leaves and the dusty, moss-damp bark of the oak trees. And with the scent came clarity.

Oh Candy, you're being stupid. This isn't just Clym – it's the whole world. The sky being the wrong color, the asphodel flowers growing out of something more like fabric than earth – if this was Clym's doing, then Clym controlled a lot more than just their apartment.

She breathed in again. Grass, and bark…then coconut-scented bathroom soap, and shampoo, and bleach. The meadow blurred, like a reflection in a lake, fell apart into ripples, and disappeared.

She was back. She looked down and saw grass seeds stuck to her new skirt, solid and real, quite different from the ephemeral sheen of the asphodel earlier. And again, her shoes were missing.

Okay, Candy, think.

She sank to her knees on the bathroom floor, hands pressed so tightly against her eyes that phantom lights flickered against the insides of her eyelids.

The food – the food of this whole world – that was what made her forget, overlaid her memories like the haze of smoke over glass. And when she'd swallowed some of her own blood…she ran her fingers up into her hair, hard against her scalp, as if trying to force her thoughts to the surface of her mind…it had cut through the haze, shown her gleams of hidden memory.

But why? Why blood?

Her fingers stilled against her scalp. Of course. It wasn't because it was *blood* – it was because it was the only thing that didn't belong to this world, didn't carry Lethe's power.

What's Lethe? Never mind. Think. Think about the food.

Oh. For the first time anger crashed down through her and surged up again, boiling. *That* was why Clym

had kept refilling her glass last night, why, this morning, he'd fed her melon and eggs and toast.

She got to her feet, the anger filling her, simmering. Spoon-feeding her, calling her baby names – it wasn't love, it was control.

From back through the apartment, the front door slammed. All Candy's muscles tightened, pulling her upright. He was back, and she was supposed to have cooked dinner. She was supposed to *eat* dinner. And the moment she did... What if she lost this new awareness? What if she went back to that dreaming, cloudy existence where she was nothing but Clym's wife, his baby doll, his little docile sweetheart?

"Candy?"

He'd come into the bedroom – she heard the wardrobe door open and the clink of him unhooking a hanger for his suit jacket.

She relaxed her hands – up until this moment she hadn't realized they were so tightly clenched her nails had left deep crescents in the skin. "Coming!" she called through the door, and then drew in a breath, trying to let it flow through her body, trying to force the tension down so it wouldn't show.

She unlocked the door and stepped out.

There was the strangest moment, then, as Clym turned, smiling, from the wardrobe – tall, dark, handsome, utterly familiar, the husband she'd lived with for a year – and she looked at him with no more feeling than if she were seeing a statue.

She had loved him – or she had thought she loved him. She'd slept with him and teased him and begged to go to work with him; had glowed with pleasure when he'd bought her something cute to wear or taken her out to dinner or shown her off to his friends.

And now she looked at him and didn't even feel pain

at realizing their whole relationship had been false, or regret at what had never really been. Not even disappointment that she'd thought she was in love and found that that was false, too.

She did feel anger, though. Oh yes, she felt enough anger to make up for the lack of everything else.

She smiled at him, teeth hidden behind her lips, deliberately crinkling her eyes so he wouldn't see the fury in them. "I'm so sorry, Clym. Dinner's not ready. I was shopping, then I walked home through the park, then I got distracted looking at my new dress."

He was staring at her, and sudden fear iced over her anger. Could he tell? Did it, after all, show in her eyes, in her tone of voice? She stood still, not daring to speak.

He pushed the wardrobe door and it shut with a slam that would have made her jump if she hadn't been holding herself tight against any betraying movements. He didn't speak, just dropped his gaze to her feet.

Oh no – her shoes. *Again.*

She forced herself not to look down, not to react. Relaxed, calm, her stomach in knots, she strolled across to the bed and reached into the bag for the shoes she'd bought that afternoon. Pulling them out, she turned back to Clym.

"Look, aren't they beautiful? They go perfectly with my dress."

His voice was heavy, cold as stone. "And yet you're not wearing them."

She smiled again, rolled her eyes a little. "Well, of course not. Didn't I say – I walked through the park, my feet were all dusty. These shoes" – she dangled them at him – "they're not having anything but sparkly-clean feet in them."

His gaze lightened a little. Not much, but Candy instantly felt her muscles sag as some of the tension left them. "You have slippers."

"Yes, but I can't wear them when I'm washing my feet!" She sat on the bed to slip the shoes on, fastened the slim golden ankle straps, and then smiled up at him. "I wasn't going to parade up and down the hall barefoot, honestly, Clym."

"Okay." His face relaxed into a smile. "So, no dinner, huh?"

"I'm *sorry*. It'll only take half an hour – "

"No, baby, it's just as well. I thought we'd go out for supper – I told Dem and Adriano we'd meet them at Nino's in an hour. Fix your face, doll, and we'll go."

Baby. Doll. She clamped down on a shudder – how weird, only this morning she hadn't minded him calling her that – and got to her feet, balancing on the high golden heels. "Of course, Clym. I'll get ready." Halfway into the bathroom, she checked, biting her lip against another shudder – this one for a very different reason. "Did you notice, has Mari gone?"

He nodded. "By the time I came in. Do your make-up in the bedroom, okay, darling? I want a shower."

The restaurant stood in a loop of the river, surrounded by a veranda of clean, white stone flags. Squat amber candles burned on the tables, a tiny shimmer of heat haze rising from each one.

Dem and Adriano had turned into Dem and Adriano and Ebon and Calla, plus Hy and Phira and Gray who turned up halfway through the meal. Tall, elegant people with long fingers and beautiful angular cheekbones, who tore heads off prawns and stabbed up olives on cocktail sticks and opened bottle after bottle of wine.

Distracted, still confused, Candy felt as if her head were swelling with the need to be alone, the need to think. She made a show of sipping her wine, put a few olives on her plate and pushed them back and forth. How much could she eat before all her thoughts would get wiped out again? And how long before they would come back? She was terrified of going back into that state of vague, unfocused fear – and even more terrified of going back to two days ago, when she hadn't been afraid, hadn't even known she should be afraid.

"Candy, *sugar*, you're not eating. Aren't you feeling well?"

It was one of the tall, dark, beautiful women. Calla? Adriano? Candy forced her face into a smile, hoping Clym hadn't heard.

"I'm fine. I am eating."

"But you're *not*. Clym, your little wife – she can't be feeling well."

From across the table, Clym looked at her. "Candy?"

"I'm fine. I *am* eating." And to prove it, she posted one of the stuffed olives into her mouth. Her throat closed, her body – now it knew what the food would do – reacting against the threat. She'd never be able to swallow it. But now half the table was looking at her, and she had to.

She made herself swallow it, and immediately felt her body relax – forced relaxation, like being swaddled, like being held down. *No. Oh no.* But she had no choice. Someone passed her the bread, someone else scooped salad onto her plate. And Clym was watching. She didn't know yet exactly what was wrong, but she knew it came from him, and she knew there was danger, and he mustn't find out that she knew.

Slowly, her hand heavy, her throat choked with fear and anger, she spiked tomato and cucumber and feta cheese, put it into her mouth, chewed, swallowed, felt the sweet, floating lethargy take her. She smiled across the table at Clym – and realized she wasn't entirely acting. Under cover of the table she dug sharp fingernails into her thigh. *Stay awake! Don't let this happen.*

The evening ground onward. Candy tried, unobtrusively, to eat as little as possible. She talked a lot, deferring to Clym, directing others' attention to him as he liked her to do.

Memory ebbed and flowed. Sometimes, she couldn't remember why it was so important not to eat, couldn't remember why her fingernails were biting through her skirt. Sometimes, it all came back to her in a shuddering rush that turned her stomach upside down, and which she had to conceal.

After one of these moments, cold with sweat, she slipped away from the table and escaped to the toilets. Inside one of the cubicles, she sat down and let her head drop into her hands. It swam with jumbled thoughts, flickers of disconnected memory. The food sat like poison in her stomach, and she felt her throat pulse with the urge to vomit.

Her head jerked up. She listened. No one had followed her in, no one would hear her. Maybe, if she could expel the food, some of this woozy, cloudy feeling would clear. Maybe she'd get through the rest of dinner without feeling terrified she was losing her mind again.

She stood up, lifted the lid of the toilet and leaned over it. Her stomach heaved but the food stayed down. And, once again, familiarly, horribly, her mind started to cloud. What was she doing here? What was she thinking? And – *oh* – she felt awful. Why did she feel so sick?

Her sense of balance went askew. She swayed heavily sideways, knocking into the cubicle wall. She clutched the hard cold metal of the toilet-roll holder, all her thoughts vanishing as nausea and dizziness overwhelmed her.

The shoes weren't helping. Clym didn't like her to take them off, but no one was going to see. And the cold, solid floor would feel good beneath her bare feet. She leaned against the wall, one hand braced against the door, the other fumbling with the tiny buckle on the inside of her ankle. The shoe fell to the floor and, thankful, she put her bare foot down, steadying herself while she undid the other strap.

Oh, that was better. She didn't dare shut her eyes – she'd fall – but she lowered her head, breathing the scent of disinfectant and pseudo-pine air freshener. She'd just stay here a moment until she recovered, then she'd be able to go back to the restaurant –

No! Memory raced up through her. She felt it like a blow to her stomach. The *food*. The food was killing her thoughts.

This time she didn't stop to think it through. She leaned over the toilet, and slid her index finger along her tongue, right to the back where, if you touched it, it would make you retch…

The vomit came boiling up her throat, all the undigested food and wine she'd forced into her body, turned sour and vile. She heard herself make a horrible croaking noise and her hand clenched on the toilet-roll holder as she was sick and sick and sick.

It left her empty. Empty and – once again – aware. She spat into the toilet, wiped her mouth with the tissue paper, breathing shallowly though her teeth, waiting for the prickle of cold sweat, the goose bumps all over her skin, to disappear.

So, that had helped. And – oh, taking her shoes off had helped, too. She'd remember that. And now, for the first time, it came home to her that she had to do something. She couldn't live like this, not daring to eat, trying to pretend to Clym that she knew nothing.

Although I still feel as if I know nothing. Something's wrong, that's all I know. My husband is controlling me and I don't remember why, or how it started, or who I was before.

Outside the cubicle, the door to the restaurant opened. "Candy? Are you all right?"

One of the women – Adriano, Calla? Candy put a hand against the cubicle wall, bracing herself, trying to think. "I'm okay! I just felt a bit faint. Give me a minute."

A moment's silence. The woman wasn't leaving. *I can't go back out there yet. I have to think what to do.*

Then a clink in the next-door cubicle – the toilet lid going down – and a scraping sound on the wall by Candy's head.

Adriano's face appeared over the top of the wall. "Candy! You've been *sick!* You're *not* okay. Just hang on, I'll tell Clym."

Her face disappeared. Candy heard the click of her heels as she hopped down from the toilet, then the outer door open and shut. *I'll tell Clym.* Yes, of course she would.

They'd been married for a year, and still, all their friends were really just Clym's friends. His colleagues, actually – no, not just his colleagues, but his *employees.* Was that part of their job, too, to notice if she wasn't eating or was hiding in the toilet making herself vomit, and to report back to him?

The door opened again, banging against the wall. The sound vibrated through Candy's head. Several heels tap-tapped across the floor. Two pairs of them, now.

"Candy? Clym is so worried. He's going to take you home. He's bringing the car round. Candy? Are you all right?"

Well, hardly. But she was stuck now. She pulled back the bolt and let the door swing open.

Adriano and Calla peered in at her, tall and gauntly elegant, with smooth olive-skinned cheekbones and sleek dark hair. Calla, though...had her coiled hair always had that scaly sheen, as if it were not hair but the entwined bodies of snakes? And had tiny flames always flickered within the pupils of Adriano's eyes?

I have to deal with people who aren't very nice, Clym had said.

Calla moved forward. "Come on, Candy. Do you need to take my arm?" From behind her ear, something like the tip of a scaly tail curled and clung.

"*No*," said Candy, then, habits of courtesy too familiar to break, "Thank you. I'm okay."

As she went out of the cubicle, Adriano swooped down behind her. "Candy, your *shoes*. Don't you want them on?"

She'd been vomiting in the toilets, her husband was having to take her home early, they were worried she needed help *walking*, and Adriano thought she wanted to put her wobbly high heels back on?

"No," she said, firmly.

"Oh, but Candy, you know that Clym – "

Candy stopped walking. "Clym what? Clym doesn't like me to go barefoot? How would you know that?"

Adriano looked taken aback. "Oh – well, Clym, everyone knows he – "

Calla cut in. "You don't want to upset him, do you, sweetie? Here, let me steady you, and Adriano will just slip them on..."

They were doing it almost before she realized. Adriano had stooped and put a slim, cool hand on Candy's ankle, raising her foot so she could slide the sandal on.

"I said *no!*" Candy snatched her foot back and Adriano overbalanced, landing inelegantly on the floor.

Calla looked appalled. "But *Candy*. You *know* Clym likes – "

Candy shook herself away from her. "*Clym likes*. Well, for once Clym can just do without what he *likes*."

Adriano came to her feet. Her eyes were flickering blue now, the flames larger, licking outside the edges of her pupils. "That's enough. Calla, hold her."

"Don't you dare!" Candy flung off their arms. "Touch me again and I'll – " *What? Tell Clym? Run away? I don't even know* where *I am*. Desperate, she fell back on playground tactics. "I'll *bite* you."

Calla laughed, coming closer, smiling into Candy's face. "Oh sweetie. You're not the only one who can bite." From the back of her head, something gave a dry rustle. Something hissed.

"No," said Adriano. "Clym would be furious. Let's just get her to him. Let him deal with her."

Calla laughed again, a dry rustle to match her hair. "You're so sensible, Adri. Come on, then, little girl. Let's get you to your...husband."

They kept close beside her as she went back out into the restaurant. It seemed unnaturally quiet. The candles burned steadily, reflected and multiplied in the dark windows all around the restaurant.

By the door, car keys dangling from his hand, Clym waited for her. In the low light of the candles, she couldn't read his expression.

The women fell behind her, but she had to walk towards him all the same. Where else would she go?

But what will I do? What am I going to do? He's the ruler here – how can I possibly not *end up doing exactly what he tells me?*

"Put your shoes on."

She'd reached him. She stared up into his face, feet firmly on the floor, and didn't move. The shoes – they really mattered. Maybe even as much as the food. Why else, for a year, would he insist she wore them, get angry if she forgot? Okay, he could probably force her to put them back on – he had plenty of support, after all – but she was damned if she was going to do it for him.

"Candy. Put your shoes on."

"Why?" she said, standing straight, feeling, oddly, taller than she had in all the high heels he'd ever bought her.

He stared at her a moment, unblinking, and she felt her face screw up slightly as if she were bracing herself for a blow.

"Because you look cheap." The words came with a sharp-edged emphasis, a twist like the lash of a whip. Intended to strike her, intended to make her flinch.

She didn't flinch. Not this time. Not anymore. She lifted her chin, keeping her eyes on his. "I do not. I look powerful. You know that, and that's what you don't like."

"*Powerful?* With your shoes off, like a streetwalker, like some cheap nymph – "

That word did strike her, but with a shock like a dash of water, like a leafy branch springing up against her face, cool and green-scented.

"A what?" she said.

He faltered. She saw him hear his last word, saw – for the first time – something like fear enter the dark face.

"A streetwalker. A *whore* – "

"That's not what you said. You said a *nymph*." And as she spoke the word, more words came, unexpectedly pattering into her mind like falling, rain-drenched blossom. "A dryad. A nature goddess. *That's* what you don't want me to look like. Why? What are you scared of? What are you hiding?"

Fury rose in his face, swamping the fear. "You don't get to speak to me like that. I'm hiding nothing – "

"Oh, you so are. There's no point, Clym. I know you've done something to me. It's why you insist I eat, it's why you're trying to make me put my shoes on. Tell me – why don't I remember our wedding? Why does our maid wear chains?"

He hadn't realized she'd noticed that. She saw his face freeze a moment, as shocked as if she'd thrown something at him. The sight sent courage shooting into her veins, bright, intoxicating.

She went closer to him, walking tall in her shoeless feet, feeling as if she drew strength through the bare soles. "I wasn't supposed to notice, was I? What else is there, Clym? What other nasty secrets am I not supposed to see? What *is* your work, that I have to be kept away from it? Who are these friends of yours you get to follow me and spy on me? Who are *you*?"

She was staring into his eyes now – *up* into his eyes. She'd forgotten how tall he was, and the bright wave of courage ebbed a little, leaving her feeling too weak, too small.

Without stepping away, without taking his eyes off her, he snapped his fingers. Except…no, he couldn't have, because there was a glass in them. A glass filled with red liquid. She'd seen something like that before and, although she couldn't remember when or where or what it had done to her, she started to shiver.

She should have stayed out of reach. She made to take a step away and his free hand shot out and grabbed her arm, fingers closing around her wrist. His eyes bored down into her.

"I'm your husband. That's all you need to know."

He brought the glass to her lips. The liquid swam in it, a brighter, sharper color than blood. And, unlike her blood, this wouldn't cut through the clouds, wouldn't shred the tapestry and let her step through, back into her own world. It smelled very sweet, like fruit and syrup. The scent woke a half memory. She had seen this before. She'd drunk this before, nearly a year ago, and that was when the world had dimmed and faded and turned into something she didn't want.

She pulled away, lips tight shut, head averted, but he wouldn't let go of her arm. He jerked her back, pinned her between him and the nearest table edge.

"Drink it, Candy. You're not happy fighting with me like this. Drink it, and we can go back to being happy."

"I don't want that kind of happy!" she flashed, then tried to clamp her lips shut. Too late. His hand came up, forced the edge of the glass between her teeth, tilted it so the liquid ran into her mouth.

No. *No*. This was how it had started. She wasn't going to let it start again.

She twisted in his arm, closing her throat against the sweet, sliding liquid, and thrust her hand, fingers clawed, at his face. His head snapped back. His grip slackened and the glass tilted, the dark liquid spilling down her chin and onto the breast of her dress. She spat after it, tried to push away sideways, get out from under his arm, but he was too strong.

He yanked her back and jammed the glass up into her mouth. Bright pain splintered into her lip, her tongue, the gums at the base of her lower teeth.

She shrieked. The blood flooding into her mouth drowned the noise, turning it into a gargled sound, and her body lost its fight, went loose against the table.

"*Candy*," he said, and let her go. She felt herself start to slide towards the floor, and reached out to grip the table, fighting the blur in her eyes, fighting to stay upright.

"I'm sorry. Oh Candy, I'm sorry. I didn't mean..."

His voice became a garbled background noise with no sense to it. She put up a hand to her mouth and pulled a wicked sliver of glass, slick with moisture, out of her lip. The skin around it clung, dragging, and the pain shot along every nerve, razor blades turning her skin to prickling ice. Liquid – sickly, salty liquid – flooded into her mouth and she swallowed instinctively, not thinking any more about what the drink would do to her, blind to everything but the pain and the fear of broken glass – *broken glass* – stuck in her mouth.

Another shard of glass in her lip, one in her tongue. She drew them out too, trying not to think how much damage they'd done, trying to do it while she was still brave with shock. More liquid slid over her tongue – warm, salty, metallic – and she swallowed again.

His voice came through the pain, pulsing, loud then soft, as if something had gone wrong with her ears. "Candy. Candy, let me help you." And his hands over hers – so cold they felt as if they burned her skin.

She jerked away, felt the floor shift under her feet, and fell. Her teeth came down hard onto her lower lip and fresh blood spurted from the open cuts. She cried out, choked on it –

"Spit it out! *Don't swallow*. Candy – "

She heard the panic in his voice – *don't swallow* – and a last bit of stubbornness rose within her like steel through her spine. She swallowed.

The pain cleared, not much, but enough so her eyes unblurred. She put her hand to her mouth and felt no more splinters of glass. She looked up.

She was facing the wall of windows that faced out onto the river, the meadows beyond it. All over them shone the reflections of the candle flames, a multitude of little amber petals suspended in darkness.

She focused on the flames, trying to pull herself together, trying to brace herself to fight, and saw the color bleach out of them, saw them go cold and bright, tiny points like specks of twinkling glass. The window lost its reflected gleam, darkened, melted away into the...

...into the sky. It was no longer the familiar landscape of river and meadow, but sky: high, clear sky, stretching away farther and farther, endlessly into the distance. And the lights were no longer candles, but stars.

The windows had gone. She was looking out of the mouth of a cave. Below her, the hillside fell away. In the starlight she could see the short, scrubby mountain grass. Wind swept in at her, scoured clean with the scent of snow.

"Stop! Stop – Candy, don't!"

But he was too late. She was already scrambling to her feet, and as he grabbed at her she flung herself out of the cave, out across the rock ledge at its entrance, onto the grass. It was sparse, now, in wintertime, and her hands brushed through the blades, straight onto the frozen-hard earth beneath.

The shock hit her like lightning, driving up her hands, her arms, all the way through her body. And memory came back, starkly lit – one flash after another.

She'd wandered here, farther and farther up the mountain, gathering narcissi, singing, and the chariot had come, its wheels shaking the mountainside. The driver had glanced at her as it thundered past, and then dragged on the reins, bringing his horses to a slithering, screaming halt.

"Candy..."

Clym came out of the cave. Behind him the restaurant, the candles, the people – all had slid away, melted into the darkness. She looked up at him and recognized the face of the chariot driver. Memory flashed again – the feel of his hand, icy on her bare arm. The sound of his cold voice.

She sprang to her feet. Even that short contact with the earth had done its work. She could feel her cuts healing, feel the power that was her inheritance pouring up through her, like tree sap wakening in the springtime.

"I said *no*," she said. "I said *no* and you took me *anyway*."

"I couldn't help it. Candy, I fell in love with you, and you wouldn't come – "

Another lightning flash. She had struggled, screaming, the narcissi falling in a scatter all around her. He'd clamped one cold hand across her mouth and nose, crushing the screams back down her throat, cutting off her breath. Bundled her into the chariot and careened down, into the darkness – darkness blacker than she, an earth goddess, could have ever known, blacker than she could bear.

"That wasn't love," she said.

"It was. It is. Candy – "

"You poisoned me! You gave me that juice – from fruit grown next to Lethe's waters – you wiped out my mind! You – " She stopped as another thought came. "You *changed my name*. You called me *Candy*. What the hell sort of name is that?"

"I couldn't let you keep a tie to who you really were. I couldn't lose you – "

"That was the shoes, too, wasn't it? Even in your damned fake kingdom, you couldn't risk me touching the earth with bare feet, couldn't risk it recognizing me and calling me home. Well, you lost. It reached me anyway. Twice I lost my shoes, did you know? The wall broke down and the earth took them, held onto them, let me know something was wrong."

He didn't speak, just stood still, looking at her.

"Does my mother know? Does she know where I am?"

He said nothing, and she read the answer in his eyes.

"She doesn't, does she? She doesn't know. She must think I'm–" She looked around, seeing as if for the first time the dry, wintry grass, the bare-branched trees, stark in the cold light of the stars. "And this – I've been gone for a year. This should be springtime. Is that what this is? Does she think I'm *dead?*"

He lifted one shoulder. "She'll know by now."

"But a *year!* A year of mourning!" She spun away from him, every moment feeling stronger; the earth's strength rising through her.

His voice came from behind her, heavy as earth on a dead man's eyes, cold as the coins they paid to cross the Styx. "Better than eternity."

She knew perfectly well he meant himself, but she

didn't care. All those others – his sycophantic colleagues, the shop girls and waitresses, poor Mari with the chain on her ankle – Lord of Death, it was his right to keep them. He'd never had a right to her. She was going home.

She began to walk down the mountain. In the distance she could see the waterfall in the sacred grove, from here nothing but a shining starlit thread, apparently motionless against the cliff face. Farther still, down in the meadow, her mother was waiting for her. Mourning, but holding onto enough hope that summer had stayed there, only there, in the meadow where their house stood.

With every step the earth welcomed her. The grass softened under her feet, grew lush with spring growth. The wind lost its cold bite, threading gentle fingers through her hair. Sweet night-time scents rose around her.

"Candy..."

He was following her. She didn't look back at him. "That's not my name."

She heard him swallow. "Persephone. Please understand. I love you."

You do not. She turned, the furious words rising to her lips. He was standing behind her, on the new grass she'd left in her wake, the entrance to his dark kingdom behind him. And his eyes, his face – they were so bleak he looked like one of his own damned souls.

She didn't say those words after all.

"I know," she said. "But you did it wrong."

And this time, when she turned away, he didn't follow her.

EDWINA HARVEY

Where is Evil?

I thought I heard a commotion out in the barn, so I took the oil lamp down off its hook and went out to investigate. Daddy and my two brothers had told me that was precisely what I wasn't to do. They were away harvesting for other farmers, trying to earn a bit of money to tide us over. We'd lost almost half of our crop this year and winter was going to be hard. We couldn't afford to lose any more chickens to coyotes, and we were down to one milking goat since we'd sold the cow.

I'd been left on my own with a list of rules as long as your arm about what a young lady is and isn't supposed to do, but mostly it listed my daily chores. This was my life. Probably the farm and the local church were all I'd ever see of the world unless Daddy married me off to someone.

All seemed quiet in the barn when I got there. I stood in the doorway and listened, but all I heard was the rustle of a rat in the hay bales.

The lamp light reflected off the amber eyes of our barn cat, Lucifer. He stared at me accusingly; I had disturbed his hunt. He tolerated me stroking his sleek, black body, and tickling the white splash underneath his chin before he slunk away, intent about his business.

Before too long I heard a cat pounce in the darkness and the scream of a captured rat ending abruptly with the crunch of sharp teeth on bone as the cat broke its neck.

"You evil cat," I called to Lucifer.

"But where is evil?" a male voice answered me from the rafters of the barn. "In the cat who kills the rat, or the rat who steals your food?

Fear as cold as ice ran down my spine.

Slowly, precisely, I held my lamp aloft and looked above.

Shiny black feathers gleamed in the lamplight. None of our chickens were black, and as I lifted the lamp higher, I realized none of our chickens had wings that big either. They seemed to spring from his shoulder blades, sweeping down in an elegant curve. I wondered how he made his white cotton shirt fit around the base of those wings, but he did. And then I wondered what he washed his shirt in to make it shine like that.

And then I remembered the fright he had given me, so I demanded: "What are you doing up there?"

Daddy had always told me to act angry when I was afraid, it might someday save my life. I figured it was someday.

"Waiting for you," came his dulcet, amused reply as he picked his fingernails with a fine-bladed dagger. "And taking shelter from the rain."

"It ain't raining," I told him, my voice still angry and defensive. "Get you gone!"

His pants were as black as the shadows, and I couldn't see his feet.

"But you haven't answered my question." His soft voice sounded petulant, but not dangerous, and I admit I was intrigued. "Why don't you come up to the hay loft?"

My mind screamed *No!* so why did I find myself standing at the base of the hayloft ladder, juggling the lamp and my long skirts?

"I can't!" I cried, after my third failed attempt. There was no way I could hold my skirts out of the way, hold the lamp and still have enough hands to climb the ladder.

"I'll come down to you then," he said, pushing himself off the rafter.

"No!" I was sure he'd do himself damage.

But as I watched, his glossy black wings opened wide enough so he sort of floated down, his shod feet landing precisely in a mound of hay.

"Are you an angel?" I asked him. Weren't nothing on Daddy's list about casting out angels.

"After a fashion," he replied, dropping down to sit in the hay, his black wings somehow folding comfortably behind him. "Come sit beside me."

My mind yelled *No!* again, and I did the opposite. I sat in the hay beside him, but left a proper space between us.

"What's your name?" I asked him.

"Lucius De Ville. What's yours?"

It was only good manners that I should reply. "Amy."

He smiled a dazzling smile at me, and I was smitten. "It's a pleasure to meet you, Amy."

Then he kissed the back of my hand. No man had ever done that to me before, and it made me feel like a queen.

"I'm still waiting on your answer, Amy. Where is evil?"

I thought about it. "I suppose evil is our barn cat, Lucifer, killing rats."

His eyes twinkled with mirth in the lamplight. I imagined rats seeing a similar look in Lucifer's eyes as he pounced on them, wondered if they begged him for mercy before he dispatched them. I was raised never to beg for anything.

"But isn't he doing you a service? The rats break the chickens' eggs and steal your grain, don't they?"

"The rats are thieves," I readily agreed.

"But the cat's a murderer," he reminded me.

I frowned. It was a quandary.

He reached out and traced my frown lines with his fingertips.

"I've never thought of it like that before," I admitted quietly, distracted by the flutter of his fingertips on my brow. "But the Good Book says – "

"Thou shalt not steal. Yes, I know; I've read the Bible many times. It also says Thou shalt not kill. At least the Commandments do. Yet haven't you broken those very commandments every time you've stolen an egg from under a hen, or stood on a bug?"

"The hens are ours, but I never – I mean – " I stammered, confronted with the idea that I mightn't have led as good a life as I'd thought. Was it really murder to stand on a bug? What if you didn't know the bug was there?

"Come now, I passed by a fine large apple tree growing on your property as I came here. The very tree of the knowledge of good and evil God forbade

Adam and Eve to eat from in the Garden of Eden. Surely if you've ever eaten apple pie you should know the answer to my simple question." An indulgent smile played around the corners of his lips.

Dear God. I was thrice guilty of sins I didn't even know I'd committed! All my life I had striven to be good, but I was a sinner like all the rest!

"You have an attractive turn of ankle," he said. "May I touch it?"

His rapid change of subject confused me, but it was a distraction from contemplating my many inadvertent sins, and it soothed what had been leading into a volatile discussion.

"Why yes, I think I'd like you to," I answered quietly. I'd forgotten Daddy's advice to act angry, but then again, I wasn't feeling afraid any more.

"So back to my original question: where is evil?" he asked as his index finger swirled around my ankle bone.

He certainly was persistent for an angel. "Evil is where we see it, I guess."

"So when the rat steals your eggs or your grain, or your cat murders a rat for theft and you don't see it, then it's alright?" he challenged me.

Like the circles he was drawing on my ankle, the answers to his question seemed an endless spiral. If I was patient, I could unravel them, like tangled strands of wool, but I was young and impetuous and I didn't want to be confronted with philosophical questions that had no easy answers.

He moved a little closer to me and asked very elegantly if he might kiss my lips. Of course, I agreed; the sweet taste of his lips upon mine sweeping away all thoughts of what was evil and what wasn't.

Then he asked if he might kiss me again, and I

again said yes. And then his body did the asking and my body did the answering, and it was *Yes!* every time as I experienced such joy, such rapture, that I never knew I was capable of feeling.

He lay on his back in the hay with his black shiny wings spread out beneath him, his open shirt and pants tousled but still upon him, while I laid resting in the crook of his arm.

"Was what we just did evil?" he asked me in the quietness.

I inhaled deeply the smell of him: incense and cloves, clean and crisp, and right. "How can love ever be evil?" I pondered, and I drowsed, protected by his arm around me.

The rustle of his wings in the hay, his embracing arm moving away from me woke me from my reverie.

"You're going so soon?" I queried, yet somewhere deep inside me I knew to let him go.

Always act angry when you're afraid, and never beg.

My hand reached for his arm and slid down it as he stood up to rebutton his clothes. I swear I saw a blue spark of light pass between his index finger and mine as our flesh stopped touching.

He bent to cup my jawline with his soft hand, tilted my head up towards him and kissed me on the brow.

"What we make with love is never evil," he told me quietly. "Never forget that." He turned and walked out into the night, the same night I'd been told never to venture into.

As I watched him leave, drops of rain began to hit the roof of the barn, heavy and slow, as if God himself was spitting apple seeds at it.

I think I knew even then that there'd be another mouth to feed by next spring. I'd have some explaining to do, and I'd probably have to lie to Daddy and my brothers, because who was ever going to believe I'd slept with an angel?

More sinning to blot my soul.

But what was evil? I've thought it over long and hard and I never came close to working it out. The only thing I discovered for certain was that if you take the word EVIL and write it backwards, it spells LIVE. And that was just what I intended to do.

NANCY KRESS

Unto the Daughters

This is not the way you heard the story.

In the beginning, the tree was young. White blossoms scenting the air for a quarter mile. Shiny succulent fruit, bending the same boughs that held blossoms. Leaves of that delicate yellow-green that cannot, will not, last. Yet it did. He always did have gaudy taste. No restraint. Just look at the Himalayas. Or blowfish. I mean really!

The woman was young, too. Pink curling toes, breasts as barely budded as the apple blossoms. And the man! My dear, those long, firm flanks alone could make you ache inside for hours. He could run five miles and not even be winded. He could make love to the woman five times a day. And did.

The flowers were young. The animals, tumbling and cavorting on the grass, were young. The fucking beach sand was young, clean evenly shaped grains that only yesterday had been igneous rock. There was virgin rain.

Only I was old.

But it wasn't that. That was the first thing that came to your mind, wasn't it? Jealousy of glorious youth, revenge by the dried-up and jaded. Oh, you don't know, you sitting there so many centuries ahead. It wasn't that at all. I mean, I loved them both.

Looking at them, how could one not?

"Go away," Eve says. "I'm not going to eat one."

She sits cross-legged, braiding flowers into a crown. The flowers are about what you'd expect from Him, garish scarlet petals and a vulva shaped pistil like a bad joke. Braiding them, her fingers are deft and competent. Some lion cubs tumble tiresomely on the grass.

"I want to give you a reason why you should eat one," I say, not gently.

"I've heard all your reasons."

"Not this one, Eve. This is a <u>new</u> reason."

She isn't interested. She knots the crown of flowers, puts it on her head, giggles, tosses it at the lions. It settles lopsided over one cub's left ear. The cub looks up with comic surprise, and Eve explodes into laughter.

Really, sometimes I wonder why I bother. She's so stupid, compared to the man.

I bother because she's so stupid compared to the man.

"Listen, Eve. He withholds knowledge from you two because He's selfish. What else would you call it to keep knowledge to yourself when you could just as well share it?"

"I don't need knowledge," Eve says airily. "What do I need knowledge for? And anyway, that's not a new reason. You've said that before."

"A tree, Eve. A fucking tree. To invest knowledge in. Doesn't that strike you as just a teeny bit warped?

Mathematics in xylem, morality in fruit pulp? Astronomy rotting on the ground every time an apple falls. Don't you wonder what kind of a mind would do that?"

She only stares at me blankly. Oh, she's dumb. I mean!

I shout, in the temper of perfect despair, "Without knowledge, nothing will change!"

"Are you here again?" Adam says. I hadn't heard him climb over the rock behind us. He has a very quiet footstep for someone whose toenails have never ever been cut. Also a quiet, penetrating voice. Eve jumps up as if she's been shot.

"I thought I told you not to talk to this ... thing ever again," Adam says. 'Didn't I tell you that?"

Eve hangs her pretty head. "Yes, Adam. You did. I forgot."

He looks at her and his face softens. That blooming skin, those sweet lips. Her hair falls forward, lustrous as night. I don't think my despair can go any deeper, but it does. She is so pretty. He will always forgive her. And she will always forget everything he says two minutes after he says it.

"Be gone! You don't belong here!" Adam shouts, and throws a rock at me. It hits just behind my head. It hurts like hell. One of the lion cubs happily fetches it back, wagging a golden tail. The other one is still wearing the lopsided crown of flowers.

As I slither away, half blind with pain, Eve calls after me. "I don't want anything to change! I really don't!"

The hell with her.

"Just listen," I say. "Just put your entire tiny mind on one thing for once and listen to me."

Eve sits sewing leaves into a blanket. Not cross-legged anymore: She is six months pregnant. The leaves are wide and soft, with a sort of furry nap on their underside. They appeared in the garden right after she got pregnant, along with tough spider webs that make splendid thread. Why not a bush that grows little caps? Or tiny diapers with plastic fastening tabs? Really, He has such a banal imagination.

Eve hums as she sews. Beside her is the cradle Adam made. It's carved with moons and numbers and stars and other cabalistic signs: a lovely piece of work. <u>Adam</u> has imagination.

"You have to listen, Eve. Not just hear – listen. Stop that humming. I know the future – how could I know the future unless I am exactly what I say I am? I know everything that's going to happen. I told you when you'd conceive, didn't I? That alone should have convinced you. And now I'm telling you that your baby will be a boy, and you'll call him Cain, and he – "

"No, I'm going to call him Silas," Eve says. She knots the end of her spider-thread and bites it off. "I love the name Silas."

"You're going to call him Cain, and he – "

"Do you think it would be prettier to embroider roses on this blanket, or daisies?"

"Eve, listen, if I can foretell the future then isn't it logical, isn't it reasonable for you to think – "

"I don't have to think," Eve says. "Adam does that for both of us, plus all the forest-dressing and fruit-tending. He works so hard, poor dear."

"Eve – "

"Roses, I think. In blue."

I can't stand it anymore. I go out into the constant, perpetual, monotonous sunshine, which smells like roses, like wisteria, like gardenia, like wood smoke, like new-mown hay. Like heaven.

Eve has the baby at nine months, thirty-two seconds. She laughs as the small head slides out, which takes two painless minutes. The child is perfect.

"We'll call him Cain," Adam says.

"I thought we might call him Silas. I love the na – "

"Cain," Adam says firmly.

"All right, Adam."

He will never know she was disappointed.

"Eve," I say. "Listen."

She is bathing the two boys in the river, in the shallows just before the river splits into four parts and leaves the garden. Cain is diligently scrubbing his small penis, but Abel has caught at some seaweed and is examining how it hangs over his chubby fists. He turns it this way and that, bending his head close. He is much more intelligent than his brother.

"Eve, Adam will be back soon. If you'd just listen ...

"Daddy," Abel says, raising his head. He has a level gaze, friendly but evaluative, even at his age. He spends a lot of time with his father. "Daddy gone."

"Oh, yes, Daddy's gone to pick breadfruit in the west!" Eve cries, in a perfect ecstasy of maternal pride. "He'll be back tonight, my little poppets. He'll be home with his precious little boys!"

Cain looks up. He has succeeded in giving his penis the most innocent of erections. He smiles beatifically at Abel, at his mother, who does not see him because she is scrubbing Abel's back, careful not to drip soapstone onto his seaweed.

"Daddy pick breadfruit," Abel repeats. "Mommy not."

"Mommy doesn't want to go pick breadfruit," Eve says. "Mommy is happy right here with her little poppets."

"Mommy not," Abel repeats, thoughtfully.

"Eve," I say, "only with knowledge can you make choices. Only with truth can you be free. Four thousand years from now – "

"I am free," Eve says, momentarily startled. She

looks at me. Her eyes are as fresh, as innocent, as when she was created. They open very wide. "How could anyone not think I'm perfectly free?'

"If you'd just listen – "

"Daddy gone," Abel says a third time. "Mommy not."

"Even thirty seconds of careful listening – "

"Mommy never gone."

"Tell that brat to shut up while I'm trying to talk to you!"

Wrong, wrong. Fury leaps into Eve's eyes. She scoops up both children as if I were trying to stone them, the silly bitch. She hugs them tight to her chest, breathing something from those perfect lips that might have been "Well!" or "Ugly!" or even "Help!" Then she staggers off with both boys in her arms, dripping water, Abel dripping seaweed.

"Put Abel down," Abel says dramatically. "Abel walk."

She does. The child looks at her. "Mommy do what Abel say!"

I go eat worms.

The third child is a girl, whom they name Sheitha.

Cain and Abel are almost grown. They help Adam with the garden dressing, the animal naming, whatever comes up. I don't know. I'm getting pretty sick of the whole lot of them. The tree still has both blossoms and fruit on the same branch. The river still flows into four exactly equal branches just beyond the garden: Pison, Gihon, Hiddekel, Euphrates. Exactly the same number of water molecules in each. I stop thinking He's theatrical and decide instead that He's compulsive. I mean – really. Fish lay the exact same number of eggs in each river.

Eve hasn't seen Him in decades. Adam, of course, walks with Him in the cool of every evening. Now the two boys go, too. Heaven knows what they talk about; I stay away. Often it's my one chance at Eve, who spends every day sewing and changing diapers and sweeping bowers and slicing breadfruit. Her toes are still pink curling delicacies.

"Eve, listen – "

Sheitha giggles at a bluebird perched on her dimpled knee.

"Adam makes all the decisions, decides all the rules, thinks up all the names, does all the thinking – "

"So?" Eve says. "Sheitha – you precious little angel!" She catches the baby in her arms and covers her with kisses. Sheitha crows in delight.

"Eve, listen – " Miraculously, she does. She sets the baby on the grass and says seriously, "Adam says you aren't capable of telling the truth."

"Not _his_ truth," I say. "Or His." But of course this subtlety of pronoun goes right over her head.

"Look, snake, I don't want to be rude. You've been very kind to me, keeping me company while I do my housework, and I appreciate – "

"I'm not being kind," I say desperately. Kind! Oh, my Eve ... "I'm too old and tired for kindness. I'm just trying to show you, to get you to listen – "

"Adam's back," Eve says quickly. I hear him then, with the two boys. There is just time enough to slither under a bush. I lie there very still. Lately Adam has turned murderous toward me; I think he must have a special dispensation for it. _He_ must have told Adam violence toward me doesn't count, because I have stepped out of my place. Which, of course, I have.

But this time Adam doesn't see me. The boys fall into some game with thread and polished stones. Sheitha toddles toward her daddy, grinning.

"We're just here to get something to eat," Adam says. "Ten minutes, is all – what, Eve, isn't there anything ready? What have you been doing all morning?"

Eve's face doesn't fall. But her eyes deepen in color a little, like skin that has been momentarily bruised. Of course, skin doesn't stay bruised here. Not here.

"I'm sorry, dear! I'll get something ready right away!"

"Please," Adam says. "Some of us have to work for a living."

She bustles quickly around. The slim pretty fingers are deft as ever. Adam throws himself prone into a bower. Sheitha climbs into his lap. She is as precocious as the boys were.

"Daddy go back?"

"Yes, my little sweetie. Daddy has to go cut more sugar cane. And name some new animals."

"Animals," Sheitha says happily. She loves animals. "Sheitha go."

Adam smiles. "No, precious, Sheitha can't go. Little girls can't go."

"Sheitha go!"

"No," Adam says. He is still smiling, but he stands up and she tumbles off his lap. The food is ready. Eve turns with a coconut shell of salad just as Sheitha is picking herself up. The baby stands looking up at her father. Her small face is crumpled in disappointment, in disbelief, in anguish. Eve stops her turning motion and looks, her full attention on Sheitha's face.

I draw a deep breath.

The moment spins itself out, tough as spider-thread.

Eve breaks it. "Adam – can't you take her?"

He doesn't answer. Actually, he hasn't even heard her. He can't, in exactly the same way Eve cannot hear Him in the cool of the evening.

You could argue that this exempts him from fault. Eve picks up the baby and stands beside the bower. Fragrance rises from the newly crushed flower petals where Adam was lying. When he and the boys have left again, I slither forward. Eve, the baby in her arms, has still not moved. Her head is bent. Sheitha is weeping, soft tears of vexation that will not, of course last very long. Not here. I don't have much time.

"Eve," I say. "Listen – "

I tell her how it will be for Sheitha after she marries Cain, who is not as sweet-tempered as his father. I tell her how it will be for Sheitha's daughter's daughter. I spare her nothing: not the expansion of the garden until the home bowers are insignificant. Not the debate over whether women have souls. Not foot-binding nor clitorectomy nor suttee nor the word "chattel." Sheitha, I say. Sheitha and Sheitha's daughter and Sheitha's daughter's daughter ... I am hoarse before I'm done talking. Finally, I finish, saying for perhaps the fortieth or fiftieth time, "Knowledge is the only way to change it. Knowledge, and truth. Eve, listen – "

She goes with me to the tree. Her baby daughter in her arms, she goes with me. She chooses a bright red apple, and she chews her mouthful so completely that when she transfers it to Sheitha's lips there is no chance the baby could choke on it. Together, they eat the whole thing.

I am tired. I don't wait around for the rest: Adam's return, and his outrage that she has acted without him, his fear that now she knows things he does not. His arrival. I don't wait. I am too tired, and my gut twists as if I had swallowed something foul, or bitter. That happens sometimes, without my intending it. Sometimes I eat something with a vitamin I know I need, and it lies hard in my belly like pain.

This is not the way you heard the story.

But consider who eventually wrote that story down. Consider, too, who wiped up the ink or scrubbed the chisel or cleaned the printing office after the writing down was done. For centuries and centuries.

But not forever.

So this may not be the way you heard the story, but you, centuries about Eve's screams on her childbed, and Sheitha's murder at the hands of her husband, and Sheitha's daughter's cursing of her rebellious mother as the girl climbed willingly onto her husband's funeral pyre, and her daughter's harlotry, and her daughter's forced marriage at age nine to a man who gained control of all her camels and oases. You know all that, all the things I didn't tell poor Eve would happen anyway. But you know, too – as Eve would not have, had it not been for me – that knowledge can bring change. You sit cross-legged at your holodecks or in your pilot chairs or on your Councils, humming, and you finally know. Finally – it took you so fucking long to digest the fruit of knowledge and shit it out where it could fertilize anything. But you did. You are not stupid. More – you know that stupidity is only the soul asleep. The awakened sleeper may stumble a long time in the dark, but eventually the light comes. Even here.

I woke Eve up.

I, the mother.

So that may not be the way you heard the story, but it is the way it happened. And now – finally, finally – you know.

And can forgive me.

AVRAM DAVIDSON

The Fisherman . . . A Tashlich Legend

He came around the corner into Dock Street and at once I noticed something odd about him – something I was aware of noticing, but was unable to pin down. The late Se[tember sun bathed his well-knit figure in soft light, and played warmly on his dark, keen face. As he came up to me, he looked at me rather intently, and would have continued by, but I suddenly put out my hand and stopped him. Then I wondered why. He gave me a sharp glance – something like the glance Mr. Cook, the High School principal, used to give the boys as he passed them in the street.

"Don't I know you?" I asked. He put down his suitcase slowly, and pushed his hat back on his forehead.

"*Attah Yehudi*?" he asked me.

"Oh, you speak Hebrew!" I blurted out.

"I speak English, too," he said. "I just wanted to make sure you were Jewish. Since you are, I am bound to tell you that you stop me at your own risk." And with that, he raised his eyebrows, as if to say, "We-e-ell? And *now* what do you want?"

"What the devil do you mean?" I asked.

"Call me by my Jewish name," he said, and then I realized *whom* it was I had stopped on the street so familiarly. He nodded his head gravely. I groped for words, and stammered something about not wanting to keep him from his business. He chuckled scornfully.

"Don't give me that," he said. "Right now they all want to keep me from my business. Blowing *shofars* every morning, distracting me with their prayers – and all the rest, just to keep me from gathering evidence." This to me took on an aggrieved note. "I've got my job to do, just like anybody else. I've got my rounds to make, and my reports to turn in, too. And now *you* stop me with that silly pretense of having seen me before. Just be careful you don't see me again, that's all." And he made as if to depart. I put out my hand again.

"One more word our of you, and I'll say the *Shema* right in your face," I warned. He blanched and gnawed his lips.

"What have you got in that suitcase?" I asked him.

He looked at me slyly. "I've been fishing," he said.

"Let's see what's in the suitcase," I directed him in pontifical tones. He started to protest, but I only got as far as "*kel melech ne –*" when his fingers were busily undoing the straps. He threw open the lid, releasing a briny odor – briny, and yet – inside was a net, and a wicker creel. He opened the creel and I peeked in. At first I could see nothing, but then as they took shape, I withdrew a little.

He reached in his hand and pulled one out. It was spikey and had a hard shell, and thousands of little hands.

"Look at this beauty," he said. "Spawned yesterday from the cast-off *aveyrah* of a communal dignitary. And this one –" he pulled out one that had no shell at all, but many tendrils that wrapped themselves around his hand " – this one came from the old mother of a middle-aged and unmarried daughter." He disengaged his hand and put these back in the creel. His next step was a curious one: he put on a pair of leather gloves. He carefully inserted one hand in, and pulled out another specimen of his catch. Its upper surface was beautifully iridescent, but the lower surface contained a double-row of ugly suckling mouths, sharp-toothed and gaping. "Here you have soething that a pillar of the community shook into the river. One of the most well-esteemed philantropists that ever sweated his employees." Back it went, and he took off the gloves, removing the rest with his bare hands.

There was one in the shape of a rosette with a single petal missing: a faint pulse of life still beat in it. "Young girl whose sweetheart told her that his intent to marry her was the same as if they were actually married. She believed him – for a while." The next one resembled a slug, but had several sets of claws that continued to tear feebly at its own body. "Head of a merchants' association – almost all Jewish – that decided to close their stores on Monday each week. They could have chosen Saturday, but they didn't." He gave me another sly glance.

"Want to see some more?" he asked. I had enough. I didn't even ask to be shown my own – I was afraid of what it might look like. He packed his catch up again and fastened the suitcase.

"Well, I'll be running along now, if you don't mind. I've got to bring these in to headquarters." He went down the street, casting no shadows in the late September sun. As I watched him, I thought of the sins which had *not* been cast away, and my heart grew heavy.

Devil's Ways

J.M. SIDOROVA

Escape Goat

Middle of nowhere,
Times immemorial.

A man was leading a goat to a precipice. When they got there and the man readied to bind the goat's feet, the goat said, "Stop right there, human man."

The man froze and stared.

"You think I don't know everything about you?" the goat said.

Goats' eyes are notoriously hard to read. And the man had been in the blazing sun since morning, walking the high desert, and admittedly had addressed the goat on several occasions – as those things go – with a criticism or simply sharing an observation. So it was easy for him to slip into a conversation with the goat: "What on earth are you talking about?" the man said.

"She had black hair and blue eyes," the goat replied. "She cried the first several times. Until you gagged her with her favorite rag doll. After that, when you came to her she would bite on that doll ahead of time."

The man stumbled back as if pushed, and sank down.

The goat said, "Shall I go on?"

"It was thirty years ago," said the man. "She was – " But he could not finish saying what she was.

"So?" the goat said.

Now the man sprang up with regained confidence, grabbed the goat's rope, and yanked at it with all his might. "I don't have to listen to this," he growled. "I paid the price! I am clean and you're going to shut your foul mouth when I drag you these five feet to this edge and you'll be dropping off this cliff and I will never again have to listen to any of that libelous venom and you will never be jabbering another scurrilous word of this to anyone else, ever!"

But the goat was suddenly impossible to dislodge, no matter how hard the man pulled and pushed. And he, the goat, did not even seem to struggle to remain in place. "Remember the pact?" said he, observing the man's efforts. "The oft-overlooked clause. Only the one who is free of sin can conduct me. Or else the whole affair makes no sense, does it?" The goat nodded up to the red yarn that was tied around its horns. "Why, it *is* a joke otherwise. And it's on you. No one forced you to take on the – dubious, if you ask me – honor. But I suppose it was irresistible. Aren't you a hypocrite." The goat said all of this while watching the man yank at the rope again and again. When the man stopped yanking and, clenching his fists at his face, screamed out in despair, the goat added, "Yeah you are."

"What if I free you," the man said tearfully. "Let me – " He reached to untie the red yarn on the goat's horns.

The goat stepped back. "Not so fast."

"Why?!"

"We have only two ways out of this. One, you go with me. Down, I mean." The goat nodded to the cliff, then studied the man's face and remarked, "Uh-huh, didn't think so. Two, then: I go with you. Into the world. And you and I, we have some work cut out for us. Once you're done with the work, I will release you. Maybe." The goat stared at the man some more and curled his lips. "This is me smiling," he explained. "Come on, human man. I *will* let you go, I truly will. Word of a goat."

Ghetto Nuovo, Cannaregio, Venice.
1637

My name is Jacob Sforno. People here at the Quarter know me as a scribe for hire. I write their business letters, love letters, birthday poems, sermons. The truth is, I protect my people. Whatever else is rumored about me is not true.

Today our community was turned from joy to mourning by the news of the disappearance of Grassin della Motta, a young man of great prospects and a son of a distinguished and prosperous family beloved by all. Just days ago Grassin had been noticed all around town in his usual happy-go-lucky disposition, and today his inconsolable father sounded alarm at the community meeting in the Synagogue, saying that Grassin had been out for two nights and two days sending no word of his whereabouts – a most unusual behavior. And as much as everyone wished we could assuage the family by a mention of a sighting of their son, no man volunteered words of resolution to the trouble, and no woman's voice from behind the chevroned wooden screen of the gallery, rose to supply a helpful tip; only lamentations and well-wishes resounded.

It is my job to observe, and my eyes were drawn to Moise Lonigo, a learned but impractical man who had been much hounded by bad luck. To wit, a few years ago this man's only son had destroyed his health engaging in alchemy and died young. And now this: Lonigo's daughter Diana, a rare beauty, had been betrothed to Grassin for two years to date only to have her future husband disappear. It was said that a match with the della Mottas would be a windfall for the Lonigos. It was also said that the unusually long betrothal was due to the old man Lonigo's inability to accrue the pledged-upon sum of money for the dowry. I couldn't help asking myself: did Lonigo look aggrieved or relieved at the news of Grassin's disappearance?

The meeting over, della Motta Sr. gave me a hand sign indicating that he wanted me at his house for a private meeting, *right now*. I nodded and headed out. Crossing the *Campo* I saw a stranger walk toward me from behind the old linden-tree in the middle of the square – only just in time to step aside to keep respectful distance. Because the stranger was a woman – by her dress and gait. But what a remarkable specimen she was, a veritable bell-tower, taller than me! A natural sense of awe made me bow. "I beg your pardon, Signora."

"Signore Sforno? A word with you, if I might."

Her voice was deep and rich, and intoned in a *motherly* way, perhaps betraying its habitual use in coaxing or instructing a child. It even managed to stir in me dormant yearnings for domesticity. I had no time to waste however: della Motta Sr. expected me. I declined, saying I was preoccupied.

"I shall walk with you then," she declared. "Just a block or two." Clicks of her heels on cobblestones readily fell in unison with my patter. "I am Signora Scaramella. I was in the gallery among the women at the meeting. Poor Diana Lonigo was not in attendance, if you must know. Her mother told everyone she'd been so stricken by her betrothed's disappearance that she'd taken to bed. Such an unraveling – even *before* the della Motta's public plea, at that. Her mother seems to think the girl *felt* that a disaster had befallen the young Signore. But surely young men can go unaccounted for for a couple of days now and then, and no one thinks they're worse for wear. Don't you agree? Were the young couple much enamored with each other, do you know?"

All the while I was inwardly cringing: Signora Scaramella was much too forward with me for an unaccompanied woman who struck up a conversation with an unfamiliar man in the street. But now I realized: she had a point. Still, I made every effort not to look interested. Doing what I do, I ought to be cautious with strangers, female or not. We'd crossed the square by then and were in front of a dark and dank *sottoportego* leading to the embankment. I stopped. "I am sorry, Signora, but I am short on time, and you said you wanted a word with me – "

She did not reply immediately.

"So?" I prodded. "A word."

"A word?"

"Yes. Proceed please. Or I must part company. I truly am in great haste."

I meant to make it obvious to her that I considered her earlier words ladies gossip or introductory pleasantries. Inconsequential. I was sure she perceived it, but she did not relent.

"Ah, Signore Sforno," she said with a knowing smile. "I already said what I wanted to say. So now you tell me: why would poor Diana Lonigo be so unraveled?"

Tall women, they often are haughty. But I was not to be toyed with. "I have not a faintest idea why. Perhaps we can discuss it another day. Have a good night, Signora, for now I must take my leave." I earnestly hoped she would be reluctant to follow me into the murk of the *sottoportego's* tunnel, and indeed she stayed behind. But to my further discomfiture I heard her speak thus: "Can you arrange that I visit with the

Lonigos? Can you introduce me? ... I only want to help!"

Of course, I was piqued: what was she? Where was she from? Why asking *me* these questions? Or rather: how did she know that *I* was the person to ask? And above all – an offer of *help*? But for the moment, I was first and foremost relieved to be rid of the strange, towering Signora – so that I could make my way to the house of my benefactor, where, I suspected, no good news awaited me.

What irony! Waiting in della Mottas' front room, all I could think of now was Signora Scaramella's words about Diana. Did the young girl know something we didn't? Then della Motta Sr. finally appeared, and my worst fears came true. The Big Signore did not look piteous, as he had at the meeting, instead he was completely beside himself, red-faced and raving. "I know it, Sforno," he said in his booming baritone, jabbing his big and hairy index finger into my chest, "I just know it! They must have thrown my son in jail. Those filthy pigs! It has to be the Council of Ten's doing. Mark my words!" He stormed back and forth, so that every chandelier pendant in the room and every silver goblet and Murano glass carafe in the cupboard shook and clinked, and then he jabbed at me again, this time stopping just short of the bridge of my nose, "You *find out* where he is and how he can be freed. You do what you have to do, you hear me? At this hour tomorrow, I want you back here – with answers!"

When someone's index finger emphasizes a point so close to my nose that I can't help blinking, I become a Doubting Thomas, in this case despite my better judgement. "But Signore – just for the sake of the argument – may there still be another explanation? A discreet romantic business perhaps? Maybe he boarded a ship to travel to – "

"Don't play an idiot," the Signore said. "I *run* shipping. Do you think I wouldn't know it if Grassin showed at the port?"

I sighed. "Is there something in particular that I need to know to... to start a conversation with those I need to... converse with? Something your son did... was doing... that I don't know about... yet?" I struggled to put it delicately enough.

The Signore stared me down. "Keep to your place, Sforno," he said. "Remember where you come from. Same time, tomorrow. With *answers*."

Oh, I remembered where I'd come from. Missteps of youth, one could say, so small yet so irreversibly ruinous. So capable of landing a young man in a dark cell of the Venetian jail, where he curls up on the floor contemplating whether he'll be hung by a leg before the St. Mark's Cathedral come morning. On a word of his accuser alone – who happens to be a Christian woman he was in love with and who he thought loved him back... Ah, and then one day (or one night, because it is still, and ever will be, dark) the lock clangs and the guard lets him go and whispers into his ear, as he stumbles by, the name of the man he should thank.

Then one thing leads to another...

My point is, how could I not do what the Big Signore della Motta Sr., my benefactor, told me to do?

Still, it was night and there was little I could do at the moment except go home and set a candle alight in my window. By design, my third story window faced the canal, the Quarter's border. Across it was a solid line of row houses just like the ones on my, the Quarter's side, only it was the *other* side, the rest of Venice. There, my little light would be acknowledged by someone – an intermediary I never met in person – behind a window that was almost a mirror reflection of mine, and a word would be sent out accordingly. By morning I'd have a meeting set up with my *contact*, the man whose job it was to know where a young Jewish man might disappear to in Venice, if he did disappear.

With this in mind, I climbed the flights of stairs to my apartment, opened the door, and came in to a surprise: Signora Scaramella! The belltower-woman sat quite comfortably at a dinner table in the room of my landlady, the two of them having a late supper of sweet and sour sardines and olives, and a pleasant conversation. I had to go through this room to get to mine, or else I would have tried to skulk in unnoticed. Instead, I endured another introduction to the "traveling Signora Judith" who had just rented short-term; all the while the above-mentioned sent me furtive glances, as if we were co-conspirators. We most certainly weren't, and I felt annoyed. At least I could get a better look at her now: she had to be older than me, in her forties, perhaps. Her face was spirited rather than pleasant, her brows were too thick and her nose too aquiline; both contrasted starkly with her motherly voice.

"How unexpected," Scaramella said to the landlady, "I thought, signora, you said this was a women-only place."

"Ah, but that's not a man, that's our Jacob! He is practically family," my landlady waved her hand at me, "and he kindly helps us with this and that."

May she be blessed above all women of the house, my landlady, but honestly, the things she could blurt out sometimes... I bowed and left the scene.

What were the odds, I asked myself, even considering that my landlady made her living by subletting to widows and spinsters in their golden years? I retired to my room and hoped to get some rest, but the idea of sleeping under the same roof with Judith Scaramella was somewhat... arousing, as in arousing me from sleep, making me restless and full of uncontrollable thoughts of puzzlement and conjecture, mainly about her, and then about Grassin and Diana. And her.

It must have been after a few bouts of drifting to sleep and waking that I padded over to my window, having lost track of time. I looked out: the night was at its darkest, yet the canal gleamed faintly under starlight. Not a ripple on it, the water seemed to stand still. Then, from the sea-side end of the canal a gondola slowly glided in. The gondolier had but one passenger – a large white goat with massive horns curved tight like perfect crescents.

The gondola docked softly right under my window. Now, I knew for a fact that there was no quay by my house, just a vertical wall; in fact there were no quays or water-level entrance doors on our side of the border canal, or else how could it be a proper border? The Jewish Quarter was connected to the rest of Venice only by three foot-bridges whose gates were locked at night, and the border canal was patrolled (even if in every generation there were young and adventurous men who beat the curfew by scrambling out of second story windows and down embankments and boating in and out – I know, I had been one of them in my time...).

At any rate, this gondola was no patrol. And it docked: no splash, no thud, just a kiss on a stone wall. And the goat somehow disembarked: he was just there in the gondola but now I saw him on a narrow walkway of the embankment between the row houses and the railing. And the gondolier stood there in the boat, keeping his balance easefully the way only gondoliers do, and counting coins as if the goat paid his fare. And more strangely yet, a tall figure in a dark cape stepped out onto the walkway from under the eaves of my building, and the goat helped it, the figure, into the gondola, and the gondolier pushed off and steered back to where he'd come from.

No quay, I repeat. None of this effortless disembarking and embarking, up and down the canal wall and over the railing of the embankment, was humanly possible. Belatedly I told myself that this therefore had to be a dream, a sleepwalking dream at worst, and staggered back to bed.

Just before dawn I was on the foot-bridge, at the gate. The guard on the other side, Giacomo his name, unlocked it for me readily. "Out for your puff pastry again, Signore Jacob?" That was our standing story: I slipped out early because I liked puff pastry and wanted to be first in line at the French bakery. "Remember to get some for us!"

"Always," I said cheerily. Who cared if he believed any of it. Though the guard was a Christian, his wages were paid by us. This made sense. It also let me slip in and out past curfew for the price of a fancy puff pastry or its equivalent in coin. "Say Giacomo, did Grassin della Motta perchance come through here three, five nights ago?"

The guard made a face of mental effort. "I don't believe so, Signore Jacob."

"Very well, thank you. Good day, my friend."

Grassin must have been using rope ladders and boats for his trips to and from, as I would have done if I were him. Off I went, toward a meeting that I had set up with my contact.

The memories of last night seemed decidedly a dream, now that I was fully awake: I most definitively had not even walked up to the window but dreamt that whole scene instead.

As a matter of fact, I, a Jew, and my Christian *contact* Giuseppe Padovani typically met in a Moslem coffee house in Rialto. Calling Giuseppe *a contact* did not describe it, but I wanted to believe that over the years I had earned a measure of his respect, and it had offset the inequity inherent to our relationship. After all, the man was employed by the Council of Ten to investigate crimes. Whereas I was – well, I…

Even at this hour I had to push through early bird shoppers and merchants. I paused to adjust to the twilight, chill, and quiet of the inside once I stepped through the door. I saw Giuseppe wave to me from a dim corner where he was reclining on a pile of faded red pillows. "How curious," he said when I sat down, "I meant to summon you myself. You must have read my mind."

"Far from it," I said at once. Giuseppe was the kind of man you did not want to hear "you must have read my mind" from, and if you did hear it, it had better be true or else you'd better grow eyes on the back of your head for your own sake. "It's a pure coincidence. I called a meeting because I have an urgent question to ask on behalf of Signore della Motta Sr."

"Ah, him." Giuseppe smiled. "Your matter will have to wait. Get your coffee now so we can talk in peace."

He told me the following. There had been a fire three days ago. A ground floor of a four-story house burned, and the flames were extinguished just barely in time to save the upper floors. There was much confusion and panic in the process. But now that the embers had cooled, questions began to warm up. "You see, Jacob," said Giuseppe, leaning toward me across our small table, "The first floor of that house was occupied by a certain Joseph Avrillo, a friar. Word is, he practiced alchemy. Nothing certain. Upstairs tenants perceived *smells* every now and then, you know. Do you follow me?"

"The fire was an alchemical accident?"

"'The striking and the novel are foremost on the mind,'" Giuseppe quoted. Then added, "But in this case I'd be inclined to agree that alchemy was involved. In some way."

"What does Fra Avrillo say?"

"Nothing. He's missing."

I did not like the sound of it at all. I finished my coffee, down to the last drop that I could extract from the gritty mash at the bottom of my glass. "What does this have to do with me?"

"My clever Jacob." Giuseppe spread his elbows far and wide on the table, and rested his pointy chin on his extended thumb, eyeing me almost mischievously. "You've heard about transmutation of metals, no?"

"Well, yes. Copper to gold, lead to silver. Right?"

"Uh-huh. Word is, the Father had been *transmuting*."

I had no idea where he was going with this.

"All right," I said tentatively, "are you saying somebody wanted in on his hermetic secret?"

"*Hermetic!*" Giuseppe mocked. "I'm saying somebody wanted in on the profit. I don't care how those alchemists do what they do – if they do it – but when someone promises to make me twelve ounces of silver out of my ten that I have to give to this someone, I call it a – what, Jacob?"

"I don't know," I said. "Hermeticism calls it adulteration."

"Will you drop your Hermeticism already? I call it 'I am being swindled out of my silver because who knows how much of it stuck to the alchemist's alembic, so to speak, and did not come back to me.' And who knows, when I return for my silver and I am told that the transmutation failed because Mercury or some other such planet went to the wrong house, did it really fail, or did the alchemist decide to pocket my silver in its entirety?"

Having said that and as sudden as he could be, Giuseppe grabbed both his and my coffee glasses and landed them bottoms up on the table with a loud thwack. I hesitated to react. Can't be too careful. "Let's see what's in your fortune, shall we, Jacob?"

I shrugged. His palms rested of the glasses while he studied me for a good while. In response, I studied his hands. He had able, graspy fingers, and the backs of his hands grew dark hairs. He lifted the glasses and inspected the drained coffee dregs in one after another, squinting like he was reading fine print. He looked at me, then back at my glass.

"What, now?" I asked.

"I see a short trip in your future," he said and rose. "Come with me, Jacob. Yes, up, up with you. Stop staring, I'm just joking. I've no idea about your future. Honestly… Come. To the burnt house we go. Time to do our inspection."

"You did not finish telling me about alchemy," I said, trailing behind him out of the coffee house.

"Yes I did. Somebody disagreed with somebody on how much metal they should be *transmuting* into profit. Hence the fire."

"Or why you told me all this and want me to go with you."

"You'll see shortly."

On the doorstep he had a tiniest of hesitations. "*You* probably don't want to be seen with *me*, no? Why don't you follow me ten steps behind."

Of course.

The first floor windows of the house were blown out, and sooty black haloes around the empty frames marked the reach of the fire. The oaken door to Fra Avrillo's quarters looked intact on the outside but its inside was charred and half-eaten by fire. The walls and ceiling of the room were blackened, the furniture had turned to coals, brass frame of the bed stood like a fence around a heap of burnt bedding, and the floor boards were covered in crunching rubble of everything else.

"There isn't much left," said Giuseppe. "Where was he doing his alchemy, huh, Jacob?" I said I did not know. He went around scouting while I stood, made glum by the sight of the place. Then the morning sun peeped through the window, and I noticed a shiny object nested in the grout line between the tiles laid around the hearth. A smooth bead, and the closer I got to it, the more perfectly smooth it seemed, like polished silver. I reached to pick it up but my fingers pinched through it, and the effect made me jerk my hand back in fright of the unexpected. My pinching had split the bead into two beads, they wobbled next to each other and then, as if by mutual agreement, fused. I nudged it again, making it quiver, jelly-like. I goaded it to roll along the grout line. I felt marvel but also, somehow, being fooled, being contaminated. I looked at my fingers.

"Mercury," said Giuseppe behind my back. "Let me." He had a brass fire poker in his hand. "Such a curiosity." He nudged with the poker, and the mercury nimbly rolled off the tile and onto the singed floor board. "You got a good eye." He prodded the bead again, and it rolled, and then, suddenly, dipped and disappeared. "Where did it go?"

We both looked for the mercury, I on my hands and knees, Giuseppe walking in circles around me, bent over, to discern if it had dashed farther than we expected. And then he said, "That's where it's gone," pointing at a crack in the floor. He crouched and traced the crack, and soon the trace outlined a trap door, heretofore barely noticeable. Where the mercury had fallen in, the crack had been widened because the fire had nibbled at the trap door.

"Well, look at that," Giuseppe said, jamming the poker into the crack and using it for a lever to lift the door. "We'll need a light."

He straightened, wiped his palms together, and left the room in search of a lantern. I waited. From time to time whiffs of cold air would come out of the dark hole in the floor as if it was breathing. The odor was complex and unpleasant. A flooded crypt came to mind. Giuseppe returned with the street torch that was kept in the holder next to the front door, and lit it with his flint and steel kit.

"Go ahead," said Giuseppe.

I'd thought something like that would happen.

"Don't look at me like that," he said. "Think of it as your apprenticeship."

A steep run of stairs led down the hole, not much more than a ladder; one was better off descending his face to rather than away from it. So I did, the torch in one hand. Giuseppe's face showed above me in the hole. At the bottom, a miasma of many burned and degraded things made my breath curdle in my throat. To my left was a moisture-weeping wall and a room extended to my right. Shelves, barrels and chests lined its walls. A huge workbench in the middle was crowded with glass and copperware and other utensils of an alchemist's trade, all of which glittered in the light of my torch like a strange, charmed city viewed from a distance. There was a kind of beauty in it. And beyond that city, once my gaze found its way through, an unburned ogling corpse sat leaning crookedly back, facing the shining display on the workbench as if it too was admiring it.

The corpse was male, that I could tell. But the details of his appearance and his decay were mercifully veiled in shadow. I pulled the collar of my shirt over my nose and looked up at Giuseppe. "There's a dead man here."

"Splendid. Do you think it's the Father?"

"I don't know. Come down and see for yourself."

Giuseppe fussed, referring to a bad knee and such, but at long last his legs replaced his face in the hole and he scrambled down halfway. He perched his behind on a rung and gestured to me to hand over the torch. From his high vantage point the light reached all of the room. "Yes, that's him."

I could hardly imagine how he could see that for certain, or how he could seem so unaffected by the smell. With Giuseppe, one never knew anything beyond doubt. A possibility that he had staged this whole experience to make some point to me could not be ruled out completely. Either way, I still stood at the bottom, Giuseppe's feet above my nose, and he blocking my only way out; and now I'd surrendered my light source. "Why am I here, Giuseppe?"

"About that," he said. He bent over, studying me intently. He held the torch loosely, resting it on one knee. "They say, one or more of your people were profiting off the money-making side of this craft here." He waved at the workbench with his free hand. "Neighbors, they pay attention to comings and goings, you know. The Father apparently had been taking students. Customers, too. And now he's a dead man. I am sure you're thinking the same thing I am thinking. Greed leads to disagreement, disagreement to a fight, and a fight ends in manslaughter. A fire to cover it all up. Right? Right."

"Or the fire started upstairs by accident and the Father down here suffocated in smoke," I said.

"Yes but that's not how it looks. Does he look like somebody trying to escape and never making it? No. And the trap door was down. Do you want to try and see if you can lift it from below if I went up and closed it?"

I recalled how he'd applied himself to the fire poker to lift the door. "No."

"Say what?"

I freed my mouth from the shirt's collar. "You are right."

"I'm glad you agree. Now. I need you to find out who at the Ghetto Nuovo had been seeing Fra Avrillo."

"What if nobody did?"

He straightened up. "We've known each other for... how long? You know how this works, it's not your first time. A whiff of this gets out... you know what's going to happen, right?" He made a pause that I could not fill. He said, "You are my informant, Jacob. So, *inform*. I need you to give me one. One Jew." He showed with a finger. "Just one. One, in exchange for the peace of all." He turned and started climbing up, with the torch. "You can drop your report in the Lion's Mouth letterbox on Calle de la Testa, like you've always done. Just don't forget to sign your name." He cleared the trap door frame and went out of my sight. I heard him sneeze and swear. I didn't move. It was as if I wanted that trap door to slam shut above me.

His face reappeared. "Are you coming or what? This place is a stink hole!"

"Give me the torch."

"What for?"

"I need to make sure it's the friar."

"Oh, for the love of God!" But he did as I asked, and I went and checked. I had never met Fra Avrillo but I knew the young Grassin della Motta well, and the corpse was not he. Why did I suddenly imagine that it would be? No particular reason other than when looking for a missing person, check every corpse you come across.

I climbed out at last.

When I next thought of asking Giuseppe about Grassin, I could think of so many reasons why it was a bad idea. Yet I also thought what would happen if I returned to the Big Signore empty-handed. I'd have to lie, and I preferred to avoid lying if given a choice. Then Giuseppe said, "I recall you had a question to ask. What was it?"

Perhaps it was the look on my face that reminded him. "I need to know if your people arrested a youth named Grassin della Motta in the past few days. If he is in one of your jail cells perchance." I thought about it, then added, "By mistake or bad luck. His father is very worried."

Giuseppe looked at me curiously. "Are you saying –"

"I'm not saying anything. A straight answer is all I'm asking for. Is he or is he not in your jail?"

"I wouldn't know."

"Are you sure?"

"Swear."

"Will you ask your people to find out?"

"Will *you*?"

"Yes."

"Then so will I."

That was what we parted on. He went his way and I went mine. I went to the French bakery. I had to stop a couple of times on the way there to compose myself, because my heart would start beating strangely and make my stomach queasy. Passers-by seemed to give me wary looks. But in the end I was lucky. They had not run out of puff pastries yet, and I bought four.

I returned with them to the Quarter. Giacomo the guard lived in a house right next to the foot bridge. I knew his wife and two children and left the purchase with them since Giacomo, off his shift for the reason of daytime, was asleep.

My landlady said I looked ill and wondered how I got so much cinder on my clothes.

I washed myself and slept some, and by afternoon I was thinking what to do next. I did not know anyone who'd been going to Fra Avrillo but as a matter of fact I did know one family that'd had a brush with alchemy: Lonigos! I'd start with paying them a visit, I decided. On my way out I ran into – Judith Scaramella.

It was a testament to the gloom and haplessness of my situation that I actually felt pleased to see her. "Ah, Signore Sforno," she said in her unforgettable voice, "I am so glad to have caught you before you left. Our hostess told me you are headed to the Lonigos. I'd like to come with you. Recall that you and I talked about them yesterday. About poor Diana Lonigo."

I was divided. The more reasonable part of me did

not welcome Judith's interference. But the rest suddenly wondered, impurely: what color and appearance might Judith's hair be? It was covered under a headscarf, of course, but the size of the bundle bespoke a full head of hair, and I imagined it dark, fine and curly, cloud-like. I said yes to her sometime during this train of thought.

"Tell me, Signora. Why do you care for Diana so much?" I said as we were walking toward our destination.

"Everyone wants to find Grassin, don't they," she replied. "I suspect Diana knows something."

"Oh." I'd expected some comment on a poor girl's sorry state. I didn't expect business.

"Or would you prefer to talk about trifles?" she observed.

I felt I was blushing and clamped up for a block or two. But then I could not help it: "And what makes you think she will tell you whatever she knows?"

"Oh, nothing in particular," she said confidently. "Just that a chat between two women can go a long way."

What could I say? Somehow, we made it happen. Scaramella went to the back to see the bed-ridden Diana, and I sat down with Moise Lonigo, her father, in the front room where, by the looks of it, the family did all their living, cooking, and working, including manuscript writing by Signore Lonigo. I feigned interest in alchemy and, stammering and apologetic, I asked whether he may be in possession of any information, from the days his son had practiced it. Any advice and referrals; I said I'd pay for it. This proved to be exactly the wrong approach with someone who'd lost his "one and only beloved son to poisonous fumes roused by his studies," in the old man's own words. Then he pleaded for me to shun the "deadly arts." He said, "May God who showed me no mercy, avert you from making the same ruinous mistake as my poor son made those years ago." And more and more of that sort. Then he mentioned Diana as an example of his continuing misfortune. He said he was afraid she'd soon die of a broken heart. He said he needed to expect the worst so as not to be crushed by it when it came. Listening to him I was considering whether, were I to double my pay for his alchemical tips, he would supply them or chase me out of his house with a broomstick. I thought the latter was more likely. I had to change my tune or leave. Time was precious, and Signore Lonigo's misery was contagious.

Just then Scaramella strode out of Diana's bedchamber in a most determined manner, followed by – Diana herself, then Diana's mother. Before I had a chance to utter anything whatsoever, the older women ushered Signore Lonigo out of the room and into the chamber they'd just emerged from.

"Signore Sforno, you need to hear what Signorina Lonigo has to say," Scaramella announced.

Even under more ordinary circumstances, getting a glimpse of Diana always made me long to be someone else: a poet, a hero, a different man, not a human being at all. And now, my poor soul simply began to vaporize into metaphors. Diana, her eyes like wells of sorrow and brows like broken wings, alighted across the table from me and whispered, "It is my fault."

"Don't judge yourself, sweetie, just tell your story," Judith said and patted her on the shoulder.

And so she did. "As you may know, I was betrothed to Grassin. It has been almost two years and there is no date for marriage fixed yet. It is a long time spent waiting." Her every utterance ended flat and hushed, as if she was running out of breath. Her eyes gazed beyond me. He pale, narrow hands lay clasped on the table, so fragile and so tempting for me to hold in gentle sympathy – though I, naturally, refrained. “He,” she nodded in the direction her father had gone and lowered her voice yet more, “cannot save the money he pledged as my dowry.” She blotted her lips together. “We are not poor. But my father has a... certain way with money. It comes and goes, and rarely stays.” She said this ignoring or oblivious of Signora Lonigo’s tightening grip on her forearm. Then she carefully took in a fuller breath of air, as if afraid that it would set her emotions flying, and said, “I was tired of sitting and waiting. Seeing my fate mishandled. Having no power over it.”

Then, with the same aloof economy of word that bespoke someone who confessed not to be forgiven but for the truth’s sake, she told us that from her late brother she knew about a certain alchemist, Fra Avrillo. Her brother had gone to him to learn the craft.

When she said this, my heart started beating twice as fast and the skin of my face felt like a shell hardened to keep my expression unchanged, while my mind did somersaults. What followed, exceeded my wildest speculations.

Diana said *she* had visited Fra Avrillo several times. Most of these times she dressed in her late brother’s clothes to conceal her delicate gender while alone out on the streets. From what this brave and willful girl had known from her brother and what Avrillo told her, she believed he could amplify the ducats for her dowry by purchasing silver and letting the alchemist do his magic on it: make more, pure, certifiable silver that could be sold for more ducats.

At first the results had been remarkable. But lately the friar had been dragging his feet. He owed Diana a big batch, but days and weeks had gone by, and no silver materialized, only excuses. She feared that she was being tricked. And that her father would discover that more than a few ducats were missing from the family’s cache. At last she grew desperate enough to hatch a daring plan. Early in the morning a few days ago she donned her brother's clothes and sneaked out to visit the alchemist. She had her brother's stiletto knife too, she'd been taking it for protection, but now that she was so upset at the friar she imagined how she'd threaten him if he did not give her her silver.

"I kept knocking on the door. I imagined so many times all the things I would say and do but never thought that he simply would not answer or would be gone. I did not know what I'd do then. So I just repeated myself over and over. Like a jammed timepiece. I knocked. And stayed. Then knocked again. I waited for a decision to come to me, which would be, I suppose, to go away, or bang rather than knock. Neighbors would hear and see me, then. But I was certain if I left now I would not find him and my money ever again. Then I thought I felt heat coming from the door. I thought Fra Avrillo might be in and doing his alchemy after all. I had my ear to the door. I imagined a magical shining in the hearth inside, and how it illuminated Fra Avrillo's face. Then, when I least expected it, the door opened very abruptly and there was Grassin. I remember a wave of heat. There may have been fire and smoke behind him in the room already but I cannot tell that for certain. I was too astonished to see him. And so was he, I think. It was just a moment or two, and then he slammed the door shut in front of me. A little while after, I started banging on the door. I don't know exactly how soon after. I was stunned. But when I was banging it was already clear to me that there was a fire inside and Grassin was there in it. I ran into the street to look at the windows, and there was fire and smoke. Some people appeared and started to haul buckets of water from the canal and throw it in the windows. But I never saw Grassin again. Because of me and my folly, Signore Sforno, my betrothed is dead by fire."

"Diana, you can't blame yourself for this," Scaramella said in a voice as sweet as a mother's embrace.

"Why would a young man flee from the face of his fiancée as if she was an angel of death unless he was up to no good there in the first place?" Saying this, Judith stared me in the eye – with a challenge, I could swear. "What was he doing there at that hour, Diana, and why would both of them not open the door when you knocked, can you hazard a guess?"

But Diana would not be consoled. "He may not have recognized me in man's clothes. Perhaps he even mistook me for my poor dead brother, and became scared. He could have been there for the same reason I was there. And ashamed of himself, when seen, just as I was. You can't make me feel better, Signora Scaramella, I still have lost him no matter what you say. And you, Signore," she finally regarded me directly, and I felt as if I was awash in her eyes, "I am told you are looking for Grassin. Look for him in the embers of the alchemist's home."

She stood up, her movements as parsimonious as her manner of speech, and went into the room her father had been expelled to. She closed the door behind her, leaving us only with the echo of her rueful words. Who'd told her I was looking for Grassin, I wondered momentarily and I stared at Judith, and she stared back, a challenge in her eyes, again. My mind was spinning like a wheel. Two thoughts in particular kept flying by over and over, chasing each other: if Grassin was indeed dead, could I give his name to Giuseppe and be done with the difficult task he'd hung on me? But if he was dead why did Giuseppe and I not find his corpse in Avrillo's living space on the first floor or his lab in the basement? Had we missed it?

I stood up and bowed to Signora Lonigo. "I am so sorry," I said. "I hope Signorina Diana recovers her spirits. No man can hold her at fault for what happened after seeing her anguish."

I yearned for a quiet moment alone, to think, but when I headed out Judith Scaramella made sure it was not to be.

"What are you going to do now?" she asked, walking in step with me.

"Why are you asking me, Signora?... And who told you I am looking for Grassin?"

"No one. But you are, aren't you?" She was as serene as I was agitated. "And I *have* helped you, admit it. Perhaps I can help you more, if you let me. There is no doubt in my mind that young Grassin's behavior when he saw Diana at the alchemist's was that of a man caught red-handed doing something worse than alchemy. And if you ask me, deep in her heart Diana suspects it too. She is simply not ready or not willing to speak ill of him."

I shook my head, my patience all but exhausted. Of course all of this had crossed my mind, I was not stupid! But my more immediate problem was how to play the next day or two: how best to re-inspect Fra Avrillo's home, what to tell Giuseppe and when, and what to tell the Big Signore della Motta Sr. so that the latter would never know what the former knew and vice versa, everyone would be satisfied, and Diana would never have to be interrogated by either one of them. That Scaramella – who had no way of knowing that Fra Avrillo was dead and that I was trying to avoid damage to our community from Giuseppe's murder investigation – that she kept patronizing me as if she had a better grasp of the situation, was wearing my civility thin. "Signora, you are a stranger from out of town and you stayed among us for how long – a few days? A week? Do not presume you know more about us than we ourselves do. Or that you can tell men you are barely acquainted with, what to do. Please do not force your company on me anymore. Not today, at least."

I turned and walked away, free of her at last. Even so, part of me knew that in her mind my outburst could well confirm she was right. And another part already chided me for being too harsh with her. Truly, this was a game I could not win.

It was with great reluctance that I went to della Mottas that night to report to the Big Signore about the progress of my inquiries. My plan was to buy time until I could examine Fra Avrillo's home again. I expected to be browbeat, and steeled myself. A servant opened the front door for me as always, but this time, ascending the house's narrow stairway between wallpapered walls with flickering sconces I felt like climbing a dangerous ravine, as if a waterfall would roar down on me any moment.

Yet, up on top the Big Signore met me with a smile on his face as wide as his dinner table and as shiny as his chandelier. "Ahh, Sforno! Here you are, you clever fox! Come celebrate with me!"

He slapped me on the back hard enough that my lungs shook inside me and I stumbled a few steps forward into the room. He continued to drive me forth with a firm hand on my shoulders. At a mahogany credenza he poured two goblets of red wine from a carafe and shoved one into my hand. He raised his goblet and downed it, then insisted that I drank up mine. I am not much of a drinker, and the wine went straight to my head.

"He is back!" the Big Signore cried. "My son is back. Everything is fine, Sforno, you can call your search off, you hear? ... You started it, didn't you, you asked around, no?"

My wine-loaded head nodded.

"Of course you did, that's my boy! Now call it off. All's well that ends well, right?"

"Wait," I said. "Grassin is back?"

"That is what I am telling you. Are you hard of hearing? Here, take this." He pulled out a drawer of the credenza, grabbed and dropped into my hand a velvet sachet heavy with ducats. "For your labors."

"Wait," I said again. I felt just like Diana had described earlier. Repeating myself, stuck on a line, too stunned to get past it and waiting for a prompt that was not coming. "Are you telling me – "

"Yes I am." The Big Signore was getting impatient. He turned and hollered, "Son! Come over here!"

In a doorway to an adjoining room there appeared Grassin, smugly glowing with health and wellness and good nature. "Hey, Jacob," he greeted me.

The Big Signore wrapped his arm around his son's shoulders and gave him a hearty squeeze. "Apparently he'd lost track of time in the arms of one very skillful signora. Didn't you? Yeah you did!"

Grassin made a face of embarrassment mixed with glee and did not deny it. "I hear you were helping to look for me. Thanks, Jacob." He reached for a handshake and my hand accepted it. We shook. I should have left right then.

But I didn't. It had to be the wine in my head, and all this glowing and gloating and shoulder slapping while in my mind I kept seeing a rueful Diana, and dead Avrillo, and myself, first expecting to be shut in the basement with a corpse and then being offered a lose-lose bargain. It had to be all this that untied a knot of my tongue and I said, "So, I take it you survived the fire then?"

"What fire?" Grassin said.

He sized me up but did not forget to smile. And this should have been plenty enough, a bucket of cold water for me. I should have said, never mind, and left in a hurry. "The Fra Avrillo's fire," I said.

Now Grassin turned to his father. "I have no idea what he's talking about." I could hear a twinge of panic in his voice. The Big Signore caught the meaning. His shoulder-wrapping arm left Grassin and lodged onto me. "Walk with me, Sforno." Now he was guiding me out of the room and the house. Down his stairway-ravine we went, the space so tight the Big Signore had to squeeze me closer to keep his hold on my shoulders. It made my walking very uncomfortable. "Who told you he was in a fire?"

"Nobody." It was a stupid answer but I had nothing better. Dread was taking hold of me. Just like many years before, my one tiny misstep was sending everything unraveling. Why oh why had I mentioned the fire?!

Della Motta Sr. stopped us at a landing. "Uh-huh. Nobody," he said. "The Lonigo girl, wasn't it? ... Yes, she. What did she tell you?"

My free hand found and held on to the railing. "She is obviously mistaken, so what does it matter. What did your son tell you?"

"Mistaken." He let go of me a little so that he could now face me. Then he grabbed the collar of my shirt and twisted it. "What. Did. She. *Say*?"

I felt the veins on my temples swelling. I stuck to silence – for the want of words, I suppose. I didn't know what my face told the Big Signore, but it must have been something of meaning to him. His choke grip on my collar turned into a loose hold on my shirt, and he pulled back a bit.

"Ah, Jacob, Jacob," he said almost in a fatherly manner. "Taking one for a pretty girl again, aren't you? And I thought you'd wised up." Now his palm patted my cheek; I winced and he pinched and jiggled it. "I've taken care of you, haven't I? And this is how you repay me? You try to play games with me and I will crush you, you understand?" Then just as suddenly his hand let go, he stepped back and studied his handiwork. He straightened my collar, erasing the signs of his grabbing and twisting, then palmed his jaw as if making up his mind. "I'll tell you how it is, plain and simple. It is a family matter and that is how it will stay. How is it my son's fault that her ne'er-do-well father can't give her to my son soon enough? Eh? Is he supposed to waste his best years? So yeah he may have got a mistress. She, that Lonigo girl, is jealous, that's all there is to it. That girl is something else,

I tell you. A cross-dressing, night-sneaking, street-walking waif, that's what she is. Mean as a rat under that sweet face of hers. Makes you want to call this betrothal null and void, don't you think? But then again, I am a family man, Jacob. So I'm thinking I might forgo part of the old man Lonigo's dowry and get this marriage done and over with. In the name of the happy resolution to our worries, why not, eh, Jacob?" He leaned in again. "Now listen carefully: if that girl squeaks but once about some crazy monk's fire and my son anywhere near it – but once! Now, or whenever. If ever she opens her pretty mouth to say anything at all about it – she is not going to like the consequences. You tell her that, Jacob. Won't you? You go and tell her. Oh, and give my respects to your landlady." With this, he gave me a shove. Not hard enough to make me fall down the stairs, but enough to make me haste to put my legs where my body was headed.

I did not go home: I did not want to run into Scaramella. And I was upset, and when I am upset I fall into temptation. I went to a certain place, a private residence in the poorer, dirtier corner of the Quarter where for those who, like me, are weak, a secret door opens to a water-level apartment, miserable and rotten, where games of chance are played. There, in that room, I spent most of the night and all of the Big Signore's ducats from the velvet sachet.

I left once out of money; it was early morning, still dark. I was so tired my senses were dulled; all I wanted was to crawl into bed. I held onto the wall climbing up the stairs to my apartment. I entered my landlady's room tip-toeing, I willy-nilly had to go through it if I wanted to get to my room, and I did not want to make any noise. What accursed congestion we live in! The landlady snored in her nook behind a paper screen room divider. And in the middle of the floor stood Judith Scaramella in an untied house-frock and white undershirt, washing her hair in a tin tub.

A long, thick, dark curtain of hair hung off to one side of her downturned face, and she drew a comb through it, so slowly, as if she were spellbound. The tub was on the floor, and the hair curtain reached almost all the way down. Now and then a water-drop off her hair fell resoundingly, like in a grotto, into a clear eye of water in the tub. She saw me and slowly straightened up, twisting her hair into a cord and letting it rest on her shoulder. I leaned onto the wall.

"What happened to you?" she whispered.

"I am a fool," I said and started to follow the wall toward my room. "A godforsaken idiot." I felt unwell.

"Wait," she said. She approached me and put her wet, warm hand on my cheek. "Who told you that?"

Her hand smelled faintly of goat's milk. Or goat's wool: I noticed for the first time that she had a length of red yarn tied around her wrist.

"It seems I've been hearing and saying these same words much too often lately. I am tired." I covered her hand with mine but I didn't want to pull her palm away. Maybe Judith suddenly reminded me of my dear, long-dead mother whom I missed so much right now. I wanted to curl up in my mother's lap. I turned my head and buried my nose in Judith's palm.

"What are you going to do about it? About Grassin?"

"It is della Motta's word against Diana Lonigo's. And that's the end of it." I did not mean to spill these beans. They just fell out of me. I'd become a bean-sack full of holes. Yet she wasn't surprised by the news. How strange that was.

"What does your heart tell you?"

"My heart tells me nothing." Embarrassingly, I was near tears.

"Do you think Diana is lying?"

"I don't know!"

"Is it because you've been betrayed by a woman when you were a youth that you're thinking every woman is a trickster?"

"Who told you – " I began but then gave up. "Oh, who cares! Enough. I am tired."

"Your landlady told me," she answered. "Women's gossip. Are you letting that long-ago incident govern your choices?"

Incident! Sometime during this exchange I stepped back and lost her comforting hand on my cheek. "You know nothing of my choices." I started toward my door.

She called again, *wait*. But I did not wait this time.

Once inside my room and having locked my door, I could not sleep. A candle was lit in the mirroring window across the border canal. Giuseppe wanted a meeting.

I don't know if Giuseppe believed me or just played along for his own convenience. Or how much seeing Diana Lonigo prior to my meeting with Giuseppe affected my decision. Either way. Giuseppe made sure that we were seen when they marched me, in shackles, to the Council of Ten's chambers in the Ducal Palace. By night, I was in a cell of the Palace prison, resting on a pad of straw. All present choices made, all future choices – forfeited. Peace at last.

I didn't *take one for a pretty girl*. That wasn't it. Yes, I'd gone to see Diana before Giuseppe. I'd told her Grassin was alive, and watched life return to her face as if I'd re-connected an artery. Then I'd shared what the Big Signore's had wanted her to know, and she listened, not a twitch of a brow marring her enlivened countenance. His offer to lower the dowry had made her happier still.

Sometime past midnight something awoke me. I lifted my head and saw Judith Scaramella. She stood very still in the corner opposite me, holding a lantern on a pole. She was dressed oddly, in a flowing robe, unfitted and undyed, and her hair was uncovered and down. I stared, then turned and closed my eyes, then twisted back and stared some more.

"Everything about you has been strange," I said, "but this is plainly impossible. I am assuming you are an apparition and I am dropping all formalities with you. I will talk – or not, or I will ignore you. At my leisure."

In unmistakably hers, rich and gentle voice, she replied, "I am not an apparition, but I don't mind if you think otherwise. If it makes it easier for us to talk." She came over, leaned the pole to the wall. "May I sit next to you on your straw? The floor is too cold."

I scooted over. The rustle of the wrinkling fabric, the little warm breezes roused by her long body folding next to me, the smell – the same faint smell of goat's wool – all of these were so very real.

She said, "It didn't have to get to this. I am sorry I could not help you enough. You don't trust women, and I happen to be one. But now that you're here and I might as well be a figment of your imagination, pray tell me: why did you choose to lay the blame on yourself instead of finding the truth?"

I certainly could answer this. Alone in a cell in the middle of the night with an apparition of a woman I barely knew. Why not?

"I was tired," I said, "of being a snitch. Living between a rock and a hard place for fifteen years. I'd reported people. Some were guilty but did not deserve the punishment they got. And for more than a few, their greatest crime was to have run afoul of the Big Signore. It only makes sense that I am here at last. Where it all started. One man for the peace of all, just like Giuseppe and the Council of Ten want."

"A scapegoat."

"Yes."

She sighed. "But what about the truth?"

"Maybe it was Grassin. But am I certain beyond doubt? No. Maybe he killed the old friar for money. Or in a rage. Maybe it was an accident. Will the Magistrates be unbiased? No. I told you, the Council of Ten is not interested in the truth. They'll have him squealing mea culpa after ten minutes in a dungeon. Meanwhile his father would have me killed. And it wouldn't stop there. Execution of his son will only make the old della Motta Sr. more ruthless."

Judith shook her head, smiling wryly. Then she glanced back at me. "What about Diana?"

Ah, Diana. "She'll get what she wants. A marriage to Grassin. Whether for love or for status and riches, I can't tell."

"And this is what made you – ?"

"No!" This came out almost in a shout. Quieter, I said, "Well, yes, but – "

"You are here because you wanted her to be happy."

"No. Because I lost hope."

"For?"

"For truth."

"I see." She hugged her bent knees and studied the tips of her road-worn shoes showing from under the hem of her robe. "I want to tell you a story about a scapegoat."

And so she did. There was a man a long-long time ago, who had once led a goat to a precipice. He did so for a Yom Kippur tradition of his town: one goat sacrificed to the Lord, one to Azazel the fallen angel turned demon who'd been hogtied under the desert for teaching humans how to compete with one another with weapons, knowledge, and pretense; hogtied while his teachings cast influence worldwide.

I knew this story, I said. Who didn't? Onto the goat meant for Azazel were transferred all the sins of the town – that was how it went.

"Why, do you think, that is?"

Because in making the sacrifice, I said, the people admitted that they had not always been good. And this reckoning was a good thing to do, more important than the goat itself.

"You are right," she said.

But as it often goes, not everyone remembered it this way. Some details had been forgotten – I too did not know that only someone free of sin could be a scapegoat-herd. Not someone who pretended not to have sinned, or convinced himself and others that he didn't, or was blind to it all along.

"That narrows the field considerably," I said.

Judith chuckled.

So, instead of serving the goat to the demon, the man had been made a servant to the demon who'd escaped into the goat.

"To do the demon's evil work?"

"Even a demon's doings and un-doings have unintended consequences," she said. "Azazel himself had been made into a scapegoat when he was punished, one for all. Have you thought of that? So, the answer to your question is no. The man I'm talking about was forced to learn his lesson by straightening the ways of others like him. That man served his time and then passed his job to another human, and so it went, from one unrepentant sinner to another, until it got to me."

"To *you*?! What did *you* do?" My skin crawled.

"I am not going to tell you." For once, her voice showed a hard edge and she looked embarrassed by that. "I am sorry. It won't help you if you knew." Then she called loudly, "Master? Did you want to show yourself to Jacob?"

The sounds came first: my cell door, a-opening, hooves a-clicking on the stone floor slowly and precisely, one mindful step at a time. A majestic white goat with horns curved like perfect crescents entered my cell. He walked in and stopped in the middle, studying me, his head cocked.

My heart started beating wildly and I grabbed Judith's forearm. I recognized him, of course. But my terror came from the almost-met expectation of the unnatural. It was indescribable, something in the way he moved. This body of a goat, one fearfully awaited, could at any moment slither like a snake or skitter like a spider.

"Do not worry. He won't do anything that would frighten you." She eased my grip gently and ran a finger under the red yarn on her freed wrist. "My time as his servant is coming to a close. After so many years. I've come a long way, haven't I?" She addressed the latter to the goat.

The goat tilted his head to rub his right cheek against his shoulder.

"Is he going to take me in your stead?" My voice barely cleared my throat.

"No." In a rustle of fabric and swoosh of air she straightened up. Without her next to me I felt a sudden, harsh chill. "A while ago he could have, but not anymore. And as a rule, if that's the case you shouldn't be seeing us, not this, not any other way." She picked the pole with a lantern and walked to stand by the goat's side. She put her hand on the goat's neck. I stared at them: they were regal. And blisteringly alien. She continued, "Unfortunately, he says you are going to die here by execution. Is that what you want?"

"How does he – " I began out of habit.

"Jacob. He knows those things."

"I… I was preparing for a life of labor on the galleys… or locked in a safe cell… Giuseppe told me that – " Suddenly – an apparition on an apparition – Judith's face seemed no longer even hers but the face of my beautiful, horrible beloved who had betrayed me. Just for one brief moment – and then Judith's words started to sink in, taking me with them. My mouth remained open, my body contracted. I hit and hit the wall with the back of my head and shut my eyes and covered them with my hands and still my tears ran and ran.

Judith, the Judith I knew, she and the goat were

next to me. "Get up, Jacob. Get up. He is going to get you out of here."

Nobody would know how I escaped. Even I could not tell exactly how I got from the inside of the cell at night to a dock at the port before dawn. All I knew was this: when I was boarding a ship sailing for England, a tall woman and a white goat were there to see me off, and the ship's crew expected me.

Before I stepped on the ladder, I asked Judith: who had killed Fra Avrillo. Did she know? She and the goat exchanged glances, and she said yes, they did. Tell me, I asked, but she shook her head, no. It was no longer my business but theirs, and finish it they would.

"So long, Jacob," Judith said. "I hope you'll never see the Master and his servant again. But if you do, it may be someone you will recognize."

The goat was looking the other way as she said that. Then he jerked his head in as if he wanted to utter a word but reconsidered. Still I thought I heard something. Not a voice but its hallucination, neither human nor animal, impossible to commit to memory.

I looked to Judith. "Did he… say something?"

"Yes. How to translate? He said: go into the world, scapegoat."

And then they took their leave, walking side by side, she resting her hand on his neck.

About the Authors

About the Authors

PERSEPHONE D'SHAUN

Persephone is a doctoral candidate in anthropology who loves incorporating her research interests into stories. A graduate of Clarion West 2009, she is currently toiling away at her dissertation somewhere in the Midwest, with dreams of spending more time writing fiction on the horizon. When not pursuing her academic goals, Persephone can be found obliterating enemies in her favorite mobile games or listening to her favorite murder podcasts.

Ben Loory

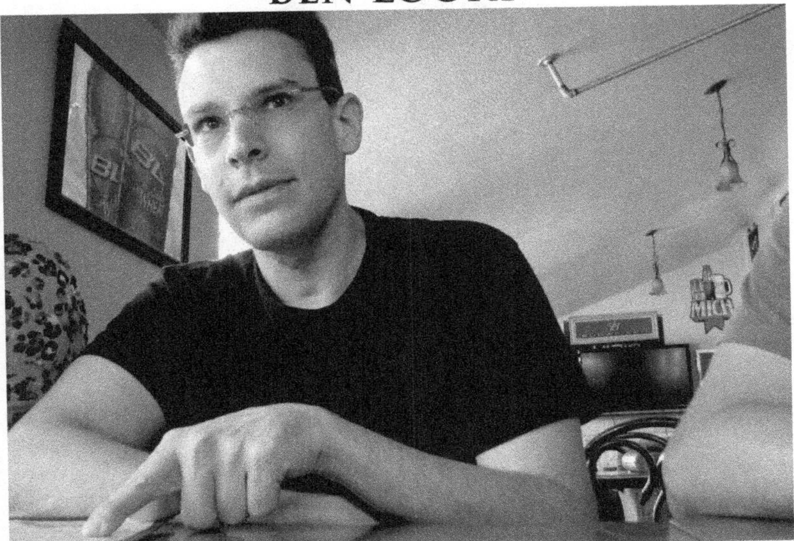

Ben Loory is the author of the collections TALES OF FALLING AND FLYING and STORIES FOR NIGHTTIME AND SOME FOR THE DAY, both from Penguin Books. His fables and tales have appeared in The New Yorker, BOMB Magazine, Electric Literature, and Fairy Tale Review, and been heard on This American Life and Selected Shorts.

About the Authors

R. S. A. Garcia

R.S.A. lives in Trinidad and Tobago with an extended family and too many dogs. Her debut science fiction mystery novel, *Lex Talionis*, received a starred review from Publishers Weekly and the Silver Medal for Best Scifi/Fantasy/Horror Ebook from the Independent Publishers Awards (IPPY 2015). She has also published short fiction in *Clarkesworld*, *Abyss and Apex*, *SuperSonic Magazine* (Spain) and several anthologies. Learn more about her work at rsagarcia.com.

MICHAEL SWANWICK

Michael Swanwick has received a Hugo Award for fiction in an unprecedented five out of six consecutive years and has been honored with the Nebula, Theodore Sturgeon, and World Fantasy Awards. He has the pleasant distinction of *losing* more of those awards than any other writer in the history of the field. He has written ten novels, over 150 stories, and countless works of flash fiction. Last summer, Tor Books published THE IRON DRAGON'S MOTHER which completes a trilogy of stand-alone fantasies begun twenty-five years earlier with THE IRON DRAGON'S DAUGHTER. Swanwick lives in Philadelphia with his wife, Marianne Porter.

About the Authors

Andy Duncan

Photo by Scott Edelman

Andy Duncan's fiction honors include a Nebula Award, a Theodore Sturgeon Memorial Award and three World Fantasy Awards, the most recent for *Wakulla Springs*, a 2013 *Tor.com* novella co-written with Ellen Klages. His third collection, *An Agent of Utopia: New and Selected Stories,* was published in 2018 by Small Beer Press. A South Carolina native and Clarion West graduate, he teaches writing in the Maryland mountains at Frostburg State University, which promoted him to full professor in 2019.

CURTIS C. CHEN

Once a Silicon Valley software engineer, Curtis C. Chen (陳致宇) now writes speculative fiction and runs puzzle games near Portland, Oregon. His debut novel *Waypoint Kangaroo* (a 2017 Locus Awards Finalist) is a science fiction spy thriller about a superpowered secret agent facing his toughest mission yet: vacation. Curtis' short stories have appeared in *Playboy* Magazine, *Daily Science Fiction*, and *Oregon Reads Aloud*. He is a graduate of the Clarion West and Viable Paradise writers' workshops. You can find Curtis at Puzzled Pint on the second Tuesday of most every month.

About the Authors

DARRELL SCHWEITZER

Darrell Schweitzer is a writer, editor, and essayist in the field of speculative fiction. Much of his focus has been on dark fantasy and horror, although he does also work in science fiction and fantasy. Schweitzer is also a prolific writer of literary criticism and editor of collections of essays on various writers within his preferred genres.

Imogen Howson

Imogen Howson writes fantasy romance and all types of speculative fiction for young adults. Her debut YA novel, LINKED, which Booklist called "a roller-coaster ride into space that just about everyone should enjoy" and BCCB described as "space-travel adventure at its best", won the YA category in the Romantic Novel of the Year 2014, and she is the winner of the Elizabeth Goudge Award 2008 and 2017. Imogen lives near Cambridge in the UK. When she's not writing or freelance copyediting, she bakes, runs, drinks coffee, and looks after a household of a vicar, two young adults, three cats, and two tiny dogs. She loves to hear from readers.

About the Authors

EDWINA HARVEY

Edwina Harvey is an Australian SF & Fantasy writer and editor. Her books *The Whale's Tale, The Back of the Back of Beyond,* and *An Eclectic Collection of Stuff and Things*, and her novelette, *Never Forget,* were published by Peggy Bright Books. She has edited *Lex Talionis* by RSA Garcia, *The Chocolatier's Ghost* by Cindy Lynn Speer and *Ashammet Desert Born* by Terry Jackman for Dragonwell Publishing. Edwina's other interests include silk painting, making ceramic art, and watching Marx Brothers movies on rainy afternoons.

NANCY KRESS

Photo by Lisa Trombi

Nancy Kress is the author of thirty-six books, including twenty-eight novels, four collections of short stories, and three books on writing. Her work has won six Nebulas, two Hugos, a Sturgeon, and the John W. Campbell Memorial Award. Much of her fiction concerns genetic engineering. Her most recent works are SEA CHANGE (Tachyon, 2020), a controversial novella about GMOs, and a galaxy-spanning space opera, THE ELEVENTH GATE (Baen, 2020). Kress's fiction has been translated into more than two dozen languages, including Klingon, none of which she can read. In addition to writing, Kress often teaches at various venues around the country and abroad, including a visiting lectureship at the University of Leipzig, a 2017 writing class in Beijing, and the annual intensive workshop Tao Toolbox, which she teaches every summer with Walter Jon Williams. She lives in Seattle with her husband, writer Jack Skillingstead.

AVRAM DAVIDSON

Avram Davidson (1923-1993) is an author of nineteen published novels and more than two hundred short stories and essays collected in more than a dozen books. He won a Hugo Award and three World Fantasy Awards in the science fiction and fantasy genre, a World Fantasy Life Achievement award, and a Queen's Award and an Edgar Award in the mystery genre. Davidson edited The Magazine of Fantasy and Science Fiction from 1962 to 1964. His last novel The Boss in the Wall: A Treatise on the House Devil was completed by Grania Davis and was a Nebula Award finalist in 1998. The Encyclopedia of Science Fiction says "he is perhaps sf's most explicitly literary author".

About the Authors

J.M. Sidorova

J.M. Sidorova is a Russian-born American biomedical scientist and author of speculative fiction. Her novel THE AGE OF ICE (Scribner/Simon & Schuster) was featured in Locus Magazine's recommended reading list, and received an honorable mention on Tor.com's best fiction of 2013 list. J.M.'s short stories appeared in Clarkesworld, Asimov's, Abyss and Apex, and other venues. Her most recent short fiction can be found in the SCIENCE FICTION BY SCIENTISTS anthology (Springer, 2016) and Gordon Van Gelder's anthology WELCOME TO DYSTOPIA (OR books, 2018). J.M. is a graduate of the Clarion West workshop.

DRAGONWELL BOOKS BY THE SAME AUTHORS:

About the Authors

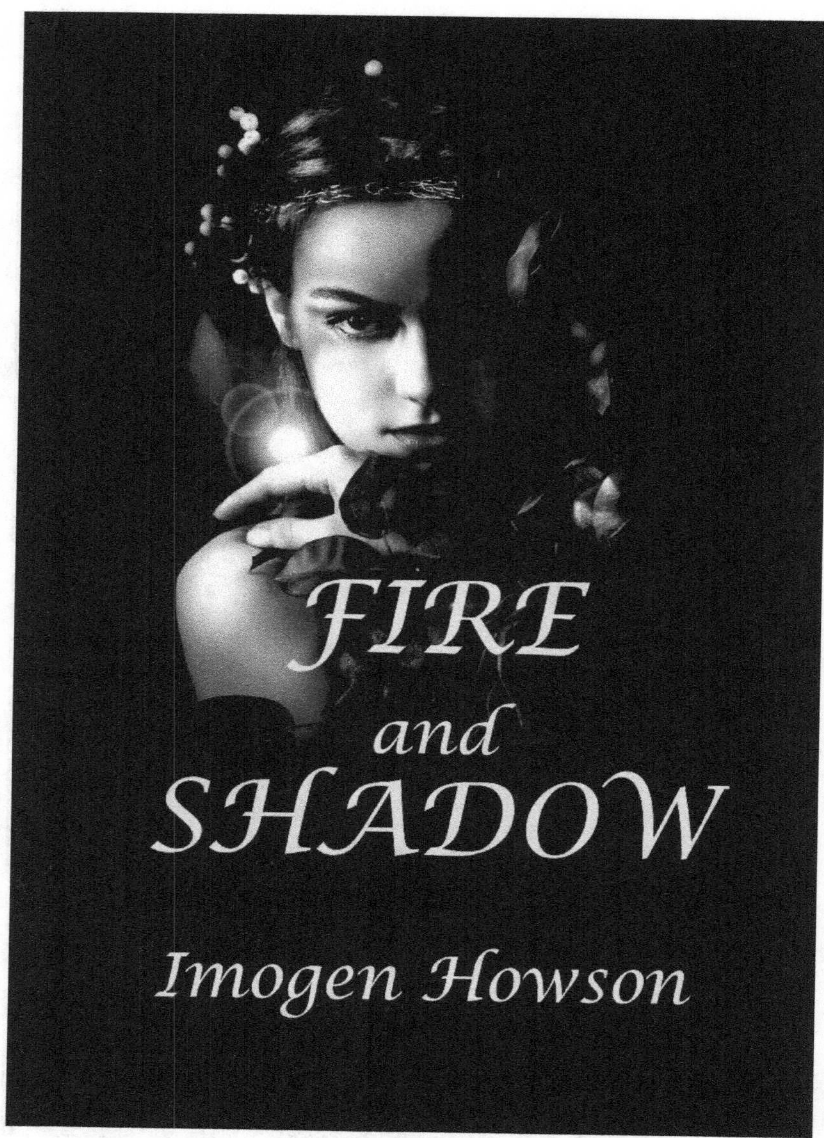

ALSO BY DRAGONWELL PUBLISHING:

About the Authors

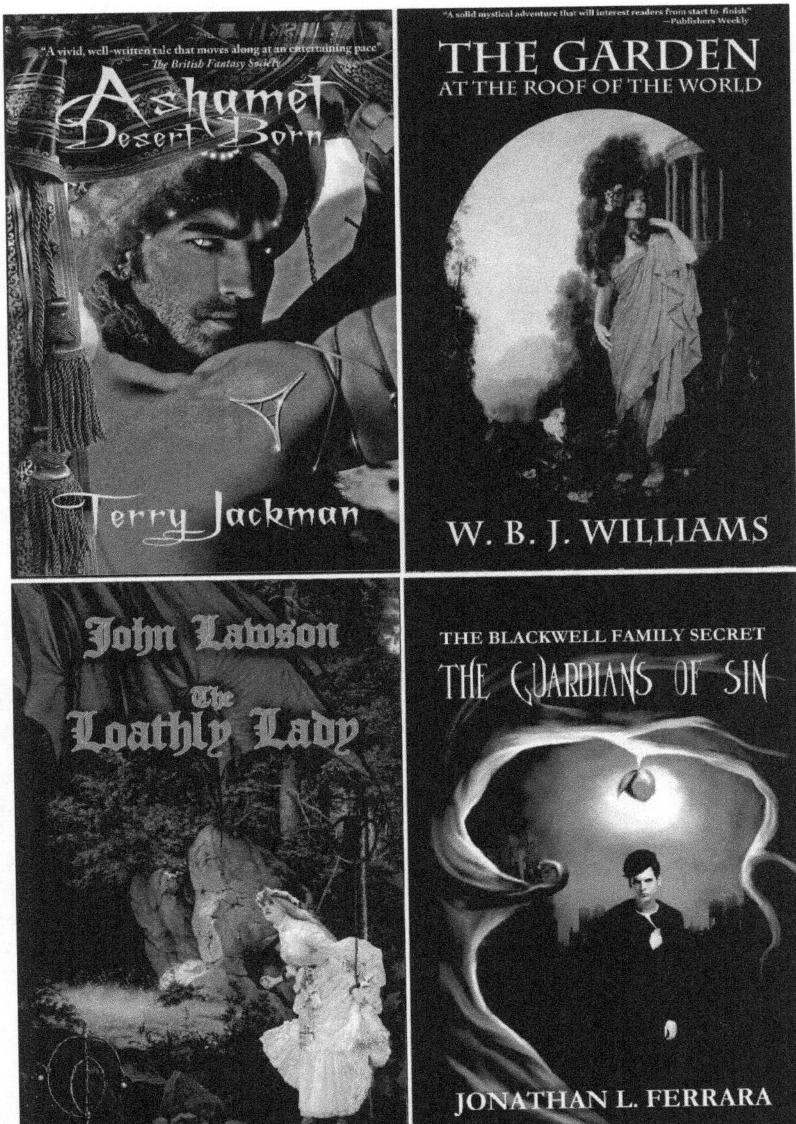
"A vivid, well-written tale that moves along at an entertaining pace"
– The British Fantasy Society
Ashamet
Desert Born
Terry Jackman
"A solid mystical adventure that will interest readers from start to finish"
—Publishers Weekly
THE GARDEN
AT THE ROOF OF THE WORLD
W. B. J. WILLIAMS
John Lawson
The
Loathly Lady
THE BLACKWELL FAMILY SECRET
THE GUARDIANS OF SIN
JONATHAN L. FERRARA

CPSIA information can be obtained
at www.ICGtesting.com
Printed in the USA
FSHW010457300720
72550FS